Terrebonne

BY ROBIN ELAINE

Days after the funeral — weeks even — I prayed for God to bring Mason back. I knew he could. I read in the Bible in the book of John that he raised Lazarus from the dead. He raised Jairus' daughter from the dead in the book of Matthew, and the book of Luke provides a horrifying account of Jesus' death and resurrection.

Matthew, Mark, Luke, and John — books splattered with such promises. I read those words over and over, knowing God could bring Mason back to me if he really wanted to. He'd done it for so many others, and I knew if I prayed hard enough, he'd do it for me too.

But he never did.

I guess God's not in the business of raising the dead these days.

He kept his reddish-brown hair short, and his full eyebrows highlighted his auburn eyes, which captured my complete attention the first time we met so many years ago. They were like sign language, communicating words his lips often didn't.

He hated that his eyes deceived him, but I was glad they spilled his secrets so easily. When they dulled slightly, they told me he was lost in thought. When the thoughts led to a great idea, the amber flecks in his irises flickered like sparks from a flint. And when he was really excited about the idea, those same flecks jumped and danced like flames from a campfire.

When Mason realized I could read his eyes, he was careful to look away when he was thinking thoughts he didn't want to share . . . or when he was trying to protect me. Toward the end, Mason looked away a lot.

"What?" he asked from his end of the couch without looking up from his newspaper.

I had been staring—admiring every feature of his face and wondering how I landed such a beautiful man for a husband.

A smile started across his face. "What?" he asked again, still avoiding my gaze.

I hadn't realized I'd been staring until he spoke, but now I thought I'd turn it into a game. I playfully narrowed my eyes and focused on him more intently.

His smile grew, but he shook the newspaper in front of him, pretending the paper had his full attention and he was paying no mind to me at all.

I leaned forward and intensified my stare, my face now inches from his, and I cleared my throat loudly. "Ahem."

Mason tossed the newspaper to the floor. "What?" he asked, laughing, his amused eyes finally meeting mine.

I expanded my smile and coupled it with a series of eyebrow

raises.

"Oh." He leaned toward me, and in one swift movement, he stretched the length of the couch to cover my body with his. He placed his warm hand on my hip, and I felt small and fragile under his full frame. "This?" he asked, placing a tender kiss on my forehead.

"And this," I said, planting a line of kisses along his jaw line.

"And this?" he asked, returning the kisses, tracing my cheek bone with his lips and working his way toward the corners of my mouth.

"Uh huh," I groaned.

"I love you," he whispered, his warm mouth hovering inches from mine.

"I love—" I began, but halfway through my reply his lips met mine and his hand moved to the small of my back.

I rolled with him, and we comfortably settled on the couch together. I buried my face into his chest as he wrapped his arms firmly around me. His arms were the only thing keeping me from toppling backward. If he let go, I'd surely fall.

"Let's just stay this way forever," I said, burrowing deeper, feeling his defined chest against my cheek and knowing I could never burrow in close enough.

"Deal!" Mason said, wrapping his arms around me tighter, securing his promise.

The heat radiating from his entire body cloaked me. I was warm and happy. I'd never felt safer and more loved in my entire life.

I closed my eyes to cherish the moment, but as soon as I did, the room grew cold. I opened my eyes to blackness, and I began falling backwards. I reached for Mason, but I couldn't find him. I swung frantically into empty air, waiting for his arms to catch me. I swiped at the darkness and screamed his name. "Mason!"

I felt his arms nearby and tried desperately to grab hold of them. "Mason!" I screamed, clawing in the darkness.

"Karla!"

"Mason!"

"Karla!" The arms encompassed my shoulders and gave a firm shake. "Karla, wake up!"

I opened my eyes to find my sister, Cheryl, staring at me with worried blue eyes.

"It's okay." Her short blonde curls framed her troubled face. "You were having a nightmare. It's okay." She sat on the edge of my bed in her pajamas.

I glanced around the dimly lit room. "What time is it?" I asked, rubbing my entire face with both hands.

She lit the light on her watchband. "Two a.m."

"I'm sorry. I didn't mean to wake you." I sat up, still trying to rub the nightmare away.

"No." She put her hand under my chin and tilted my face to look at her. "*I'm* sorry. I'm sorry you're going through this. It's not right. None of this is right." She wrapped her arms around me and pulled me to her, holding the embrace for several seconds before pulling back. "Do you need anything?" She gently squeezed one of my hands in hers. "A glass of water? Anything?"

I shook my head.

"I love you," she whispered, kissing my forehead before getting up and turning away quickly. She crossed the room to the door and paused in the light of the hallway. "Let me know if you need anything," she said, keeping her back to me in an attempt to hide the tears I'd already seen.

"I will."

"Karla?"

"Yes?"

"Please don't shut me out. Let me help. Okay?"

"I will. I'm fine."

But we both knew I wasn't.

I lay back down and thought about the dream. *Was* it a dream? I closed my eyes. No, it wasn't a dream. It was a memory.

"Let's just stay this way forever," I'd whispered.

"Deal!" Mason had replied.

Remember that, Mason? We had a deal!

But Mason broke our deal. It wasn't his fault. It was God's fault. But Mason was gone all the same.

Mason had let go—he'd been forced to—and just as I knew I would, I fell.

I was still falling. I was flailing! But it wasn't because of Mason. Not this time. This time—the reason Cheryl was here—was much more terrifying. Apparently, taking Mason wasn't enough. After the grief God had already put me through, he still felt the need to—

I shook the memory away. I didn't want to think about it. I squeezed my eyes shut and willed it to go away. To not be true.

But it was true, and the memory was persistent. I kept reliving it over and over. If I had known, Isaac and I would have stayed home that day. We would have never ventured out into a world that would swallow us up—that would leave more questions than answers and pile heartache on top of heartache.

I thought about that day and my stomach ached. Guilt gnawed at my gut, and I felt like I was going to puke.

And for what? A rusty lantern? An old nutcracker?

It wasn't worth it. I wanted to take it all back. I wanted to erase the entire day and give back all the treasures that drove us to go searching in the first place.

And more importantly, I wanted back what God had taken. I knew by now he was never going to give Mason back, but I was done letting him steal from me. I was done letting him play games. Done! This was all out war, and I was not backing down. Not this time.

"Okay," I said, looking up. "Let the games begin."

CHAPTER 1

Rusty Lanterns

"What?" I whispered. "What do you want?" I turned the gold band on my left ring finger and waited for an answer. The flea market was too crowded for anyone to notice I was once again talking to an inanimate object.

A few years ago, I would have paid no mind to the lantern, but now objects like the lantern captured my full attention—objects that were old and had a story to tell. Last week, while strolling through a hole-in-the-wall antique store, I found a large mirror with a four-inch-thick frame and I had to have it. The beautiful gray wooden frame was embossed with thick, hand-carved, swirling vines. Its reflective glass was tarnished, giving it a distinct quality most mirrors lacked. I walked over to it and, without checking the price, carefully picked up the hefty treasure. Carrying it with some effort to the counter, I promptly paid the two hundred and fifty dollars the clerk requested.

"Two hundred and fifty dollars? Are you mad?" the young girl in line behind me had whispered. But I didn't feel the regret that often comes with an impulse purchase. I would have paid four hundred dollars for it if that were the price; that was how badly I wanted it—how badly I *needed* it.

And now, the lantern was beckoning the same way. I had to have it. I picked it up and caught my breath at the overwhelming delight I felt just to have it in my hands. I examined every detail. Its metal base was coated in rust and its hourglass-shaped globe was layered with dust. The remains of a dry, tattered wick poked out of its burner.

"Okay." I hugged it to my chest. "Let's go home."

An old man stood nearby whittling on a short piece of wood, so I assumed the ten-by-ten space where the lantern had been temporarily housed was his. Even as he slouched his tall, lanky body against the hood of a rusted and dented blue Ford truck, he appeared to be much taller than my five-foot-seven frame. His wrinkled fingers were wrapped firmly around the wooden handle of a short-blade knife. His light blue jeans were held up with dark blue suspenders stretched over a red plaid shirt peppered with wood shavings. A gray beard framed his wrinkled face and held the remains of his last chew.

He glanced quickly at the lantern, then set his attention back on his piece of wood. "Forty," he declared, indicating he wasn't the negotiating type.

I found a spot on one of the tables cluttered with iron pots and pans and sat the lantern down so I could dig for my wallet.

Seeing I wasn't going to argue about the price, he laid his whittling project down. "Do you know what that is?" he asked, nodding to the lantern as he dusted wood shavings from his shirt.

"A lantern," I answered swiftly.

"It's called a dead flame lantern," he explained. "Likely made in the 1800s. It was one of the earliest portable kerosene glass globe lanterns produced."

I took longer than necessary searching for my wallet, providing ample time for him to tell me more about my treasure. It had belonged to his grandfather. Family members had rummaged through his grandfather's barn after he died and took everything they felt had value. They left the lantern behind, oblivious of its worth.

I pictured the lantern sitting on the barn's dirt floor. I pictured it waiting patiently for me.

". . . ninety-seven when he died," the old man was saying. "Yes sir, my grandpappy lived a long life." He shook his head with an amused laugh. "Stubborn though, that man."

He wasn't talking about my lantern anymore, so I quickly pulled my wallet out of my purse to pay. My hand had been on it the entire time waiting for the right moment.

"Pops found grandpappy lying on the ground by his truck

one winter. Crazy ol' gus had gone off and drove himself to town to get a bag of dog food for a mangy ol' stray." The old man was rambling now. "He wouldn't wait for someone to drive him," he said, shaking his head again. "Impatient, stubborn fool." He tried to sound annoyed, but the pride in his voice deceived him. "Found him, deader than a door nail, hugging a fifty-pound bag of dog food. Slipped and hit his head, I s'pose."

I pulled two twenties from my wallet and handed them to him.

"Ain't that someth'n?" the old man said, taking the money. His cataract-blue eyes seemed to stare into the past. "The war couldn't kill him, and influenza couldn't kill him, but that fall sure killed him." He shook his head. "Just like that," he snapped his long, wrinkled fingers, "and he was gone."

I flung my purse over my right shoulder before picking up the lantern. "Maybe just like that," I replied, cradling the lantern and snapping my fingers as well, "was best."

The old man's tobacco-stained jaw dropped open, and I turned and walked away before he could respond.

What did he know about death? *I* knew about death. *I* knew about goodbyes. All goodbyes were bad, but long goodbyes were the hardest. Especially when you didn't believe it was goodbye in the first place. Especially when you prayed for God to change things so it *wouldn't* be goodbye, but God ignored your prayers.

I quickly swiped a tear from my cheek with the back of my hand, angry that God had seen it.

I continued walking around the flea market. A milky white vase with hand painted pink flowers briefly caught my eye, but it was too recent a piece for my liking. A small dresser with tiny decorative pull knobs would have been beautiful, but someone had refinished it, naively erasing its story. I spotted some black boots crumpled under a table piled high with military coats and hats. I walked over to them, imagining they had once trampled the blood-soaked ground where freedom was once threatened; but as I got closer, I realized they were newer than I'd first thought.

A young girl with blonde, stringy hair caught my gaze and quickly scooped the boots up to display. "They were my great, great grandfather's," she beamed, stretching them out for inspection. "He wore them in World War I."

I waved her off, annoyed she was telling such a lie. But I instantly forgave her; the poor thing had probably been told that lie her entire life.

I walked the complete loop of the flea market without finding anything else that beckoned me. I made my way to my car and gently buckled the lantern in the back seat before hopping into the front.

As had become my norm, I kept my eyes peeled on the way home for other places that could be hiding another of my treasures. Popping in on estate sales and flea markets, rummaging through antique stores, and searching for out-of-the-way spots had become an obsession lately. I didn't understand why, but I felt accomplished, even when I left a place empty handed . . . and the times I left with a treasure felt magical. It was exhilarating to stumble upon an object I didn't know I was looking for—to wander through a place, not hoping I'd find a specific item but that a specific item would find me. And when it did—when it whispered to me—it was surreal. I'd stand holding it, mesmerized by the thought that countless others had picked it up or passed it by hundreds of times. Some never gave it a second thought, while others thought they were making a conscious decision to not buy it because it was chipped or cracked or too expensive. But really, they didn't purchase the item because it didn't belong to them. It belonged to me. I just hadn't come for it yet.

I arrived home after finding no more places to treasure hunt and carried the lantern up the stairs to the guest room currently serving as my treasure chest. I placed the lantern gently on the floor next to other items I'd collected, but I quickly decided it didn't belong there, so I picked it up and placed it inside an old crate hanging vertically on the wall. The crate made an ideal shelf for the lantern.

I smiled. The lantern was home. The crate and the lantern made a perfect pair. They belonged together . . . just like Mason and I belonged together.

Why did you want that lantern?

"I didn't," I mumbled. "It wanted me." I twisted the gold band on my left ring finger.

Well, whatcha gonna do with it?

I shrugged. I didn't dare look up from the lantern to search for Mason's eyes. I knew I wouldn't find them. Hearing him and seeing him were two different things. I knew that.

Well, maybe you'll figure it out.

"Or, maybe I won't," I said, shrugging again.

You will. I felt Mason standing directly behind me. *You always do.*

I stepped backward toward his voice, longing to feel his warm chest against my back. I took two steps, then three, before bumping into the wall.

I slid down the wall and crumpled to the floor—the pain of emptiness filling my entire soul. I squeezed my eyes shut as tears found their way down my cheeks, as if squeezing them tight enough could wring out the pain. But nothing could wring out the pain. Nothing could take it away. Nothing could even dull it.

I sat crying, my heart full of anger at a God who took . . . and wasn't done yet.

CHAPTER 2

Then, There's Isaac

"Not today!" I thumped my fist to the carpet as I sat slumped on the bedroom floor. I was talking to a higher power who seemed to enjoy toying with me every chance he got. I purposely focused on the treasures surrounding me—treasures so infused with life from their pasts they somewhat masked the overwhelming gloom of death that was present.

I forced myself to think about each object and the time in which it was at its prime. Those were good days. Days when people woke up early and went to bed tired. When people worked hard for their daily needs and took pride in their work. I imagined hands that tilled the soil, planting and nurturing each seed; and I pictured those same hands harvesting their blessings and preparing meals for their families around a table without cell phones or laptops. And after dinner, they sat around the fireplace reading and playing music, or crocheting or mending a torn shirt.

And they talked. They truly talked to each other—not via text messages or emails, but with their mouths and their eyes.

And how they valued every belonging! Things didn't get thrown away because they were old or broken. In the days when my treasures were born, store owners refilled their grain sacks again and again. Iron workers melted down scraps of metal and reshaped them into something new. Everything had purpose and meaning. Everything had value.

I looked around at the things in my room—things that were broken but had survived. They'd been used to their utmost and then passed down, each time acquiring a new story to tell. Each time, leaving a new footprint. They were only pieces of wood, glass, and metal, but I was learning more from them than I had learned in an entire lifetime of experiences. My lantern, for example. I imagined it once lit the way for a soldier as he returned from the battlefield to his new bride. Or perhaps it was once cradled in the hands of a small child as he tiptoed into the night to check on a newborn calf in the barn. And my mirror! How many generations of women had it stared at, reminding them time and again of their beauty?

Having the precious items in my midst made me long for such days. Days that were meaningful. Days that had purpose.

I thought of my world—a world that had changed me into someone I didn't want to be. Any place within where grace once dwelled had been swallowed up by an anger I was desperately trying to tame. Not because I wanted to. In truth, I wanted to absorb the anger. I wanted to embrace it and become one with it. But I couldn't, because being angry didn't stop the repeated chime of the doorbell announcing another concerned churchgoer. It didn't stop the incessant ring of the telephone or the endless barrage of sympathy cards—all of them scribbled with "I'm sorry for your loss."

And being angry didn't bring Mason back.

So, I held on to the small flicker of grace burrowed in the darkness of what was once me. That grace, however small, was the only thing keeping me from throwing entire casseroles on persistent church ladies each time I opened the door to one of their fat, smiling faces.

And then, there was Isaac. If not for Isaac, I would have gladly doused that last ember of grace with salty tears and surrendered to the sound of hissing coals as darkness closed in.

But there was Isaac. Thank God there was Isaac! He was the only reason I continued to acknowledge God at all. When Mason died, I wanted to be done with God . . . to ignore him the way he ignored me; but I feared if I did, he would take Isaac the way he took Mason. The relationship between me and God was one of submissiveness and fear, not love and respect.

Isaac. I smiled when I thought of him. He was the reason I

got out of bed each day—the reason I kept things running in a world that would one day go on running without me and pay no mind I ever existed. One day, I too would be gone, and I'd leave no footprint. There'd be nothing for someone to hang on their wall in the years to follow that would bring them the same comfort my treasures brought me. I'd only leave memories, and memories didn't count. I knew that for a fact. I tried to let memories comfort me when Mason died, but it was impossible. I couldn't wrap my arms around memories the way I could Mason's body. I couldn't smell memories the way I could smell Mason's cologne on his freshly-shaven neck each time he leaned in to kiss me good morning. No, memories didn't count. Only material things counted. Things I could hold onto. Things I could hang on a wall or sit on a shelf. Things like my lantern and my mirror.

I heard the front door open and close, then thump, thump, thump as Isaac ran up the stairs.

Dear, sweet Isaac. He was Mason's footprint, I suppose . . . and the only piece of Mason I could still wrap my arms around.

I stood to greet him as he bounded into the room, but he immediately noticed the lantern and bypassed my outstretched arms as he made a beeline toward the wall to inspect the room's newest addition.

"Cool!" he said, removing the lantern from its nook. His light brown bangs hung in his eyes as he examined the lantern closely. He tossed his hair to the side and tilted the lantern to look at the bottom, carefully adjusting it in his hands to support its glass globe. "Does it work?" he asked.

"Probably not." But I smiled, having no problem imagining a time when it had. "Maybe with a new wick and oil . . ."

"Where'd you get it?"

"Sweet Springs."

I watched him examine the lantern further. As he held it up to the light streaming through the window, the sunlight caught his eyes, revealing their color. Today, they were green. Sometimes they were hazel. Sometimes blue. Isaac's eyes behaved like a chameleon, taking on whatever color he was wearing, and today he was wearing a green hoodie sweatshirt with brown shorts.

I stared at his features as the light caught each one of them. He had a pronounced chin still round with baby fat, and the bridge of his nose and cheeks were peppered with reddish-brown freckles. He was only nine years old, but he already had every feature of Mason's and not a single visible characteristic of mine.

His bangs brushed the tips of his eyelashes, and he tossed them to the side again. His face expressed the same awe for the lantern I'd experienced upon finding it.

I smiled. I never encouraged Isaac's interest in antiques. It just happened. In the beginning, I thought treasure hunting would be my private pleasure—something just for me—but every item I brought home captured Isaac's attention just as it had mine, and he handled each piece with genuine curiosity. After my first two antiquing trips, he asked if he could go with me. We'd since spent many Saturdays strolling through old homes and off-the-main-road stores searching for treasures. Isaac's first purchase was a rusted cow bell.

"I have to go to Morgantown this week. Wanna go?" I asked. It was August, and Isaac's last week off before school started back.

"What do you have to go to Morgantown for?" he asked, carefully placing the lantern back in its place.

My job as a fundraising coordinator for the West Virginia branch of Maximum Capacity, a work innovations company based in New York, required I attend a great number of business conferences and seminars each year. The events were long and often repetitive of the ones before, which made my job both easy and boring. I was frequently invited as a guest speaker where I shared with attendees the latest and most innovative ideas being introduced daily in the workplace. The majority of the attendees were there to receive promotional training, or they were business owners looking for the newest and most ground-breaking technology to use in their business, but some of them were there with ideas and concepts of their own—ideas they hoped to have implemented in work places—and they came to Maximum Capacity for help.

Entrepreneurs came from all over the world, each with their own revolutionary business idea with no notion of how to bring it to fruition. It was my job to befriend them, gain their trust, and then make just enough changes to their concept that Maximum Capacity could assume part ownership. It was a good deal for everyone involved. Our company had the reputation and resources needed to create and duplicate inventions and ideas and introduce them into work places—large and small, new and established, domestic and international—and entrepreneurs had the creativity. We needed their ideas, and they needed our finances and connections.

It was a dream job for many, but I'd been doing it for so long it had become monotonous. Even new and innovative ideas, after a while, were only slightly improved versions of ideas and concepts already on the market. Still, it was a good job and had brought good things into my life. The best of which was Mason.

I'd been working at Maximum Capacity for two years when Mason and I met. I was working my way up the corporate ladder by attending any and all conferences and seminars Maximum Capacity wanted to send me to. It was the last day of a three-day technology exhibition in Benson, Missouri, and I was standing at the hostess station of the hotel's restaurant waiting to be seated when Mason walked in.

"Reservation for Garrison," he said to the hostess, pulling the cuffs of his shirt down below his dinner jacket and tugging at his collar uncomfortably. He glanced at me, smiled, and nodded hello.

I smiled and nodded back, but I looked away instantly, quite perplexed by the color of his eyes. They were a strange but beautiful auburn, a mixture of golden honey and liquid rust. They were a color I'd never seen before, and they drew me in instantly. I stared uncomfortably at my feet, then glanced back up to find he was still staring at me. I smiled again, and so did he.

"Oh no," the hostess said, her face twisted in confusion, then fear.

Mason and I both looked at her.

She fidgeted with her name tag that read "Hattie," then ran her fingers through her layered blonde hair. "Oh no," she said again, becoming more anxious.

I didn't know what was going on with Hattie, but I felt uncomfortable just staring at her. She was obviously having a bad day and didn't need an audience, so I turned to Mason. "Are you here for the technology exhibition?"

"Uh, no," he answered, looking amused. "All that new stuff that's only new for a month or so before something else new comes along." He made quotation marks in the air each time he said "new."

I raised my eyebrows, miffed that a young man would have such dislike for new technology.

He obviously read my expression well and quickly moved passed the subject, clearing his throat. "I'm here for the teachers' conference. It starts tomorrow. Thought I'd get here early."

I nodded and smiled.

"I'm a history professor," he continued, fidgeting with his collar again and staring at me with those fascinating eyes.

"Ooohh," I said dramatically. "That would explain your disdain for all things new."

"I suppose it could." When his lips smiled, so did his eyes. They were completely mesmerizing.

"Um, excuse me," Hattie interrupted, nearly in tears.

I startled and tore my stare from Mason to look at Hattie.

"I am so sorry, but . . ." her face twisted in apparent frustration and panic. "I accidently booked both of you for the same dinner reservation. I thought I was reserving table seven for you at the first seating," she explained, looking at me, "and for you, sir," she continued, turning to Mason, "for the second seating. I accidentally booked you both for the first seating."

"Oh," Mason and I simultaneously responded.

An awkward moment passed.

"You know what?" Mason finally said. "It's okay. I'll go unpack and come back for the second seating." He held out his hands in a "ta da" manner. "There, problem solved."

A tall, slim man wearing a black jacket and a black bowtie was hurrying toward the hostess station with impatience clearly strewn across his face.

"But," she said, looking anxiously at the man, then back at us, "you don't understand." The man was halfway across the restaurant and approaching the hostess station quickly.

"I'm going to get fired," she whispered. There was real fear in her voice. "I'm not good at the computer, and I keep messing up. The manager said—"

"Is there a problem, Hattie?" the man asked as he approached.

Hattie's look of horror told me immediately he was the dreaded manager who'd likely threatened to fire her pending another slip-up.

Hattie nervously fidgeted with some papers on the hostess station. "Um—" she began.

"Everything's fine," Mason answered before Hattie had a chance. He wrapped his arm around my waist and smiled at the manager. "She was just showing my wife and I to our table."

I don't know whose eyes were bigger, mine or Hattie's, but I recovered quickly and returned Mason's embrace. "It's a lovely restaurant you have here," I said, hoping to distract the manager. "If I was a betting girl, I'd say you helped with the décor. Am I right?"

The manager looked down at his feet modestly. "Well," he said, looking back up and motioning with his hand to one of the walls, "I did suggest the color palettes."

"Chosen to make one hungry, I suppose?" I winked.

"Well—" the manager grinned.

"It must be working because I'm starved!" Mason said, patting his stomach dramatically.

"Oh, of course." The manager stepped aside. "Please, enjoy your meal."

Hattie walked us to our table and mouthed the words "thank you" as she placed the menus in our hands.

Mason gave her a wink and we laughed about the incident over appetizers. By the time our dinners arrived, we were laughing about everything—families, jobs . . . and life in general. I was fascinated with Mason's ability to be funny without losing his air of sophistication. And he easily flipped the switch to well-informed when it came time to discuss politics and religion—both topics we were in total agreement on. When the entrée plates were taken away, I ordered dessert. Not because I wanted it, but because I didn't want the evening to end.

Afterward, Mason walked me to the front desk, where I asked the hotel clerk to extend my stay for one more night. He had asked me to dinner for the following evening, and I eagerly accepted.

The second night of conversation was even better than the first, and we were inseparable from that night on. Two months later, Mason asked me to marry him. Two months after his proposal, we eloped—much to the dismay of our friends and families. But those first few months set the tone for our entire marriage. We dove into a life together, feet first. We did things our way, by our rules. We didn't overthink too many decisions. We just lived life day by day, moment by moment.

Meeting Mason had been a perk to working at Maximum Capacity, but there were other perks, as well. The company had always been good to me. When Mason got sick, they were very sympathetic. They booked conferences and events that were close to home so that I didn't have to be away from Mason and Isaac overnight; and eventually, when Mason got really sick, I stopped attending conferences altogether. Instead, Maximum Capacity assigned me the task of researching information for a book intended to help businesses find solutions for keeping productivity and employee morale up in an ever-changing world where computers and technology were replacing them.

A Zillionaire Gets No Zzzs quickly became a bestseller, much to everyone's surprise. While I wasn't legally due any royalties, since my research and writing was as a hired employee, Maximum Capacity recognized my contribution by regularly paying me bonuses reflecting book sales. The bonuses allowed me to spend more time with Mason during the last year of his illness. Really, they could have kept me from ever participating in another conference, but my therapist recommended I start attending them again after everything had, as she put it, "settled down," so I did. She said I'd heal quicker if I "got back out there." She lied. I didn't heal quicker. In fact, I hadn't healed at all. But when you switch therapists three times, hoping one of them will have some real answers, and each makes the same recommendation, what is one to do?

"Mom?"

"Hmmm?" I asked, shaking away the memories and forcing myself back to the present.

"Why are you going to Morgantown?" he asked again.

"Oh. I have a conference. But I only have to attend the morning session, so we could take the back roads on the way home and see if we can find any places to browse through."

"Sure." Isaac smiled. "Sounds fun."

"It's a date, then," I said, catching him as he tried to dart out the door. I wrapped my arms around him tightly. He groaned, but returned the hug, wrapping his arms around my waist and burying his head.

I stood there with my arms around a piece of Mason, with all my treasures surrounding us. The moment lasted only seconds, but it felt like eternity. There really is such a feeling as eternity—when the world grows silent, then blurs away. When worries disappear and thoughts of what are to come cease.

I glanced again at all my finds. In another life, I wouldn't have given them a second thought. In another life, I would've called them dust collectors or trash bin fillers. In that life—the one I shared with Mason—I wouldn't have needed them.

But I did need them. I needed them more than I could ever know . . . and by the time I understood why, there was no reversing everything that had happened. By the time it began to make sense, none of it made any sense at all.

CHAPTER 3

Leaves

We woke early to make the four-hour drive to Morgantown, wishing too late we had driven up the night before. I was the first speaker of the day following the keynote speaker, and we planned on leaving right after lunch. That would give me plenty of time to take the leisurely route home in search of antiques.

I was surprised at the large crowd in attendance given that the conference was on a Tuesday. When it was my turn, I dutifully gave the speech I'd memorized from years of repetition, clicking through my PowerPoint presentation and inserting comedic relief when needed. When finished, I took a seat beside Isaac.

"Can we go now?" he whispered.

I reminded him he'd agreed to stick around through lunch, and I encouraged his patience by sharing how I'd seen the staff preparing plates of the largest chocolate chip cookies I'd ever seen for the lunch hour.

We both had difficulty sitting through the morning speakers; by the time we broke for lunch, my mind was already rummaging through items I hoped to find at an antique store on the way home.

The conference and dining sides of the conference room were separated by a curtained wall during the speaking portion of the conference, and about a half hour before the lunch break started, the aroma of pork and chicken seeped through the curtain, making Isaac's belly growl loudly, causing both of us to work really hard at stifling laughter. The more the smells permeated the room, the louder Isaac's belly growled.

As soon as the conference host dismissed us for lunch, Isaac headed straight for the dining side of the conference room where two large buffets, each draped with white tablecloths and covered with meats, steamed vegetables, and salads, were set up in the middle of the floor. Two round tables at each end displayed individually plated desserts of chocolate brownies and cheesecake. The promised platter of over-sized chocolate chip cookies acted as a centerpiece. On the far wall, a table held two coffee urns, a clear urn of sweet tea, and several small pitchers of water.

Isaac jumped in the quickly forming buffet line, while I scanned the crowd for people I'd not yet met in hopes of making the required connections with potential new clients. Two women in nearly-matching business suits stood talking in a far corner. I headed toward them, plastering a friendly smile on my face and extending my hand pleasantly as I approached. We shared introductions, then business cards, and I moved on to the next person.

I networked quickly, knowing Isaac would no longer be pacified after he finished scarfing down the baked chicken and mashed potatoes he'd piled on his plate. I was talking to a married couple who were in the startup phase of their new business when I noticed him starting on the cookies, and I knew I was running out of time.

I said goodbye to the couple as I handed them my business card. I headed toward Isaac, but halfway across the floor, a short, plump, pleasant-looking woman who smelled like fresh rose petals stepped into my path. Her hair was dark brown and teased high on the top and sides, while red glasses framed her jolly face. A bright gold chain dangled from the glasses and got lost in one of the fat rolls around her neck. She wore a black blazer and a long red skirt that came just to the top of her matching red heels. The blazer hung long enough that it covered her round stomach and thigh area. Other than the stretched fabric around the buttonholes indicating they were one breath away from popping, she looked very classy. We'd met before at some point, but it had been years ago and I couldn't remember in what capacity. I recalled her first name was Nancy, but her last name escaped me.

"Karla! It's so good to see you!"

I smiled in acknowledgement, hoping that would suffice given the fact Isaac had just finished his cookie and was now standing at the entrance door to the conference room expectantly motioning at the exit door. Nancy, however, had other plans, stopping my forward progress by hooking her arms under my armpits and around my shoulders as if we were best friends.

"I was so sorry to hear about your husband," she said, pulling out of the hug. Her stiff hair left a stickiness on my cheek I didn't like, and the smell of Aqua Net hairspray shrouded the smell of rose petals that initially made her charming.

Here we go again. Another someone who doesn't really know me, apologizing for something she knows nothing about. 'Your husband.' She probably doesn't even know his name.

Nancy put each of her hands on my cheeks and looked up at me with the same stare of condolence I'd seen hundreds of times. "So sorry," she repeated.

Isaac stood in the doorway tapping an imaginary watch on his wrist and making no attempt to hide his impatience.

"Thank you." I put my arms on her wrists and removed her hands from my face. "I really need to go, though. My son is with me," I nodded in his direction, "and we have somewhere we have to be."

She glanced over her shoulder. Isaac raised his eyebrows and gave a quick nod, and she waved excitedly as if she'd known him for years. "Well, then," she said, turning back to me. "I'll let you go, but if you need anything," she squeezed my arm, "anything at all, you just give me a call."

She didn't offer her phone number. She either assumed I already had it, or she didn't mean for me to call. The latter was likely the case, which was fine with me. I accepted her comment as a "goodbye" and hurried past her to Isaac.

We shared our annoyance by exchanging eye rolls. "Let's get while the gettin's good," I said, grabbing his arm and ducking out like two kids sneaking out of an adult party we weren't supposed to be attending in the first place.

We found the car in the parking lot quickly and got on the road before anyone else could interfere with our mission. A long drive was just what I needed after a morning of forced smiles and filthy handshakes.

As planned, I avoided the interstate, taking the curviest, narrowest roads I could find while keeping in the direction of home. About an hour into the drive, the road narrowed. It was still two lanes, as apparent by the faded solid double line down the middle of the road, but it was missing the white lines that usually trace the edges of the roadway.

The drive was beautiful. Sunlight flickered through the canopy of trees, highlighting remnants of orange and yellow leaves already scattered on the roadway. It was mid August in the Appalachian Mountains, but the days had been mild and the evenings cool and crisp, contributing to an early autumn.

It seemed the seasons had been out of whack for years—off by a month or so. When I was Isaac's age, it always snowed on Christmas. Always. Sometimes, it even snowed on Thanksgiving, but by Easter, it was sunny and warm. That wasn't the case anymore. We often had snow on Easter. Mason had once joked if we hid white eggs instead of colored ones, they would never be found until the snow melted.

Although they had many theories, scientists couldn't say with certainty why summers were being cut short—why winter so rudely invaded spring—but Mason said it was simply God's plan.

Despite the seasons being out of whack, West Virginia was still one of the remarkable states where one could clearly discern the four seasons—spring, summer, autumn, and winter—and enjoy the splendor each one brought. It was one of the most beautiful states on the map, and I was glad Maximum Capacity allowed me to work outside their New York headquarters and live instead in the Appalachian Mountains where Mason and I chose to make our home.

I cracked the window and inhaled the crisp air of early autumn. Autumn was my favorite time of year—when the leaves turned bright hues of red, purple, yellow, and orange, and then fluttered to the ground to decorate the undergrowth and road-ways.

I stared at the recently-fallen leaves beautifying the road-way and woods around me, and a notion came to me I had never considered before. The thought shattered the tranquility of the moment. A sensation of horror rose in my chest as the realiza-tion of *why* the leaves were scattered sunk in for the first time.

"They're dead," I whispered as soon as the thought came to me, making it real . . . and wrong. How can that be beautiful? The leaves changed as part of their dying process—a beautiful cover to hide something ugly—then, each was taken away by the wind or the rain or whatever decided it had a right to take it, leaving a gaping hole where it once hung.

What if the leaf didn't want to die? What if it had clung des-perately to the tree branch and begged, "No! Don't take me! I'm not ready!"

The sound of Isaac's breathing distracted me from the awful thought. I looked at him fondly. He'd dozed off a few miles back and was now sleeping peacefully in the passenger seat, his long eyelashes fluttering. Dreaming.

As I drove out of a turn and into a straight stretch, my eyes were once again drawn to the patchwork of colors garnishing the mountains far ahead. Orange, yellow, and purple leaves were clinging to trees along the mountainside. Just minutes ago, it was beautiful . . . but now, all I could think about was how tightly those leaves must be holding on. Thousands of leaves not ready to let go.

Good for you! Don't let go. Hang on!

I was so mesmerized by the thought that the road directly in front of me blurred. By the time I saw the deer dart in front of my vehicle, it was too late. Years of driving experience were forgotten as impulse took over. I swerved, but the deer turned and ran back in front of my vehicle. I jerked the wheel in the opposite direction. Tires squealed against the pavement as I slammed on the brakes, but I was unable to avoid him. The right front bumper clipped the deer's back end with a loud thud, and I caught a glimpse of brown as he tumbled down the passenger side of the car. His antlers and hoofs thumped against the doors as he hit. The front right tire dropped off the road and onto the shoulder, and I struggled to hold it steady until the car finally came to a halt.

I sat with my foot still on the brake and my knuckles white on the steering wheel, shaking.

Isaac!

I looked over, prepared to comfort him, only to find him still asleep. He hadn't moved. I unclenched my fists and raised my trembling hands to my face. I shook my head in both disbelief and amusement, the sight of him peacefully dreaming partially washing away the drama of what had just happened.

I realized I was still halfway on the road, so I let off the brake, straightened the wheel, and let the vehicle roll to the side of the road, clear of any vehicles that might pass by. I flipped on the hazard lights and took a few deep breaths before getting out to inspect the damage.

I closed the car door gently so as not to wake Isaac and stood on the passenger side of the vehicle with my eyes temporarily closed, mentally preparing for the damage I knew I'd see. Slowly, I opened my eyes, but the shock came from what I *didn't* see. There was no damage! Deer hair poked out of the crevices all along the side of the vehicle, and a white powdery substance coated the Accord's red paint, but there wasn't a single dent or scratch on the entire vehicle.

I examined it closely, running my hand down the side. Nothing! I was confused. The sound of crumpling metal as the deer hit was still fresh in my mind. Had I imagined I'd hit him harder than I actually had—my senses heightened in the moment?

I got back in the vehicle, bewildered, and slammed the car door shut without thinking.

Isaac sat up in his seat. "Hey!" he said, immediately wide awake with excitement. "You found one!"

I followed his gaze to a sign on the side of the road just a few yards ahead. It was a small sign with the words *Crawley Antiques* painted in faded red letters against a pale-yellow background. Below *Crawley Antiques*, a red arrow pointed to a dirt road that angled off from the paved road. The sign was predominantly hidden behind overgrown brush. Had the deer not jumped out in front of us, I would never have seen it.

"So I did," I said, trying to hide my surprise.

I decided not to tell Isaac about the near-calamity he'd slept through—partly because it didn't seem necessary, but mostly because, knowing Isaac, he'd be upset he missed the whole thing.

I turned the car onto the dirt road, and about a hundred yards down, I spotted the promised antique store. I halted the car and took a minute to take in the view. Beautifully-faded barn boards not yet defiled by a paintbrush covered the outside of the building. Two paneled windows, one on each side of a green screen door, balanced the front of the store charmingly. A metal roof, speckled with maroon rust, extended out onto four wooden posts that ran directly into the ground, creating a porch-like area with a dirt floor. A narrow strip of patchy green grass separated the store's porch from a parking lot.

Brightly colored leaves were scattered everywhere—on the roof, the grass, and all over the graveled parking lot. I smiled. If not for the distraction the leaves had caused just prior to the deer, we'd have never found the store in the first place. The irony of their now-welcoming presence was not lost on me.

Large items cluttered the front of the store—too many to take in all at once—and several smaller items were tucked away under the protection of the covered porch.

"What do you think?" I asked.

"Doesn't look very big," Isaac answered, a bit disappointed.

He was right. At first glance, it didn't seem very big, but I leaned to the side and noticed the side of the building indicated it was fairly deep.

"I think it's bigger than it looks," I said, raising my eyebrows and restoring his excitement.

I let the car drift down the remainder of the road, and I turned into the empty parking lot, positioning the vehicle to face the store about twenty yards from the entrance. The empty parking lot led me to believe the store may be closed, but a sign on the store read, "Come on in," so I held out hope.

I turned to Isaac, who was looking at me with a mischievous smile while rubbing his hands together briskly. "Here we go," he said, and he was out of the vehicle before I could get the key out of the ignition.

I followed suit quickly and locked the door with the car remote. At the sound of the second beep, indicating all four doors had locked, Isaac turned to me, anticipation spilling out all over his face. "Can I go ahead?"

"Yes, but not too far. And do not leave the building or go to the bathroom without letting me know," I answered sternly, reminding him of the rules.

Isaac rolled his eyes, but nodded his understanding. Then, he darted across the parking lot and disappeared through the screen door of the store.

I took my time walking across the parking lot, taking in all my eyes would allow. A large, rusted red farm tractor sat at the left corner of the building with an old wash basin full of colorful flowers balanced on its oversized back tire. A tall water barrel stood near the front door with an old Coca-Cola crate full of green canning jars sitting on its top. Birdhouses hung from various metal hooks along the front of the building. Additional birdhouses sat atop wooden posts stuck in the grass that bridged the parking lot and store. A long, cracked bench that had presumably once made its home in a church sat to the right of the door. A plaque was mounted on its back with the words, *Let the weary rest,* carved into it. Below the words, *Isaiah 28:12* was written.

I gave the rest of the items outside the store—an outdoor

metal bench, a concrete water fountain, a canning jar drying rack—a quick glance before grabbing the small metal handle of the screen door. A surge of electricity shot through me as I gripped the handle—not an alarming amount, but a rippling vibration. The sensation was more than that of being shocked via static electricity, but it didn't have the intense spark that caused one to flinch. It pulsated through my fingertips and traveled up my arm to my chest. I'd never felt anything like it before, and I wondered for a brief moment if I was having a heart attack. But the sensation passed quickly, and I was too excited about what I might find inside to give the phenomenon any more attention as I pulled open the door.

CHAPTER 4

Crawley

The feather-light door slammed shut behind me, and a gold bell tied from a string above the door clanged loudly, announcing my arrival.

A kind-looking elderly woman with graying hair and silver glasses looked up from behind the counter. She smiled warmly but didn't yell out the annoying "Welcome!" that many store owners do. I liked her already.

I returned her smile and breathed in the sweet, musty air. It was a delightful smell and one I missed if I went too many days without it. A mixture of dirt, dust, and rose petals.

But it wasn't only the smell that greeted me. The entire space gently wrapped its arms around me as one welcomes an old friend. Dim lights from bulbs overhead mixed with streams of sunlight as it spilled through the doors and windows, providing a perfect glow to the space—a perfect warmth not found anywhere else.

Isaac and I—the Antiquing Aristocrats, as we jokingly had come to call ourselves—had different shopping techniques. He darted around quickly from item to item, as if he couldn't look at everything quickly enough, while I walked slowly, making sure to give every item in every space an opportunity to speak to me— to know I was in the room, in case it had been searching for me.

How we each shopped didn't matter. Both our shopping techniques were correct. His worked for him and mine worked for me. What mattered was that, by becoming the Antiquing Aristocrats, we had discovered an antidote to help with healing—something of which we'd been deprived.

I looked around, momentarily overwhelmed by the smorgasbord of items. While most antique stores had sections divided off for various vendors, antique dealers, and crafters, this store didn't. Usually, one could tell a vendor's interest by the items bunched together in their stall; one vendor might choose to fill their corner of the store with beeswax candles and candle holders, while another might fill their space with old quilts, pillows, and rare books. But this store was different. This store felt as if the items were the collection of one individual. Nothing was arranged in any particular order. Glass plates and uniquely shaped pitchers, normally found encased in curio cabinets or shelved in armoires, were scattered along the worn wooden floor. Colorful oil paintings, typically hung carefully from hooks on the walls, sat propped up against hope chests and travel trunks. Other than the paths cleared for walking, the place more closely resembled an attic, where items had been haphazardly placed and forgotten, than a store.

I scanned the distance of the space as far as my eyes would allow. Large pieces of covered furniture sprouted up like proud mountains across a country landscape. I strained my eyes to see further, but no matter how much I strained, I couldn't see the back wall of the building. The thought of how big the store might be suddenly scared me.

"Marco?!" I called out.

Marco Polo was a childhood game that had become my security blanket over the years. Mason and I played it first, long before Isaac was born. If we got separated while shopping, either by accident or intentionally, one of us would call out "Marco" and the other would reply "Polo." We were able to pinpoint each other's location in the store and continue shopping peacefully. When Isaac got old enough to wander off on his own, we began playing the game with him.

"Polo!" Isaac's voice called out from my close right.

I released a comfortable sigh and began my leisure walk through the store. I spotted a headboard standing six feet tall to my right covered in brown leather with perfectly spaced nail heads trimming its shape. Directly in front of it was its matching footboard, which was made smartly into a bench. I imagined a young girl sitting on the benched-footboard lacing up her white ballroom shoes.

Lying in the floor nearby was a silver rose-embossed brush and mirror set, and I watched the girl pick up the brush and brush her hair, fifty strokes, before pinning it into an intricate updo.

"Look, mom!" Isaac came running up with something in his hand.

I blinked the girl away. "What is it?" I asked, glancing down at what he'd found. It was a small nutcracker, about the size of his palm. Time had not been its friend. Paint had faded so severely from its face that it was left with only its right eye. The paint of its once-bright blue suit had also faded, displaying patches of solid wood beneath, and the soldier's cracked crown gave an eerie testimony of his maltreatment.

"It's an old nutcracker." He thrust it out for observation, a large smile across his face.

"Old is an understatement. How about abused?"

He turned it over for my inspection. "There's no price on it."

Why nutcrackers, I didn't know, but Isaac had collected them most of his life. He picked up his first one when he was two years old while riding in the shopping cart at a retail store. I was hurriedly finishing up my last-minute Christmas shopping when I carelessly parked the cart too close to one of the shelves full of Christmas decorations. Isaac's chubby little hand curiously plucked a tiny green nutcracker off the shelf and refused to let it go. Too into the Christmas spirit to deny him, I told the cashier to ring it up; but Isaac wouldn't loosen his grip long enough for the young lady to scan it. She ended up coming around the counter and scanning it with her hand-held device while Isaac gave her the death stare for fear she was going to try to take it from him. He'd gotten a new nutcracker every year thereafter. Actually, he'd gotten more than one a year, as his collection was now at thirty-something and he was only nine.

"It's probably not too much. Keep it with you and we'll ask the price when we're finished shopping. I'm sure you'll be able to afford it."

"Will *you* buy it for me?" he asked, always one for holding onto his own savings and preferring to spend mine.

"Tell you what," I answered. "Since you had to sit through that boring conference, I'll buy it for you. How's that sound?"

"Even if it's a hundred dollars?" He smirked.

"It won't be a hundred dollars. But yes, even if it's a hundred dollars."

He gave me a hug and mumbled a quick "thank you" before dashing down the aisle to continue his hunt.

I smiled as I watched him navigate the aisle, then disappear out of sight. I realized, looking at the store's disarray, I wouldn't be able to leisurely stroll through items as I was accustomed to doing. I'd need to take more time than usual and move things around, ensuring I'd see everything . . . and everything had a chance to see me. I began picking things up, aware of a deep fear that the one item that brought me here might be buried so deep I'd never find it.

A pile of folded linens lay on top of a rollback desk. I flipped through them gently. The fabric of each was very delicate—white doilies and handkerchiefs with hand-stitched colorful flowers on their corners. They were beautiful, but none of them especially caught my eye.

But something else did. Or *someone*. There was an old man in one of the aisles. He was tall and slim with a white, balding head. I felt him before I saw him because he was staring at me intensely.

I returned his stare, and when he made no attempt to avert his gaze from mine, I smiled, but he didn't return the courtesy. Finally, after a few seconds, he twitched his nose and hurried away.

"Marco!" I cried out, disturbed by the man's strangeness.

"Polo!"

I released the breath I'd unknowingly been holding and pushed away my paranoia. *It's just an old man. Poor thing. I probably made* him *nervous.*

I continued shopping. A Norman Rockwell plate hung on a white door. It was a portrait of an old man sitting with an old lady in front of a fireplace, each of them holding small cups and saucers. I knew the plate well; it was one in a series of four, and the only one I already owned. It was passed down to me by my Aunt Nina, who said she gave the other three plates to her "other three favorite nieces." The four plates would probably never be together again.

I searched on, stepping over items, reaching into cabinets, and poking around on shelves. I opened the doors of a buffet hutch and drew in the robust aroma of old wood and varnish. I'd heard some people detest the smell, but I inhaled it like it was the cure for a relenting headache others hadn't found the cure for yet. I fumbled through the small items inside, but nothing captivated my attention.

I spotted a sizeable black hope chest with brown, leather-strapped buckles stretched across its dome-shaped lid. I lifted the lid and inadvertently caught a glimpse of my watch, realizing I had no idea how long I'd been rummaging through items. I hadn't noticed what time it was when we arrived, so I had no way to gauge how long we'd been in the store . . . or how much time had passed since I'd last heard from Isaac.

"Marco!" I squatted down and sifted through the items piled inside the hope chest. I moved a hand-stitched quilt aside only to find more quilts. The quilts were heavy. They all had plain brown backs, but the patchwork on each of the fronts was unique and colorful. Some of them had intricate patterns and some were simple block patterns, but each was exceptional in its own way. Hours and hours of time and work must have gone into making them. I pulled one onto my lap and stared at the pattern made to look like a flower garden. I ran my fingertips over one of the flower's triangle petals. It felt old, yet crisp and new at the same time. I imagined it draped over the bed of a young bride on her wedding night.

I folded the quilt, laid it back in the hope chest, and shut the lid. I started to shuffle through some items on the floor at the base of the chest before realizing I hadn't heard Isaac answer me.

Or had he?

"Marco?" I called out again, this time standing up to listen for him.

No answer.

I made my way to one of the aisles in the center of the store and called out again, "Marco!"

Still no answer.

The store was big and deep. If he was at the back of the store, he probably couldn't hear me. "Marco!" I called out as I walked toward the back of the store. But there was no resounding "Polo."

A pang of worry came over me and I quickly pushed it aside. Parents always worry. They worry if their child doesn't come out of the public bathroom as quickly as they think they should, or they worry if their teenage child doesn't call at four o'clock to let them know they arrived at soccer practice safely. But it's almost always unfounded. The restroom child had to wait for a stall in the bathroom, or their teenage child calls at five after four instead of four o'clock on the dot. I had no logical reason to worry.

"Marco!" I called out loudly, walking more briskly, stopping along the way to check between each aisle and search anywhere he might be. "Isaac?!"

I finally reached the back of the store, both relieved and dismayed—relieved to find the store had a back, and dismayed because Isaac was nowhere to be found.

I stopped and listened for him. I listened without moving, hoping to hear him rummaging through items or running down an aisle, but the only sound was the humming of a halogen light bulb flickering overhead.

Maybe he had to use the bathroom and couldn't find me to let me know.

I looked for a sign indicating a bathroom was nearby; first walking slowly, then more quickly, hoping to see a bathroom door. Or Isaac.

"Isaac?" I yelled. "Isaac, where are you?"

There were no doors leading to a bathroom. There were no doors leading anywhere—not to an office or a storage room, or even one that might lead outside.

Okay, this is actually good. This means he went to the front of the store, and we just missed each other somehow.

I jogged the distance to the counter where the nice lady had smiled at me when I entered. I was trying very hard to control my fear and think logically, but the closer I got to the front of the store, the more I knew something wasn't right. I *felt* it. It wasn't a deep feeling down in my gut, but a feeling that surfaced quickly and crawled all over my skin. It overwhelmed my entire being, urging me to panic . . . to hurry up and find him.

The lady who had been at the counter was no longer there.

I glanced around the room quickly, my eyes searching every darkened corner and my ears intently listening. I didn't see anybody—not the store clerk, not the creepy old man who'd made me uneasy . . . and not Isaac.

"Isaac!!" I screamed as loudly as I could.

There was no echo from my cry.

There was no answer from Isaac.

There was nothing. Only silence.

He went to the car. That's where he went.

I was afraid to leave the store for fear he would come looking for me, but I knew I had to check the vehicle. I ran outside in a hurry, glancing back and forth from the store front to the car the entire time in case he came out the door while I was in the parking lot.

From a distance, I couldn't see him in the vehicle, but the sun was reflecting on the car's windshield, making it difficult to see inside. As I got closer, I unlocked the door with the remote.

I unlocked the door. I froze in my tracks and looked down at the remote in my hand. He couldn't have gotten in the car with the doors locked. I knew it was true, but I forced myself to take the last few steps and open the door anyway.

Any glimmer of hope that he would be lying down napping in the back seat, having gotten tired of waiting on me, faded and I begrudgingly accepted the disappointment I had set myself up for.

I ran back to the store, panic-stricken, dead leaves crunching underfoot, and the bell above the door mocking as the screen door slammed shut behind me.

"Isaac!" I yelled once more, only to make real what I already knew. Isaac was gone.

CHAPTER 5

The Search

The store clerk reappeared at the sound of my screams, and we searched the store together with the same result—no Isaac.

Two police officers arrived at the store a half hour later. They searched the store thoroughly, looking under covered items and in anything that was large enough to hold a nine-year-old boy. Finally, they called for backup; and over the next several hours, twelve more officers arrived—two of them with search dogs. After searching the entire store again, they spent hours searching the woods around the store, looking for cliffs or drop-offs where Isaac might have stumbled.

They searched all the places I'd already searched. They called out his name in vain, just as I had done.

While the officers searched, one young female officer questioned me repeatedly. "Where were you traveling from? What time did you arrive at the store? Did you see anyone else in the store?"

I answered her questions as best I could. I told her about the store owner and the old man. I told her no other vehicles had been parked in the parking lot when we arrived. I told her I didn't know what time we'd arrived.

"How long had it been since you last saw or spoke with your son before you noticed he was missing?"

That was another question I didn't know the answer to, and I diverted my eyes in shame when I told her. How long had it been since Isaac had brought me the nutcracker, excited about his find? It could have been minutes. It may have been an hour. I'd lost track of time those moments after we last spoke—too focused on rummaging through items, looking for my next treasure.

"Did you hear anything out of the ordinary?"

Again, I didn't know, but I had somberly shaken my head no.

But what if there *had been* something out of the ordinary, and I had been too immersed in my world of antiques to hear? What if Isaac had called out, and I hadn't heard him? What if he had kicked over a vase or a lamp as he was being drug out of the store, mouth covered, trusting I would hear and come running?

Three weeks later, the thought still haunted me—not just at night when sleep wouldn't come, but during the waking hours, as well.

And the man haunted me—the tall, balding man I told the police about. The one who had made a brief but disturbing appearance just before Isaac went missing. The creepy old man who was also missing, and who police doubted even existed because the store clerk told them she never saw him. She'd claimed only Isaac and I had been in the store that day; but it was hard to believe she hadn't seen or heard him . . . not with the clanging bell over the door announcing everyone's arrival and departure.

And now the woman was missing. She was not just the store clerk, but also the store's owner. After she'd given her statement to the police, she closed her store indefinitely. I knew, because in the three weeks since Isaac's disappearance, I had been to the store four times, making the forty-five-minute drive just to sit in the parking lot and stare at the store where yellow police tape still surrounded the search area. I sat there for hours, willing Isaac to walk out the door and across the parking lot. Willing him to get in the car and laugh, "Gotcha, mom!"

The claim that the store owner hadn't seen or heard the man, and the fact that she and the man were now both missing, led me to believe they were in cahoots with each other. Of all the scenarios I played out in my head, it was the only one that made sense. For whatever reason, they had conspired to take Isaac.

The notion brought a surprising, yet eerie, comfort. After all, the woman would never hurt a child. She was too elderly and kind. She was gentle. I recalled the tenderness of her frail hand rubbing my back as I sobbed and we waited for the police to arrive. She'd whispered soothing words that were just gibberish at the time, but they flowed sweetly from her lips. So, if they had taken him, he was alive somewhere. Unhappy, perhaps, but alive.

It was the only thought that kept me sane as I stood in Isaac's bedroom missing him beyond words. The hope that he was alive was the only thing keeping me from swallowing an entire bottle of sleeping pills and curling up for an infinite sleep on his bedroom floor.

I looked around his room. It was full of his favorite things—a hodgepodge of all the items that made him happy. His dark blue ceiling was covered with more than two hundred forty glow-in-the-dark stars he and I had strategically placed into actual constellation patterns. He was only six years old then, standing on the top bunk of his bed as he reached to the ceiling, announcing he was going to be an astronaut one day.

The astronaut dream was short lived. It died the moment he first stepped onto a football field. From that day forward, he swore he'd one day run the ball for the St. Louis Rams.

The football trophy he won that first year served as a book end for a row of children's story books sitting on the bottom of his bookshelf. They were his favorites when he was younger. We used to read them together before bed every night . . . but we hadn't read together in years. The books didn't mean much to him these days, but they had priceless meaning to me. I imagined one day I would read them to my grandbabies. I told him as much once, and he laughed hysterically at the notion I'd ever be a grandma.

What if he was right? What if I'd never be a grandma? What if we never found him so I could be? I hadn't yet come to terms with the fact that I was no longer a wife, and now I had to accept that I was no longer a mother and would never be a grandmother?

I refused to believe it, and I allowed my mind to be distracted by other items in Isaac's room. I scanned his bookshelf. The top shelf held the taller trophies he'd earned over the years playing every sport imaginable—from T-ball to basketball to football—but there was no mistaking which sport was his favorite; the number of trophies featuring a helmeted runner holding a tucked football far outnumbered the others.

"You gonna play basketball again this year?" Mason had asked Isaac one day while passing the football in the front yard.

"I guess," Isaac had answered with a shrug.

I'd been sitting on the front porch steps watching.

"You don't sound very excited," Mason commented. "You don't like basketball?"

"It's okay. It passes time 'til football season comes back around."

I smiled at the memory as I ran my fingers across the bottom of one of the trophies.

The three middle shelves were reserved for his collectibles—items that seemed odd to me, but found meaning with him. Seashells. Rocks and amethysts. A shark tooth. A Magic Eight Ball. Figurines of Abraham Lincoln.

I ran my fingers along the items, touching the pointed beard on a miniature statue of the Abraham Lincoln Memorial that Isaac had gotten while on a family vacation to Washington, D.C. I smiled, thinking of how he'd explained that Lincoln was his favorite historical character because of the stories he'd read of Abe's honesty and his loyalty to his family.

My smile faded. *Isaac was a good boy. Why had I let this happen to him?*

I picked up the Eight Ball. How many questions had we asked it? How many times had it been right with answers like "Probably" and "Undecided?" I struggled with the idea of shaking it gently and asking the question I needed answered: *Where is Isaac?*

"Only God knows, really," Isaac once said, relaying what he'd been taught at Langston Baptist Academy where he attended school for several years before Mason died. After Mason died, I enrolled Isaac in public school. I decided the faith-based school didn't need my tuition money if they were going to use it to spread falsehoods about how good and kind God was. More importantly, Isaac didn't need his head filled with lies of how death is not a bad thing, but a new beginning.

"Yes," I had replied to Isaac's Eight Ball comment, "but doesn't God sometimes communicate through things like clouds and burning bushes?" At the time, I still believed God *did* communicate in strange and unusual ways.

Isaac smiled. "But an Eight Ball, mom? I don't think so."

I put the Eight Ball back. Isaac was right. Even if God chose to communicate, he wouldn't do it with an Eight Ball. Besides, it'd been my experience that God didn't choose to communicate at all these days.

Additional smaller trophies sat atop his dresser, and medals dangled from his top bunk bed. We'd removed the bottom bunk from his bed years ago and turned the empty space underneath into a fort by hanging a curtain from the top bunk. Isaac and his best friend, William, had spent many nights camping in the indoor fort. Like the children's books, Isaac had outgrown the fort a long time ago and he now used the curtained space to hide stuffed animals he secretly still cherished. He also tossed sports balls behind the curtain in his weekly rush to clean his room.

I picked up a Spalding football from the pile. It was the fourth football I'd purchased over the years. His first had busted apart at the seams from the hours of tossing he and Mason had done, the second had been left in the yard, exposed to the elements one too many times, and the third simply disappeared one day. I tossed the ball in the air and watched it spiral back into my hands, remembering how Isaac had been a natural on the field. He ran a 93-yard touchdown in the first game he ever played, and he finished last year's season by scoring the two-point conversion that won his team the championship.

I laid the ball back in its place and spied the cast that had been cut away from his left arm some years ago. He broke it on the first day of football practice that year, landing on it in such a way that both the ulna and radius twisted and snapped. He'd gotten up after his fall, despite his arm dangling in a distorted s-shape, and finished the drill. It was a horrible day. Mason and I had both run to him on the field, but Mason got to him first. He scooped him up in his arms and, without saying a word, raced with him to the vehicle. Mason jumped in the back seat with Isaac, so I instinctively climbed behind the wheel and drove to the hospital where Isaac was quickly attended to and cared for.

I blinked, large hot tears streaming down my face. We had both been there for Isaac that day, but neither had been there for him this time. Mason couldn't be, and I simply hadn't been. Mason would have been there for him had he been able to. He'd have done a better job protecting Isaac than I had. He'd have never let this happen.

I failed him! I failed both of them!

"I'm sorry!" I screamed, throwing the cast at the wall and accidentally hitting a framed picture that had been sitting on the nightstand by Isaac's bed. It came crashing to the floor, face down. I picked it up and ran my thumb over the beautiful faces staring at me through the frame. It was a picture of Mason and Isaac when Isaac was four. Mason was squatting beside Isaac, and they were holding fishing poles near a river bank. I touched Mason's cheek. "Please help me. Do you know where our son is?" I blinked another tear, shaking . . . afraid to ask the next question: *Is he with you?*

I didn't ask. I couldn't. I closed my eyes and willed Mason to send me a sign that Isaac was okay. I squeezed my eyes tight and listened, disappointed that the only sound I heard was the pounding of my heart in my chest.

And then, suddenly, whispers . . . the kind some say is the conscience and others say is the very core of your soul hissing. It was so loud! Whisper upon whisper—so powerful and numerous that none of the whispers made any sense, each drowning out the other.

Then, the whispers were silenced by the sound of a scream. Isaac's scream. He called out to me in the darkness—his boyish tone ricocheting off the walls of my heart, punching like a fist to my chest, and then disappearing beyond earshot . . . beyond my reach . . . and the hope I'd had just moments earlier disappeared with the sound of Isaac's screams.

And there it was—the last living part of me gone. I knew it. I felt part of me die when Mason passed, so I knew what internal death felt like. I couldn't go through it again. There wasn't any part of me that would survive this time—not my desire to fight, not my desire to believe, and certainly not my desire to live.

Death is a process, even internal death. It always starts with faith. With Mason, I'd had faith God would heal him. This time, with Isaac, I'd had faith I would find him within a few short minutes, and then, within a few short hours. I even had faith that he'd be found safe within a few short days. But that hope gradually succumbed to reality.

Next is anger—anger that nobody is doing anything fast enough. With Mason, I was angry at the doctors for being slow with a diagnoses and treatment . . . and for not providing the right medications that could heal him. With Isaac, I was angry that the police didn't find him quickly. Everyone knows the longer it takes to find a child, the slimmer the chances of finding them at all. And there was anger at God for allowing such horrible things to happen in the first place.

And finally, grief. So much grief! Grief when Mason died, and now grief that I hadn't been able to keep Isaac safe—that he was somewhere needing me. Or worse, that he was gone . . . just like Mason . . . and I'd never see either of them again.

There was a process to internal death—steps one goes through—and I had reached the end.

A tear rolled down my cheek, and I wiped it away with the back of my hand just as the doorbell rang. Like the toll of church bells calling mourners to a funeral, I knew the bell chiming meant nothing good. I felt it, so I took a deep breath and waited.

CHAPTER 6

Lies, All Lies

I heard Cheryl downstairs scurrying across the floor to answer the door.

Cheryl was my only sibling. She was younger than me by two years, but she had taken on the role of older sister too many times to count. Unlike me, she had never married, nor had children. She was an artist who performed the duties of her craft from the sanctity of her home studio. She was very talented and made more than enough on the sales of her paintings to provide a decent income.

Not only was she talented, she was beautiful—in appearance and in spirit. Her curly blonde, shoulder-length hair framed her round face. She had bright blue eyes she'd inherited from our paternal grandfather, and a beautiful smile I can only assume she inherited from an angel. She was so stunning.

In addition to her beauty, she had an infectious laugh that came from deep in her soul. Except now. There wasn't anything funny about what was happening now. There was nothing to find humor in—nothing to bring about a smile. She knew it as well as I did, so she didn't even try to make me laugh. Not once.

Instead, she'd been here since the day Isaac disappeared, doing everything for me. She cooked and cleaned. She woke me from nightmares and comforted me as best she could until daybreak. She answered phone calls and doorbells.

Once, I heard her return a call to Maximum Capacity and tell them I'd be out for an "indefinite amount of time." I would have never returned their call. Returning to work was the last thing on my mind, but Cheryl knew the things that needed to be done and she did them . . . just as she had when Mason died.

During the day, I lay in bed and listened to her moving

around downstairs, keeping the house in order. Sometimes I'd hear her talking to people just after the chime of the doorbell or the ring of the telephone. I'd hear their muffled voices, and then I'd hear the visitor leave, or I'd hear Cheryl hang up the phone because she was kind enough to turn them away, knowing company wasn't what I needed right now.

Still other times, when I knew for certain there was no one at the door or on the phone, I'd hear her muffled words between soft sobs: "Please," and "I have faith in You." I knew who she was talking to, and I believed with all my heart it would do no good. It hadn't done any good when I'd made those same desperate pleas for Mason.

"How is she doing?" I heard voices downstairs and recognized immediately that one of the voices was Pastor Dan. He'd been our family's pastor for the past fourteen years.

Turn him away like you've done everyone else, Cheryl. Turn him away. I don't want to talk to him!

"The same," Cheryl said. "You can talk to her."

No! I don't want to talk to him! Tell him to leave!

But I heard Pastor Dan's footsteps on the stairs, and then I heard him go down the hallway to my bedroom.

"Karla?" The creaking of my bedroom door told me he'd opened it to find I wasn't there.

I heard him walking toward Isaac's room. "Karla?"

I hurried out and closed the door behind me. I couldn't stop him from invading my space, but I wasn't going to let him invade Isaac's.

I closed the door and walked over to a bench situated in the dormered window of our Cape Cod. Mason had enlisted the help of Isaac to custom-build it years ago. Isaac was too little to be much help, but together they'd spent about a week on the project.

I sat down and rubbed my hand over the dark-stained oak, recalling how Mason had explained each step to Isaac, even though Isaac was too young to retain the information. The memory brought a smile, followed closely by sorrow. *Must everything remind me of what I've lost? Must I constantly be tortured?*

Pastor Dan's heels made a clicking sound as he walked the rest of the way down the hallway and stood at the bench in front of me. His shiny black shoes came into sight as I sat hunched over, and I followed his form from his shoes, past his light brown slacks and dark jacket, to his necktie. I stared at it for a few seconds—it was navy with silver crosses printed all over it—and finally, my eyes landed upon his face.

It seemed odd that Pastor Dan had been our pastor for more than a decade and was not yet in his forties. According to his sermons, he started preaching when he was twenty-two, having known his entire life he'd been called to spread the word of God. Serving God must have provided an easy life for him, as his short brown hair showed no signs of the gray that usually appears around the fourth decade of life. He took off his Harry-Potter-like glasses and unbuttoned his jacket as he sat down beside me. He sat quietly for what seemed like eternity before finally taking my hand in his. "I want you to know I'm here. I've been praying, and if there's anything else I can do—"

Like what? What could he do? Surely he knew from his many years of comforting the sick and afflicted that there wasn't anything he could do in a time like this. Nothing that could make me feel better or help in any way. Surely he'd asked a hundred people the same question a hundred times: "Is there anything I can do for you?" and surely he'd been given the same answer each time.

Could he take away cancer?

No.

Could he stop a wife from cheating on her husband?

No.

Could he bring back a loved one from the dead?

No.

I knew he had a duty as a pastor to ask, but I still didn't want or need him to; and for a brief second, I felt sorry for him. He was just doing his job, hoping beyond hope that someday someone would say, "Yes, Pastor, you *can* help." Hoping that one day someone would say, "Yes, I would love for my church family to prepare meals for me or clean my home. That would make things *so much better*."

But what he fails to realize is that the sick of heart don't care about clean homes or full stomachs. They only care about having their futile prayers answered. They want Pastor Dan to do for them what God won't. They want him to bring back their loved one or heal their illness.

Pastor Dan squeezed my hand. "Karla? Karla, did you hear me?"

He was getting on my nerves already. I was heartbroken, not deaf. I was angry, not stupid. In fact, he *could* do something for me. He could leave me alone. He could spare me whatever words of wisdom he came to share and be on his way.

"All hope is not gone," he said. "We are all praying, and I know God is listening."

I wiggled uncomfortably and tried to pull my hand from his, but it felt numb.

Didn't he know I had no doubt that God was listening? *That* was the point. I *knew* God was listening. I *knew* he heard my cries and desperate pleas. He heard them and chose to *ignore* them. In just two short years, he had taken everything from me. And why? What had I done to deserve it? What had Mason done? Or Isaac?

"God knows your pain," he continued, placing his free hand on my shoulder, "and he's going to help you through it."

The sermon Pastor Dan was churning out was familiar. He'd preached it when Mason died. He said God understood how painful it was to watch Mason suffer and die because God had watched his own son suffer and die when he sent him to die on the cross for our sins. He said, because God sent his son to die, there is life after death for all those who believe. He said one day I'd see Mason again.

The words had brought some comfort right after Mason's death. Not enough to return me to church, but some.

Now, they meant nothing.

I blocked out Pastor Dan's words, turning his voice into a distant hum. I didn't need to hear again the same words I'd heard two years ago—words that didn't change or fix anything. But try as I might, I couldn't block him out completely.

". . . loves you . . ." Pastor Dan's words kept poking through the barrier I'd put up. "God lost His son, too."

Anger swelled inside me, and I jerked away from him with so much force even I didn't know where my strength had come from.

Pastor Dan startled back.

When did God lose his son?!

If I asked the question out loud, Pastor Dan would tell me that God lost his son when his son died on the cross, but that was a lie! God never lost his son. Jesus went from the cross straight into his father's arms. They were together in the beginning when God created the heavens and the Earth, and they're together still today, so not once has God gone without his son. Not once! Even when Jesus walked this Earth in human form, God was with him. They talked many times. No matter where Jesus was or what he was doing, God saw him and watched over him.

I was sick with the truth that was becoming so evident.

"Karla?!" There was worry in Pastor Dan's voice.

My mind raced. *God was never without his son! Never!! But I was supposed to go without mine?!*

"Karla?!"

My mind was rambling now with a truth that was becoming clearer. *Yes, God watched his son suffer and die, but they were never apart. NEVER! So how could he possibly know how I feel?*

He couldn't!

I was trembling with anger. My entire body was shaking.

"Cheryl!" Pastor Dan screamed. "Somebody!" He sounded panicked . . . as if he didn't know what to do with me.

I ran to my bedroom and slammed the door shut. I turned the lock to keep out anyone who might try to come in. I paced the floor and frantically twisted the gold band on my finger. I wanted desperately to make untrue the truth I'd realized, but instead, the truth was becoming clearer with every passing moment.

I sat on the edge of my bed and tried to calm myself, but the more I realized God had no idea what I was going through, the angrier I got.

Ever since Isaac's disappearance, the one thing that had brought any level of comfort was believing I'd find Isaac. God and I weren't on speaking terms, but I believed he knew my pain—that he, too, had lost a child—and that he wouldn't allow that to happen to *me*. Not after all he'd already taken.

I recalled how blessed I felt when I found out I was having a son—the same gift God gave himself. But God gave himself a son for keeps. He gave me a son just to take him away. God didn't know what that pain felt like because God's son was never taken from him.

Unlike God—who could always look at his son and see that he was safe—I couldn't look in on Isaac or talk with him daily. I didn't even know where my son was! A day did not pass when God didn't know where *his* son was!! A day did not pass when God was not able to speak with his son and know he was safe.

No, God didn't understand. He couldn't.

Anger raged inside me. It burned in my stomach and boiled up into my face, moistening my cheeks like steam from a furnace. The heat spread all over, searing my entire body, making me nauseous and disoriented. For a moment, the room turned black, and I thought I was going to pass out. I shook violently, unable to control the burning sensation flaming throughout my entire body.

I hated God. He was not a loving God at all. He was a selfish God who wouldn't give to me what he'd given to himself—a relationship with my loved ones that could never be severed.

"Karla!" Pastor Dan was pounding on the door. "Cheryl! Get help!"

God was an Indian giver. That's exactly what he was. And I

hated him!

I looked up, imagining God sitting on his gold, jewel-encrusted throne, his son sitting to his right. Behind them, a cloudless blue sky and the sound of children playing all around them.

I watched God lean in toward his son and whisper, and I heard them laughing.

He was mocking me!

"Go ahead!" The words spewed off my tongue and onto my lips in a white froth. *"Sit there with your son while my son is missing. Laugh and have a glorious time."* My teeth were clenched so tightly I couldn't tell if I was actually saying the words or just yelling them in my mind. *"I don't need you!"*

I stood up, keeping my eyes on the vision I'd created—that I knew existed. I shook my finger, pointing and blaming. *"I don't need you. You hear me? I don't need you! I will find my son all by myself!"* My fingernails dug into the palm of my hand, my accusing finger now clenched into a fist. *"And you will not take him from me again. Do you hear me?! You WILL NOT take him!"*

I heard Pastor Dan fiddling with keys outside the door. Cheryl must have given them to him.

"Karla, honey," she was saying. "It's okay. I'm here."

I had to get out of here. I grabbed my jacket and heard my car keys jangle in the pocket, still there from my last drive to Crawley Antiques. I opened my bedroom window, stepped out onto the roof covering the front porch, and quickly shuffled to the edge. The ten-foot drop looked more like twenty, but I hesitated for less than a second before making the jump. I allowed my knees to buckle upon impact to protect my legs from absorbing the full shock, and then used the momentum to roll forward to distribute my weight. The tactic worked and I jumped to my feet unscathed.

I was already backing out of the driveway by the time Cheryl poked her head out of the upstairs window.

"Karla!" she screamed, but I was already gone.

CHAPTER 7

Return to Crawley

I drove to the store, parking in the exact spot I'd parked days earlier, determined this time to retrace the entire day . . . to find something that had been overlooked. The yellow police tape around the building had become detached in several places and was flapping in the wind. It reminded me of a haunted barn on Halloween. Isaac wouldn't like it; he was not a fan of haunted houses or scary movies.

I got out of the car and made my way toward the store. I stopped, remembering Isaac as he rubbed his hands together anxiously before running on ahead. I could see him plainly, as if he were still standing in front of me, his face exuding his excitement at finding an antique hideout, eagerly anticipating what might be inside.

I remembered my excitement, as well. Part of it stemming from the same anticipation as his, and part of it from seeing Isaac so happy.

But today, walking up to the door, a different feeling taunted me. A feeling that crept inside my stomach and lay there like rotting meat. It soured my stomach and I fought the urge to vomit. My legs, my arms, my face . . . everything grew hot and numb at the same time. Beads of sweat surfaced across my forehead and upper lip. I knew the sensation. I recognized it immediately. I'd felt it when the doctor gave us Mason's diagnosis. I felt it when Isaac disappeared. And here it was again. Pure, unequivocal fear.

I willed my legs to keep walking. Each step felt as if blocks of cement were attached to my shoes. But I kept moving forward, keeping my eyes on the store's entrance. Keeping my eyes on the goal in front of me.

Finally, I arrived at the screen door, recalling the slight quiver of electricity I'd felt the first time I entered the store. I paused to wipe the sweat from my palms before reaching for the handle. No tremor. No shocking vibration surging through my hand and arm.

I'd brushed off the wave of electricity that had coursed through me during the first visit; but this time, I was acutely aware of its absence . . . as if whatever life had been flowing through it was now gone.

It bothered me. I *wanted* to feel that sensation. I needed to retrace every part of the day—everything had to happen exactly the same as it had three weeks ago—and the fact that I hadn't even made it through the door yet and nothing felt familiar instantly brought me down.

I forced myself to keep going. Isaac needed me. I pulled open the screen door—the screen door that weeks earlier had been feather-light and now seemed so heavy. It was like pulling on dead weight, and I held the heavy door to my back as I put my hand on the door knob of the solid inner door that had been open during my first visit.

Please don't be locked.

I tried the knob, and it turned easily. *Not locked.* I breathed a sigh of relief. I turned the knob the rest of the way and started to open the door when I remembered the bell that dangled from a string above the door.

If the bad people are still here and have Isaac, you don't want them to know you're here.

I opened the door and quickly grabbed the bell in my fist to silence it from announcing my arrival. I clinched tighter and gave the string a firm tug; it broke easily, and I stepped the rest of the way into the store, catching the screen door with my free hand to keep it from slamming.

For all the searching that had taken place for Isaac, everything in the store appeared to be exactly the same as it had been the first time I had entered—nothing having a place of its own, and random pathways scattered here and there.

I quietly laid the bell on the counter and began walking in the same direction I had walked weeks earlier, retracing my steps.

"Isaac?" I whispered when I reached the exact spot where I had last called out to him and he had answered. Last time his voice had reached me, providing a peace I was unaware of until this time when his voice did not fill the store.

"Isaac?" I whispered more loudly, hoping for a reply I knew wouldn't come.

I walked farther and stopped. *And this is where I was standing when he came running to me, holding the nutcracker.* I glanced around. *What direction had he ran afterwards?* I closed my eyes, concentrating.

I remembered! He ran into the aisle to the right. I opened my eyes and stared in the direction he'd gone.

I started to step forward, then hesitated. *This is where everything changed.* I stared at my feet. *This was the last spot I knew Isaac to be okay—to be safe.*

I took a shaky breath. Stepping forward meant all of this was real—that Isaac was truly gone. Stepping forward meant reliving that day where from this point forward I had no memory of his smiling face. This was the last place I'd seen that face. This was the last place I'd felt his warm palm brushing mine as he laid the nutcracker in my hand. I didn't want to step forward into a time when I couldn't see him anymore.

I took a step back and turned the gold band on my ring finger nervously. "What do I do, Mason?"

You can't change history.

I closed my eyes and saw his smiling, care-free face. "You would say that. You love history."

No, I love you.

I smiled.

But history is history. You can't change it. And you can't reverse it. All you can do is move past it.

"How?"

Open your eyes.

"I don't want to."

Open your eyes. On three. One.

"I don't want to."

Two.

"I'm not ready."

Three.

I opened my eyes to an image of Isaac running down the aisle—an image so clear I could have sworn it had just happened. I followed after him, turning right at the end of the aisle as he had done. Then I paused, wondering where he had gone next. I closed my eyes and inhaled deeply.

Where did you go, Isaac?

I opened my eyes and looked around.

I know my child. Think like Isaac.

I scanned the room, searching for something that may have caught his eye—something he may have gravitated to—and I saw it! A chunk of tarnished gold was poking out from under a flowered scarf on a bedside table, and I knew immediately what it was. I had seen dozens of them on Isaac's bedroom book shelf and dresser. It was a trophy!

I pulled the trophy out from under the scarf. The engraving on a gold plate at the base of the trophy read *Earl Nicely, Wide Receiver, Talcott Falcons, 1923.*

Isaac had held it. I knew it. I had no doubt about it. I held it in my hand and felt warmth radiating from it as if Isaac's hand had recently been wrapped around it.

I took a few steps forward, confident I was traveling the same path Isaac had. "I'm here," I whispered. "I'm looking for you, sweetie . . . but I need your help."

I walked down the aisle until I had the choice to either walk straight or turn to the right. I paused, examining my options.

Which way did you go?

I closed my eyes, trying to *feel* him . . . or *hear* him . . . but I felt and heard nothing. I opened my eyes, determined.

Which way?

I looked down the aisle to my right, scanning as far as my eyes would allow. Then, I looked at the path straight ahead. The items straight ahead were large recognizable items. There was nothing mysterious about them. But the items to the right were smaller and numerous, with only a few large pieces of furniture here and there. It was hard to tell what one might find if they rummaged through such items. It'd be like treasure hunting. Yes, he would have gone to the right, curious about what might be hidden there. I walked to the right with confidence.

I followed the aisle as it curved around to the left, feeling more confident, but as it bore further around, it came to a sudden dead end. I felt cheated—like a mouse in a maze that had correctly completed the task but hadn't gotten the reward.

I wiped a bead of sweat from my brow with the back of my hand and looked around. Surely, Isaac had come this way. It's the path that made the most sense. He had to have been here. There were no other reasonable options.

I investigated the space further. There were no doors or windows where anyone could have gotten in or out, but maybe there was a secret door somewhere. The notion was something I'd only seen in horror movies, but wasn't I in a horror movie? Didn't the possibility of a secret door seem just as feasible as all the other unfeasible things that had happened?

I walked up to the wall and began running my hands along the boards, pushing on each one to see if any moved. I knocked and listened for an echo—a sure sign something might be on the other side, like a hidden room.

When the walls didn't reveal anything, I got on my knees and began running my hands across the floor, feeling for air coming up through the cracks of the wood . . . or for loose boards.

Sliding my hands across the floor, I reached under every piece of furniture, feeling carefully and moving my hand slowly to avoid splinters. As I ran my hand under a large piece of covered furniture nested against the wall, my fingers bumped something small, hard, and round, sending it rolling wood-on-wood across the floor. I jerked my hand away and pulled it to my chest.

My heart pounded. I knew instantly what it was, but *could it be?*

I reached under the covered piece again, stretching out my fingers to where I thought the item had come to a stop. Finding it, I curled my hand around it and pulled it out.

It was the nutcracker Isaac had brought me! I jumped to my feet, overjoyed. I held it to my chest, knowing it was the last thing Isaac had touched. He had wanted it so badly! I had told him to hold onto it . . . that I would buy it for him.

Suddenly, reality caved in around me. *I had told him to hold onto it. He'd wanted it so badly*. Isaac would have never laid the nutcracker down. He would have kept it close, maybe even put it in his pocket for safe keeping.

The tears came without warning, and I fell to the floor like a puppet whose strings had been cut—the joy of finding the nutcracker shattered by what it meant.

I sat there for what seemed like an eternity as the building grew dim from the impending night. I was exhausted—physically and mentally. I sat on the floor with my back resting against the piece of covered furniture that had sheltered Isaac's treasure as the darkness continued to seep in . . . and I cried. I cried weakly—not stemming from the deep sadness that had long ago found a home in my soul, but with a complete loss that encompassed death and defeat in one deadening emotion. He had won. God had won.

I cried until my body had no more tears to give. Then, I sat in silence as particles of dust and dirt dried in the residue from my tears and turned my face to stone. I dropped my head to my knees and I waited. This is how they would find me—a cemented statue of grief so hard to look upon they'd have to hide me from the world for fear the world would at once witness for the first time a shelled human.

Get up! A whisper. *Get up and keep looking!*

"I can't," I mumbled, my face buried in my knees.

Get up!

"I can't," I repeated.

You must. You can't give up!

"There's nowhere else to look. There's nothing else I can do."

GET UP!

The voice was loud, as if someone were standing directly in front of me, and I jerked my head up to look.

Get up. The same voice, but this time gentle and kind. It came from nowhere and everywhere at the same time. It wasn't there, yet it was.

"Okay," I said aloud as I mustered my strength and stood up slowly. I unclenched my fisted hand and gave the nutcracker one last glance before shoving it deep into my front jean pocket. "Let me think. Finding the nutcracker is good. It means I'm looking in the right place. And I found it because I followed my instincts. That means I can trust my instincts. Okay, I can do this."

I grabbed a corner of the fabric covering the furniture that had hidden Isaac's nutcracker, finding a somewhat-clean section to wipe my face. But when I pulled it to me, the entire covering slid to the floor, exposing the furniture underneath for the first time. It was a large mirrored armoire, and I jumped at the ghostly image it revealed before realizing I was looking at my own reflection. I leaned in for a closer look. Dark circles surrounded my red-rimmed eyes. My hair, pitch black and straight, had not been washed for days, and my cheeks were gaunt from eating only nibbles of bread and sips of tea to pacify my sister. Would Isaac even recognize me when I found him?

I started to turn away disgusted, but as I did, I caught the reflection of something moving behind me. I snapped my head quickly. "Who's there?" I demanded, looking over my shoulder and sounding more frantic than I wanted to.

My eyes searched the dim outlines of furniture and other items in the growing darkness of the room. I stood very still—partly too scared to move and partly hoping whatever or whoever was there would move again. But they didn't.

I turned and looked in the mirror again, staring past my reflection at the room behind me where I'd seen the movement.

Nothing.

"The shadows of the night must be playing tricks on you," I said to my reflection, attempting a laugh.

I turned to walk away a second time, but the movement came again! I jerked my head more quickly, intent on catching him or her . . . or whatever was in the room with me, but there was nobody.

I turned back toward the mirror slowly and leaned in closer, looking deep into the mirror's glass, forcing everything else to blur, focusing fully on the spot where something or someone kept moving.

There it was again—a movement! Being this close to the glass, I was able to see the movement clearly; and I realized it wasn't coming from behind me . . . it was in front of me! I jumped back in horror. How was that possible!?

I stumbled backward, not taking my eyes off the spot in the mirror that kept moving, but the longer I stared at it, the longer it stayed still. I chanced to move slightly and, when I did, it did as well. I furrowed my brow and stepped forward. I moved from side to side, allowing the little bit of light that was left in the store to shift on the mirror's surface, and I instantly felt foolish as I realized what was happening. There was a smudge on the glass—or perhaps an imperfection—and the light reflecting on the spot each time I moved made it *appear* that something was moving behind me.

I laughed nervously and stepped closer to the mirror, amused. Which was it—an imperfection or a smudge? I reached out to touch it, but just before my fingers made contact, I realized exactly what it was . . . it was a fingerprint!

I pulled my hand back quickly, not knowing what to do.

It's Isaac's fingerprint.

I was confused. Hundreds of people had been in this store,

anybody could have touched the mirror.

It's Isaac's.

But what if it isn't? What if it has nothing to do with Isaac? What if it's the fingerprint of some random person who admired the armoire and considered buying it?

It isn't.

But what if it is? I couldn't stand the thought of getting my hopes up because of a false lead.

I stared at the fingerprint. It was tiny—about the size of a nine-year-old boy's. What if it's Isaac's? Should I call the police?

I stood staring at it and began to shake. The idea that it might be Isaac's print overwhelmed me. If I touched it, would it be like touching Isaac? I closed my eyes and reached out, my fingertips yearning to touch the last place Isaac's hand had been. I imagined my fingers touching his as my fingertips grew warm. I pulled my hand back to my chest, imagining I was pulling Isaac back to me, and I opened my eyes.

"How?" I mumbled, startled by what I saw in the mirror—frightened and fascinated at the same time. Circles were spreading across the mirror where I'd touched it the same way a pond reacts to a rock being thrown into its waters. I shook my head, not believing what I was seeing, and I watched the small circles morph into larger circles, then fade away.

How can that be? My head lolled, dizzy from the idea. I was going crazy! I had to be. But—

Touch it again.

"Mason?"

Touch it again.

"I'm afraid."

Touch it again.

I moved my hand forward, pausing in midair. I *was* afraid. I was terrified! Not that the mirror would react again, but that it *wouldn't* . . . proving my sorrow had finally driven me insane.

Touch it.

I felt my arm moving forward, as if someone were guiding

it. I felt my fingers skim the warm glass, and I saw the wake left behind where my fingers had been.

I pulled my hand back and rubbed my fingers to my thumb. They were wet! The wonder of it consumed me.

"Isaac!" I screamed, plunging head first into the glass.

CHAPTER 8

Lost

My head throbbed. I was laying face down with my eyes closed. I vaguely remembered slamming my head into the mirror. After that, everything had gone black. Had I knocked myself out?

I heard voices. Someone must have come looking for me. But how did they know where to find me? And how long had I been unconscious?

My head ached too badly to think, so I lay with my eyes closed and focused on the pounding in my head, willing it to stop.

The voices grew louder. They were getting closer. Surely, they'd see me lying on the floor.

But what if they didn't? What if it was too dark in the store and they couldn't see me?

I opened my mouth to cry out, *I'm over here!* but my words were stifled by a mouthful of what felt like gravel. Ignoring the excruciating pain in my head, I pushed up on my hands and spit the granules out, then I laid my head back down, too tired and confused to attempt yelling again.

I felt something tiny and sharp digging into my skin as I rested my cheek on the floor. I was too tired to open my eyes, but the surface beneath my cheek didn't feel like the hardwood floor I'd crawled around on at the antique store. A frightening thought occurred to me; what if the tiny shards digging into my cheek were pieces of broken glass? I'd slammed my head into the mirrored armoire pretty hard. What if I'd shattered it? What if I'd hurt myself more than I realized?

Just lie still. Help is coming.

I heard feet shuffle beside me.

"Ma'am?" A man's voice. "Are you okay?"

"She had to have already been there." Another man's voice,

heavy with an air of uncertainty. "She was there. Didn't see her is all."

"Ma'am?" Again, a man's voice, this time kneeling very close. I felt a firm hand on my back.

I slowly opened my eyes, but I instantly squeezed them shut again before blinking several times, unable to comprehend what I was seeing. The ground, level with my line of sight, was covered with pieces of broken gray and pearled seashell. I shook my head, confused.

I messed up my senses when I slammed my head into the armoire, that's all. Give it a minute. The imaginary seashells will fade away to the hardwood floor of the antique store soon. Just give it a minute.

I laid my head back down and closed my eyes again. But I felt another gentle shake and heard the voice again, "Ma'am? Are you okay? Can you open your eyes?"

I raised my head and turned my neck carefully toward the sound of the voice before forcing my eyes open again.

Sunlight from behind the man's head blocked his face from my sight.

Where did the sun come from? Seashells. Sunlight. If there was any doubt before, I knew now without question that I wasn't in the antique store anymore. Perhaps someone had brought me outside after finding me unconscious.

I rolled over, intent on sitting up, but mounds of fabric tangled around my legs as I rolled.

Had they laid blankets on me to keep me warm—to keep me from going into shock after my injury?

I rested my head on the ground and raised my hand to my eyes to block the sun and get a better look at the man who was tending to me. Was he a police officer? An EMT worker? The sun was so bright, all I could see was an outline of his body, so I pushed up on my elbows to get a better look. But I instantly pulled away in surprise when I finally saw him clearly!

"Easy there," the man said, placing his hands in the air the way one does with a frightened animal to show they mean them no harm.

I stared in disbelief. The man was dressed in clothes I'd only seen in old movies! I squeezed my eyes closed and rubbed my temple. *Wow! I must have really done a number on my head. I'm hallucinating!! Shake it off, Karla. You can't afford to go crazy right now. You need to find Isaac.*

I shook my head, determined to regain my senses. I tried to sit up further, but winced at a dull pain in my ribcage. I laid a hand on my ribs and felt something wrapped tight around my waist . . . under my clothing. *My head should be wrapped, not my ribs!*

I looked down. Someone had changed my clothes! I'd been dressed in blue jeans and a Rolling Stones t-shirt when I fled to Crawley Antiques, but now I was wearing clothes that looked like they were from the Victorian period. Someone had dressed me in a pale blue dress with a full skirt and pointed bodice; and under the bodice, I felt the unforgiving steel strips of a corset . . . explaining the pain around my rib cage.

I struggled to a seated position, pushing the air from the fabric of the dress as it ballooned in my lap like a parachute.

I picked up a handful of the crushed shells from the ground and sifted them through my fingers, allowing them to settle back to the surface where they formed a loose, but well-made road. The road stretched out to my left down the middle of a field filled with wilted brown grass and bright purple flowers, and I wondered at the contrast of the vibrant flowers against the dead weeds. How were they able to survive the sweltering heat that had killed the grass and was already causing me to sweat?

I wiped my damp forehead and turned my head in the other direction, shielding my eyes from the bright sun with one hand. My eyes were still adjusting from going from the dark antique store to the bright outdoors too quickly; but if I squinted, I thought I could see a town or city in the distance. I put my other hand to my brow to block the sun further and thought I saw buildings sprouting up from the horizon. If so, they were too far away to tell how big they were or how large the town might be— if the town existed at all. It could be a figment of my imagination, brought to me courtesy of my distraught and broken brain.

The man, who was still kneeling at my side, leaned in, blocking my view of the maybe-there town.

He certainly was real, or at least a figment of my imagination that didn't seem to be going away any time soon. "Are you okay?" he asked again, beginning to sound worried.

I picked up a dime-sized piece of shell from the road and squeezed it as hard as I could. Yep, it was real.

"Well?" a voice from behind the man inquired.

I dropped the shell and looked up, leaning sideways so I could see around the kneeling man to where the voice had come from.

Two men were sitting on horses, but their backs were to the sun, so I couldn't make out their faces. I could barely make out that one was holding the reins to a third horse, which I assumed belonged to the man kneeling in front of me.

I shifted my weight and struggled to get to my feet, pounding at the parachute of a dress in my lap.

"Whoa," the man said before I could stand. "Why don't you just sit for a spell."

The two men on horses trotted around to my left.

"Well?" the man persisted. "Is she okay or isn't she?"

I looked to the voice. He sat comfortably hunched over the horn of his horse's saddle, staring down at me.

With the sun no longer shadowing their bodies, I could see each of the men was wearing the same type of getup as the man in front of me. I was again taken aback by their appearance.

"Take it easy," the man kneeling by my side said, putting his hand gently on my shoulder.

Shaded by the sun behind him, I still couldn't see his face, so I looked once again to the two men on horses. The man hunched over his saddle was wearing a short dark jacket with snug brown britches and a brown wide-brimmed hat. Short strands of straight blond hair poked out from underneath. He looked to be in his early thirties, and he sat staring at me with a half-smile.

The other man fidgeted on his horse. He was younger, probably in his mid-twenties, and as he removed his hat to wipe sweat from his forehead with the back of his hand, he revealed a full head of straight dark hair. "How is she doing?" he asked, straightening his hat back on his head.

"Just a minute," the man kneeling beside me answered without turning to look at either of them. It occurred to me he hadn't taken his eyes off me since he knelt down by my side.

"Do you hurt anywhere?" he asked softly.

Do I hurt anywhere? How about everywhere? I hurt everywhere!

"No," I answered, making another attempt to stand.

"Don't get up," he said, lightly placing both hands atop my shoulders. "That was quite a—"

But I ignored his instructions and continued my feeble effort.

"Okay." He shrugged, seeing I wasn't the obeying type. "Let me help you, then." He placed two supportive hands under my right arm and pulled me to my feet.

I welcomed the help. My legs felt as though they'd fallen asleep, and when I was finally able to balance my full weight on both feet, my toes cried out in pain. I winced and lifted my skirt to find ivory, tiny-heeled boots with sharp-pointed toes squeezing my feet. The boots came mid-shin and had thin white shoe-strings laced uncomfortably taut around my ankles.

Really? It was bad enough my ribs were scrunched, but my feet had to be, as well?

I dropped the bottom of my skirt back over my shoes and rubbed my head.

"Did you hit your head?" the man asked, reaching for me as if hitting my head automatically meant I might fall.

"I—I think so."

"Should I fetch a doctor?" Concern grew quickly in his voice.

Even with my added height from the uncomfortable heels, he was a good half foot taller than me. I squinted against the sun and tilted my head to get a better look . . . struck temporarily speechless by how handsome he was! His face was tan, framed with wavy locks of pitch-black hair. His eyes were a dark, deep brown—like mahogany-stained wood I once saw trimming the doors and stairways of a house Mason and I toured together on a trip to Colonial Williamsburg.

Most things that brought back a memory of Mason angered or saddened me, but this was different. The stranger's eyes were warm and kind, and I found myself staring deep into them, unable to look away.

He must have noticed because the concern that had moments ago been so evident on his face faded and was replaced with a modest smile of perfectly-aligned white teeth.

I looked down, embarrassed.

He tugged at his dark coat that hung mid-thigh over his light trousers as he squared his shoulders and cleared his throat. Despite having no knowledge of where I was or what was going on, I knew his dress suggested he was a man of great wealth and sophistication.

I forced a smile. "No. No doctor," I finally answered. "Thank you. I'm—I'm good."

"You sure? You don't look so good," the younger man on the horse commented.

"I beg your pardon?" I shot a glare at him, very much offended.

"Oh, no ma'am," he said, putting his hands in the air defensively. "I didn't mean you don't look good. I meant you don't look good."

The other man on the horse laughed, still casually hunched over his saddle.

The younger man on the horse looked embarrassed and child-like. I felt sorry for him. He was acting as clumsy with his words as I felt in my body right now.

I smiled. "I'm sure I do look a mess," I said to comfort him, putting my hand to my hair . . . then tapping it all over, confused. *When did it get put into a bun?*

"Not at all," he said. "You don't look a mess at all—"

"Not at all," the man in front of me chimed in swiftly before the young man could say another word. He once again displayed a flawless smile. "The name's Lawson," he said, stretching out his hand, palm up, the way a prince greets a princess.

I instinctually laid my hand in his, feeling momentarily like royalty. "Karla. Pleasure to meet you." I stared at him, once again swimming in a sea of mahogany.

"*Are* you okay?" he inquired, his face still masking a touch of worry.

I dropped my hand from his and forced myself to look away. I was reeling inside. None of this made any sense. I recalled finding the nutcracker Isaac wanted to buy. I recalled the mirror—how it had altered under my touch—and I recalled diving head-first into it. But then, nothing. It didn't make sense.

I felt the blood drain from my face, and I stumbled back, dizzy; but Lawson wrapped his arm around my waist and caught me.

I clasped his forearms, feeling his firm muscles through his coat.

"Why don't you sit back down for a spell." There was no hiding the uneasiness in his voice and concern on his face.

"No, I'm fine." I was here to find Isaac. There was no time for sitting.

"I think she's going to puke, Lawson," the older man teased. "You better stand a clear!"

I glanced around Lawson to catch the man's eye. He was staring at me with a playful smile.

"She looks awfully pale," the younger one commented. "I mean—" he corrected quickly, obviously concerned he'd say something offensive again, "you look beautiful, but pale." He looked down, flustered.

"Thomas, you're not helping," Lawson said, while the older man laughed again. He obviously had a good sense of humor, finding nearly everything laughable. "That's my brother, Thomas." Lawson nodded to the younger man.

Thomas must have felt he'd said enough already because rather than speak again, he simply tipped his hat.

"And the loud one," he nodded to the one still playfully holding my gaze, "is our good friend, Jackson."

Jackson removed his hat and placed it to his chest, displaying a full head of tussled blond hair. "Ma'am," he said with a wide grin.

I nodded to each of them and quickly diverted my eyes back to Lawson. I realized he was still holding me, and I pulled away quickly, directing my attention to dusting off my dress.

"Do you need a doctor?" he asked again.

"Um," I stumbled with my words, trying to make sense of it all. "Um, no, thank you. I'm fine. Just took a little tumble there, that's all. I'm okay."

Lawson placed his hat back on his head. "We could give you a ride into town." He nodded to his horse.

"That won't be necessary. I'm fine."

"Are you sure? That was quite a—" he hesitated. "That was quite a nasty fall you took."

We stared at each other for a few awkward moments. There was a look on Lawson's face that indicated he felt as strangely about our encounter as I did, but I didn't have time to read more into it than that. I was starting to feel better and was overcome with the idea that Isaac might be here somewhere.

I smiled with genuine gratitude. "No. Thank you, though."

The awkwardness lasted a few seconds longer, as if he was waiting for me to say more.

"Very well," he said abruptly, taking the reins from Jackson and mounting his horse in one swift movement. "Good day to you, then." He tipped his hat and pulled on the reins to move his horse around me before starting down the road in the opposite direction of town.

Thomas and Jackson did likewise, tipping the brims of their hats as they circled me.

I smiled graciously, nodding farewell, and watched until they were a good distance down the road before attempting to take a few deep breaths. Of course, my corset forbade it.

I'd dreamt of Victorian days—of wearing lavish dresses with ribbons and lace—but my dreams were always full of refinement and grace; they never contained the harsh truth of discomfort.

I turned toward the town. It was a good distance away, but not too far to walk, and it seemed the most logical place to start my search for Isaac.

The road leading into the town was narrow. The crushed shell that had loosely paved the road on the outskirts of town became so firmly compacted as I got closer that it felt like concrete under my feet. I debated many times which would be more uncomfortable: walking in the tiny pointy shoes that strangled my feet, or walking barefoot on the crushed shell. In the end, the shoes won—not because of comfort, but because I didn't want to draw attention to myself. If the townsfolk spotted me running around town haphazardly *and* barefoot, they would likely lock me up in an asylum . . . if they had one . . . and I couldn't risk anything keeping me from finding Isaac.

As I walked, I recalled each and every event that led up to my being here. Isaac disappeared. I went looking for him. I found the nutcracker in the antique store. The mirror moved. I came through it.

I kept saying it to myself, reminding myself it was true—that it happened.

And I understood clearly what all of it meant. It meant Isaac was here . . . because if I came through a mirror into another world and time, so did Isaac. That's why we couldn't find him.

It all made perfect sense. Even though, in truth, it didn't make any sense at all.

CHAPTER 9

Found

I walked down the middle of town where both small and large buildings stood unevenly next to each other. The large buildings were not the large skyscrapers found in New York City; rather, they were buildings I'd only seen in history books. The tallest building was only four stories high. And even though the style of the buildings indicated they would have been built a hundred years ago, they looked as though they were just built yesterday with new wood, fresh paint, and flawless glass.

The bottom of my dress dragged in the dirt and shell as I walked, despite my efforts to keep them lifted. Occasional hat tips from men and head nods from women greeted me as I made my way from the street onto the raised cobblestone sidewalk running parallel with the buildings, carefully steering clear of the horse-drawn carriages that muddled the street.

Smells of spicy foods filled my senses as I passed by store fronts and restaurants. I breathed in the sweet, pleasant aromas.

"Karla!?"

I froze. *Had someone called my name? Impossible! How could they have? Who could know me here?*

But I heard the voice again, louder this time and filled with excitement and surprise. "Karla!"

The voice came from behind me. I turned to find a slim young girl with brown shoulder length curls crossing the street toward me, dodging carriages and waving her arm. She looked to be in her mid-twenties.

"Karla!" she called out again as she reached me and threw her arms around my neck. "You're here!" She held my face in her hands for a moment, then kissed each of my cheeks. "You're really here! We didn't expect you so early."

Expect me? We?

"Why did you not telegraph that you were coming? We could have met you."

If I had known I was coming, I would have let you know, I thought. *Or perhaps* you *could have let* me *know I was coming.*

"Um—" I began instead.

She stood waiting for a response.

"—I didn't know myself what day I might arrive," I continued.

"No matter," she said, hugging me again, "you're here now." She placed both her hands on my upper arms and glanced over my shoulder. "Karla!" she cried out, sounding astonished as she looked about. "Did you travel alone?!" But before I could answer, her eyes narrowed sternly. "You know how Grams feels about women traveling alone!" Then, a mischievous smile stretched across her face, and I could see the thought of my breaking the rules intrigued her. "It will be our little secret." She winked. "Oh, won't everyone be happy to see you! Did you arrive on the boat?"

No, I arrived thorough a mirror.

"They've come a long way since the Anglo-Norman, have they not?" she continued. She wrapped her arm around my waist, pushing me forward as if we were running late for an important meeting. She kept glancing at me like she thought I might disappear if she let me out of her sight. "Oh, I can't believe you are really here!" she said again, hugging my waist.

We went back in the direction from which she had come, crossing the street quickly to dodge the horse-drawn carriages.

Many of the buildings lining the streets were tall and narrow, and the smells and sounds of the busy town were all around us. As we turned from the larger street onto a smaller one, I noticed a sign that read "Good Street."

I took a chance, fishing for more information, "Everything has changed so much."

"Oh yes," she said excitedly, in the same manner old women welcome the opportunity to share new gossip. "Moneybags

Mr. Grinage bought out Mr. Belanger and sold that property over there to Mr. Jones. Do you know Mr. Jones? Francis Jones?" She continued as if the answer was of no importance. "He built the inn there." She nodded in the direction of a building on the corner. "It's been an invitation for all kinds of shenanigans." She eyed me when she said "shenanigans," as if she would share more with me later.

She rambled on, telling me about all the changes that had taken place. I was listening carefully, but it was taking time to process it all . . . as if each piece of information was lined up, waiting patiently for my brain to pay it any mind.

We didn't expect you so early.

Everyone will be so happy to see you.

They've come a long way since the Anglo-Norman.

The Anglo-Norman? Why did that sound familiar? I began to recap all the history conversations I'd had with Mason throughout our marriage. Mason was always filling our dinner time with fun historical tidbits that fascinated me. Even more fascinating was watching Mason's face when he shared the stories. He loved understanding where we came from and how the past laid the foundation for the future.

Anglo-Norman? Anglo-Norman? Come on, Mason, help me.

The Anglo-Norman! I remembered! The Anglo-Norman was a ship that had exploded on its maiden voyage, killing around two hundred people. What year did that happen? I searched my memory and listened to Mason tell the story. It was during the California gold rush, Mason had said.

But the gold rush was in the 1850s, wasn't it?

Impossible! I began to shake, and I clasped my hands together to hide it from the girl who was still jabbering away.

"Why did you mention the Anglo-Norman?" I interrupted.

She didn't slow her pace or look at me, but she tilted her head in confusion. "What?"

"The Anglo-Norman," I repeated. "Why did you bring it up?"

She stopped suddenly and turned to me, cupping my hands

in hers like a nest encompasses a fragile egg. "Oh, Karla dear, you didn't know anyone on it, did you?"

"No," I said cautiously, "it was a long time ago."

Relief replaced concern as she hooked her arm in mine like a giddy school girl and we began walking again. "Some people would argue that six years is not that long ago, actually."

I stumbled to a halt. *Six years?! The Anglo-Norman exploded six years ago? It wasn't possible!*

The girl moved her arm to my waist to steady me. "Are you okay?"

Six years? That meant I was walking streets that only existed in the 1850s. But how could that be? I struggled to take a deep breath, my corset once again protesting.

But then, why was I surprised? Didn't my clothes and my surroundings cushion me against any surprises? But still—

"Give me a minute," I said, placing my hand on my stomach, breathing slowly.

"Am I walking too fast?" the girl asked.

"No. Just give me a minute."

I began gathering my thoughts and putting them together piece by piece. *Remember the nutcracker. The nutcracker was by the mirror. The mirror moved—I came through it. Isaac must have come through it, too; and that means Isaac is here somewhere.* I nodded. *You have nothing to lose by being here . . . by allowing this.* I closed my eyes. *You have nothing to lose and everything to gain.*

"Okay." I took a breath and opened my eyes. "I'm ready." *Let's go find Isaac.*

"Are you sure?" the girl asked. A genuine look of concern shrouded her face.

I nodded.

We began walking again, and she kept a tighter grip around my waist than she had moments earlier. "How thoughtless of me walking so quickly. You must be exhausted. Here you've traveled all this way and you only just arrived." She squeezed my waist as we walked and looked at me with pure joy. "It's just—I can't believe you're here, and I know everyone will be so happy to see you. Of course," she said with a knowing smile, "I know who you're most anxious to see."

Say Isaac, I pleaded. *Please say Isaac.*

But she didn't.

CHAPTER 10

Grams' House

The noises of the town faded into the distance. The buildings of obvious business slowly transformed into rows of shotgun houses—tall, narrow, and close together—then, into massive properties with more distinction. We walked for quite some time as the properties got further apart, and the road appeared less traveled.

Finally, the girl pointed off in the distance to a large home with an expansive yard. "Well?" She stood smiling at me, watching my expression.

"Well what?" I asked, but she just rolled her eyes playfully and marched us onward down the final leg of the trip.

A long narrow pathway lined with bright flowers led from the road to the house, but the girl ignored the path and instead steered us directly onto the lawn, cutting across the property to the front porch the quickest way possible. As we walked across the lawn, surrounded by towering trees and peppered with hundreds of orange and blue flowers, I was in awe of the home's beauty. Six round columns stood with their feet at the base of the front porch and towered past the second story wrap-around balcony. Above the balcony, three projecting dormers sat atop a square hipped roof. Atop it all was a small cupola—a crown for the majestic home.

Mason had described such historic homes to me in his storytelling, but it didn't compare to seeing one in person. "It's beautiful!" I said, awestruck.

As we stepped onto the porch, the girl yelled out, "She's here! Karla's here!" and she ran into the house, behaving anything but ladylike as she lifted her skirt to free up her legs for running.

I stood on the porch, running my fingers across the chiseled design along the bottom of a window, but my fascination was cut

short as squeals and laughter were accompanied by two girls—
one younger than the other—barreling out the front door in my
direction. The younger of the two, probably around fifteen years
old, got to me first and wrapped her arms around my shoulders.
She pulled away long enough to kiss each of my cheeks, then
hugged me again.

"You're really here?" she said, not letting go. "Helen said it,
but I can hardly believe it!"

So the girl who chaperoned me through town was Helen.

"Do let me say hello, Emma," the other girl said, pulling at
the younger one.

"Oh, okay, Ann, you don't have to pull on me." Emma reluctantly let go, but she didn't take her eyes off me. She had long,
blonde, wavy hair that was pulled up on the sides with a blue
ribbon that perfectly matched her blue dress, suggesting they'd
once shared the same fold. Her eyes matched the blue ribbon,
and her long eyelashes blinked several times as if in disbelief
that I was standing in front of her.

Ann hugged me tightly, then pulled away, her face inches
from mine. Her light brown hair was swept to one side and hung
over her left shoulder in loose curls. She looked to be about seventeen or so, and her pale, yet radiant, face framed brown eyes
that sparkled with excitement. "You look wonderful!" she said.
Then, her look turned to one of worry. "How was it traveling
alone? Was it terribly awful?"

Before I could answer, Helen intervened. "She wasn't alone!
She was with me," she said, grabbing me by my waist and ush-
ering me into the house. "And she's very tired, so let's let her sit
a moment."

She opened the front door and my awe of the home's beauty
continued. The inside of the house was magnificent! The entry
hallway showcased a grand circular stairway with decorated bal-
usters and a thick handrail. To the left appeared to be a parlor
with a large entrance door with embossed silver hinges and a
similarly-embossed round doorknob with gold trim around its

outside edges.

Helen guided me into the room, and Emma and Ann trailed close behind. She steered me across a floral-print rug that covered a large portion of the dark hardwood floors toward a red velvet sofa with a lavishly sculpted back that sat against the parlor's far wall. Behind the sofa was the large window I'd seen from the home's front porch. Helen sat on the sofa with me, and Emma and Ann curled up in the floor at our feet, still unable to take their eyes off me.

I looked around the room. Its craftsmanship was overwhelming. Moldings, obviously hand-carved, graced the tops of the doors and windows. A large mirror hung over a stately fireplace with a black marble mantel. A chandelier hung artfully from the tall ceiling with excessive detail.

"What a beautiful chandelier," I commented, staring at it intensely.

Helen followed my gaze. "It's a gasolier, actually; it has yet to be changed over. Uncle says he's hesitant to do so because it is so exquisite just as it is." She pointed out each detail. "See the cherubs? They represent love. And the flowers, friendship. The fruit," she said matter-of-factly, "is for hospitality."

I smiled. "Where is Grams?" I asked suddenly. I didn't know why, but for some reason I was anxious to meet her. It seemed she was head of the house, and I had a distinct notion she could answer all my questions.

As if on cue, a tall slim woman with gray hair pulled tightly back into a bun came to the door. She appeared to be in her mid-seventies, but she looked healthy and prominent. She was wearing a crimson dress with a high neck. The dress, while simple, was trimmed with satin and had a netted fabric covering.

"What is all the fuss?" she asked, sounding more curious than upset.

"You see!" Emma answered, jumping to her feet and pointing to me.

"Goodness me!" Grams exclaimed, a surprised look on her

face. She stepped quickly across the floral rug with her arms spread as if she were going to hug me.

Emma clamored to her feet and got out of the way as I stood to greet her; but just before Grams reached me, she paused. She flattened the front of her dress with the palms of her hands, as if composing herself, before taking the last few steps in my direction.

"Karla dear," she said, kissing both of my cheeks. "When did you arrive?" She stared at me with eyes that were warm and welcoming.

"Um," I started, but Helen was anxious to tell the story.

"I found her on Main Street," Helen said. "I could hardly believe it when I saw her! I had to look twice!! But when I called her name and she turned around . . ." she trailed off.

Grams gave me a stern look, "Were you traveling alone?"

I looked to Helen, who gave a slight shake of her head, assuring me she hadn't said a word. "Well," I began, "I—"

"Ladies should never travel alone," Grams interrupted sternly. "It is not acceptable to be unaccompanied. However," she said, staring blankly forward—the way one does when looking into the past, "it does happen sometimes. Unfortunately."

She redirected her gaze to me and smiled, hugging my shoulders. "And you've arrived safely, which is all that matters. Although—" she said, deep thought apparent on her face again. She paused for an awkward moment, as if she had something else to say. "No matter!" she continued suddenly, clasping her hands in front of her. "Emma. Ann. Spread the word, we shall have a grand gala tonight to celebrate!"

Emma and Ann ran out of the room squealing with excitement.

"Helen," Grams said, "could you let Jeremiah know? Ask him to find the fattest hog we have and prepare it."

"Yes, ma'am." Helen straightened to a soldier's stance and saluted.

"Goodness, Helen. Could we behave less ladylike?" Grams

asked, as Helen trudged off in a stiff march like a toy soldier.

It was just the two of us now, and we sat together on the velvet sofa.

Grams took my hands in hers. "How are you, dear?"

How am I? What a question. I was enchanted. I was curious. I was anxious. I was excited. I was scared. How do I sum all those things up? "I'm a bit tired," I answered honestly.

She patted my hand, "Yes, well, that's to be expected. Why don't you go upstairs and rest. We'll wake you for supper."

I don't want to rest. I want to find Isaac.

Of all the things I was feeling, the one thing I wasn't feeling was confused. I knew Isaac had to be here, and I was determined to find him.

"Evelyn!" Grams called.

A short, plump black woman appeared in the doorway. "Yes, ma'am?"

Evelyn wore a solid brown dress that hung limply to the floor with a long, white apron tied around her lumpy hips. A brown headwrap was swathed around her head, hiding any hair she may have had. It was difficult to gauge her age. She stood, somewhat hunched over, with dark, wrinkled hands crossed high on her stomach.

"Would you show Miss Karla to her room?"

Evelyn nodded, leaving her head bowed a little longer than seemed necessary.

"And," Grams said, clapping her hands together, "we're having a feast tonight! Can you see what Jeremiah needs help with? I'll join you in the kitchen later."

Evelyn nodded again.

Grams turned to me. "Get some rest, dear. You'll feel better when you wake."

Evelyn motioned to the hallway. "This way, Miss Karla,"

"But—"

"Go on now," Grams said gently. "We'll have plenty of time to talk later."

Her soft tone and gentle urging made me feel comfortable and safe, and I obediently stood from the couch to join Evelyn.

I followed Evelyn out of the parlor and back into the entry hall to the stairs. Each stair was wide and thick and solid, made of marble slabs. I took them slowly, allowing my hand to drag on the wide handrail. This close, I could see the intricate details on each baluster. It played tricks on my eyes, making me think the fine details could not possibly be made of anything but lace. I touched one of the winding vines. Nope, not lace. Mahogany.

We reached the top of the stairs, and Evelyn led me to a room down a broad, high-ceilinged hallway. She opened a door to the third room on the left and stood in the doorway with her hands folded neatly in front of her. "Dis is yer room, Miss Karla."

I started into the room, but paused and turned toward Evelyn, who had already started back down the hallway.

"Evelyn?" I called.

She stopped and turned toward me. "Yes, Miss Karla?" she asked, walking back in my direction.

I had so many questions. What year is it? Where are we?

Evelyn reached me and stood waiting patiently.

"Have you seen Isaac?" I asked.

A look crossed Evelyn's face I couldn't decipher. A look of empathy? Of concern? Did she think I was crazy?

"Not today, ma'am," she said.

Not today? What did that mean? Had she seen him, or hadn't she?

"Is there anything else, ma'am?" she asked.

I shook my head.

I watched her turn and walk back down the hallway, then scurry hurriedly down the stairs. She *did* think I was crazy. She was probably on her way to tell Grams right now.

I went into my room. A large bed canopied by thin, white curtains occupied a large area of the space. A fireplace, less grand than the parlor fireplace but still wonderfully detailed, graced the far wall, and a high-back flowered chair sat in front of the fireplace with a small round table to its side. Two large windows with heavy red drapes were perfectly spaced on the other wall, and on the wall adjacent to the bed was an oak armoire. Beside it, a small mirrored vanity with a dainty wooden bench.

I walked over to the bed where obvious sleeping clothes lay, but I was too tired to bother with them as I climbed onto the bed using the small step stool at its middle. I lay on the bed, my mind restless and my body weary. I couldn't sleep. How could I sleep?

And yet, I couldn't stay awake. My eyes, which had been widely taking in all they had seen, grew heavy. I closed them only to blink, but they didn't reopen.

I saw the tree in the distance. It appeared like an oil painting across a water-colored field, its hues of orange, red, and purple lighting the tree like an iridescent candle. I stood in awe at its beauty. A warm autumn sun cascaded across my face as I drifted closer to the tree.

Then, a breeze began to blow—gentle at first, as a few of the colored leaves drifted from the tree's branches and onto the wind. But then, the gentle breeze turned rough and turbulent, and the leaves struggled to keep their grip against its cruel intent. The air twisted and twirled around me, ripping at the leaves.

"Stop!" I yelled, my hair whipping into my screaming mouth. "You're tearing them up! Stop!!"

Then, a figure appeared under the tree. "Peace. Be still." The voice came from the figure, yet it didn't; it came from everywhere. It echoed all around me. It sounded familiar, yet strange.

The wind continued to swirl and destroy as it escalated in strength and force.

Again, I heard, "Peace. Be still."

And again, the wind did not obey. It grew furious as it ripped leaves and twigs from the tree, casting them away as if they were nothing—as if they had no value or importance.

I fought to keep my hair from my face and the debris from my eyes as I squinted through the storm to the figure near the tree. I couldn't make out who it was. They looked familiar. I leaned in, squinting harder and shielding my face from the accumulating debris being thrown through the air.

A large branch came swirling in my direction. I started to duck, but I was distracted by the figure under the tree who raised one hand high in the air.

What are they doing? I leaned in closer just in time to greet the branch as it slammed into my forehead, and everything went dark.

CHAPTER 11

Lawson Returns

"Karla. Karla?"

I felt someone shaking my shoulder. I hesitated to open my eyes. I couldn't remember falling asleep, but I remembered where I was when I laid down, and it wasn't anywhere I had ever been before. What if I opened my eyes to find Cheryl waking me from another dream? I kept my eyes closed.

"Karla, wake up."

It didn't sound like Cheryl's voice. Slowly, I opened my eyes to find Emma sitting beside me on the bed, a large smile on her face.

"You have a gentleman caller," she said with so much excitement one would have thought the gentleman caller was for her.

I sat up on one elbow, rubbing my eyes with my free hand. "Who is it?"

She shrugged. "I don't know. But my, is he handsome!" She clasped her hands to her chest and batted her eyeslashes.

She looked at me, still in the dress I was wearing when I arrived, and scrunched her nose. "Goodness, Karla, how tired you must have been." She paused for a minute, then shrugged matter-of-factly. "Well, at least he'll not be kept waiting while you dress." She wrinkled her nose again as she looked at my hair and patted it gently. "You may want to tidy your hair, though; it's a terrible mess."

She jumped off the bed and headed out the door. "Do hurry. He's waiting in the parlor."

I crawled out of bed and, after finding everything I needed to freshen up in the room's armoire, I reluctantly made my way down the stairs to the parlor, but there was no gentleman caller to be found.

I sat on the red velvet sofa. *So, this is what it feels like to be a lady in waiting,* I thought humorously. *Or was that what they called a friend to the queen?* I shook my head, smiling at my own ignorance.

A few quiet moments passed before Emma's loud whispers broke the silence. "Pssstt! Karla! Karla, where are you?"

I walked to the parlor door. "Emma?"

"There you are!" she whispered. "What are you doing in there?"

"You said someone was waiting for me in the parlor—"

"I said a *gentleman* is waiting for you. He's in the *gentlemen's* parlor," she said, pulling my arm in the appropriate direction. "This way."

We walked across the hall to a room equally as exquisite as the parlor we'd just left, but it was evident as soon as I stepped into the room that the room was tailored specifically for men. Despite having large windows similar to the ones in the ladies' parlor, the room was dark, with rich wood and brown leather furniture. One entire wall was lined with floor-to-ceiling bookshelves lined with black leather-bound books. The fireplace on the far wall was just as grand as the one in the ladies' parlor, but rather than a mirror hanging above it, a sizeable painting of a man standing in a polished suit graced the wall. The man was holding a cane he clearly didn't need, providing him an air of refinement.

In front of the fireplace, sitting in leather high-backed chairs, were two men with their backs to us. They were talking in pleasant, low tones and sharing a laugh.

Emma cleared her throat to announce our presence, and both men stood quickly and turned to look at us.

I recognized one of the men as Lawson, the man who'd offered repeatedly to fetch a doctor when I first arrived. The other man, I didn't recognize, but when he saw me, he hurried across the floor to greet me with utter joy across his face.

"Karla!" he exclaimed, kissing each of my cheeks, then hugging me tightly. He placed my hands in his and stared at me in disbelief just as all the others had done. He had a full head of peppered gray hair and a friendly, wrinkled face. He stood about a foot taller than me, and I stared up at his welcoming smile.

How is it they all know me, and I know none of them?

"It was all I could do to keep from waking you when they told me you were here," he said, giving my hands a slight squeeze, "but Grams would have none of it until supper."

He moved to my side and escorted me across the room to Lawson. "Do you recognize this fine young man?" he asked, gesturing to Lawson.

I nodded. "We've met."

"He's rather persistent, for reasons that elude me, to see that you are okay." The man looked suspiciously back and forth between the two of us.

Lawson stood tall, but appeared a bit uncomfortable.

Neither of us said a word.

"Karla?" the man pressed. "You *are* okay, aren't you? Is there anything I should know?"

I shook my head, staring down at my feet awkwardly. I looked up for a second to find Lawson looking down at his feet, as well.

"Very well," the man said after a long silence. He clasped his hands together. "I'll let you converse then, shall I?" He turned to Lawson and shook his hand. "Young man," he said.

"Sir," Lawson responded.

He turned to me with the same affection one has for their own child. "Okay?" he asked.

I smiled and nodded.

"It *is* so very good to see you." He hugged me again and planted a kiss on my forehead before leaving the room.

I turned to watch him walk out, noticing for the first time Emma was no longer in the room. It was just Lawson and me now. I turned to face him.

He fidgeted with the hat he held in his hands and looked

down at his feet awkwardly. "Um." He cleared his throat. "Well, it um, it seems you are well, so I suppose I'll be on my way." He placed his hat back on his head and walked toward the door. "Ma'am," he said, tipping his hat as he walked by.

I couldn't let him leave. He'd said I'd taken a nasty fall. What had he seen? How much did he know?

"Lawson, wait!"

He turned and looked at me. "Yes?" he asked with just as much anticipation on his face as I presumed was apparent on mine.

"Um ..." It was my turn to stumble with my words.

He took a step toward me. "Ma'am?"

I laughed. "Ma'am," I repeated softly, amused at the idea of his calling me ma'am considering we were seemingly the same age.

"Something funny?" he asked, my smile already becoming contagious across his lips.

"It's Karla," I said. "You can call me Karla."

"Karla," he corrected.

We stood staring at each other, another awkward silence passing between us.

"So, it is true!" Helen poked her head in the door, and I was grateful for the interruption. "Hello." She held out her hand to Lawson in ladylike greeting. "I'm Helen. It's a pleasure to make your acquaintance."

Lawson took her hand in his and bowed a gentlemanly hello.

She shifted her gaze to me. "Emma said you had a gentleman caller." She made no attempt at hiding her delight over the visit.

We all stood in silence for a very brief minute, thanks to Helen's recognizing the awkwardness.

"It's a beautiful day," she suggested. "Why don't the two of you take a walk in the garden?"

Lawson responded quickly. "I *could* use some fresh air," he said, turning to me. "If you'd do me the honor?" He held out his arm.

"I, too, could use some fresh air," I said truthfully. I hooked my arm in his and we walked into the entry hall. Helen slipped me a small fan as we passed by, accompanied by a playful smile and wink.

We walked out the main door and onto the lawn. Lawson seemed to know exactly where he was going as he led me into the side yard and onto a small, pebbled pathway. The blue and orange flowers scattered along the front lawn were abundantly clustered along each side of the path. The path circled a cement water fountain that was not shy of the same artistic details I had seen throughout the house. Massive trees surrounded the garden, many of them loosely holding Spanish moss.

I spoke first. "You did not tell . . . um . . ." *Oh, shoot! What was the old man's name?*

"No," he said, apparently knowing what I was going to ask, saving me the embarrassment of not knowing the name of someone who obviously had so much adoration for me. "I didn't feel that Mr. Darap should worry."

"That was kind of you," I said, making a mental note of the old man's name. "Thank you."

Lawson didn't say anything for a few moments as we walked in silence. Then, he stopped abruptly and turned to face me. "*Are you okay?*" he asked.

Here we go, I thought. *Time to find out what happened.*

"Why wouldn't I be?" I forced a lighthearted laugh.

"Well," Lawson seemed to be choosing his words carefully. "You fell—" He trailed off.

I waited, but when it was obvious he was struggling with his words, I tried coaxing. "It is so hot," I said, spreading out the fan Helen had given me and waving it dramatically. "The heat must have made me dizzy. I can't truly remember. Did I trip over something, do you know?"

I could tell Lawson was uncomfortable. "Not exactly," he

said. "Neither my brother nor Jackson saw you until you were on the ground, but—"

I gave him time to continue, and when he didn't, I urged him to go on. "But?"

"Well," he said, sounding a bit shaky, but sure. "You fell from nowhere. You weren't there, and then you were. I don't know how to explain it."

Should I tell him?! He, if anyone, would believe me, right? He saw me appear out of thin air, didn't he?

But what good would it do to confide in someone who wouldn't know what to do with the situation either? Why drag him into my world?

Besides, what if he was testing me to see how much I knew about what was happening? Who could I trust, really?

I laughed and waved my fan in front of his face, "I do declare, Lawson, I believe *you're* the one who may have gotten too much heat. You're hallucinating!"

The look on his face told me he wasn't going to push the issue. "Do you suppose this July heat could really do that to a man of my stature?" he asked, squaring up his shoulders.

He was joking now, trying to lighten the conversation, but I caught that he'd said "July." Finally, we were getting somewhere. It's July. Now, I just needed to figure out July *where*.

I turned the fan back on myself. "Is it always this hot here in July?"

"In Terrebonne Parish, you mean?" He shrugged. "It's a little hotter than usual, I suppose."

We were in Terrebonne Parish! Wherever *that* was. Pieces of the puzzle were coming together. It's July 1850-something in Terrebonne Parish. This walk was proving more beneficial than I'd expected.

Now, just tell me where Isaac is, and I'll be on my way. That's the only information I care about, really.

Lawson took out a pocket watch. "We should be heading back," he said, putting the watch back in his pocket. "I hear there is a grand gala awaiting you tonight."

"So I hear," I replied, allowing him to steer me around a bed of lilacs. "Will you be there?"

"No."

"No?" I asked, surprised at the disappointment in my voice.

Lawson apparently caught it, too, but he looked down at the ground to hide his smile. A true gentleman.

"It's only for family and close friends, I think."

I didn't argue. I didn't know protocol for such things, and I wasn't about to add to his suspicions about me by saying or doing the wrong thing.

We walked in silence, and when we popped out of the garden, Ann came running across the lawn. "There you are! I've been looking for you everywhere!" She grabbed my hand and pulled me anxiously. "Come. Emma and I will help you get ready for the gala."

She looked briefly at Lawson. "Good day, sir," she said, dismissing him, as if spending any more time with him would be inappropriate.

I shrugged my shoulders at Lawson as she pulled on my arm.

Lawson folded his arms across his chest and chuckled as he watched Ann drag me away.

CHAPTER 12

A Gala for Two

"Ow!" I groaned as Ann pulled tightly on the strings of the dress she'd chosen for me, lacing up the bodice.

"Hold still!"

"I can't, as I find breathing far more important," I answered.

Emma laughed while Ann continued the task at hand.

"If women's dress reform continues to advance, you'll be breathing comfortably in britches soon enough. I hear it is the latest trend coming," Ann said. "But for now, we need to get you dressed in appropriate attire." She gave the strings one last tug and tied them neatly. "There! All done."

I turned around to face her. "Well," I said, holding my arms out for inspection, "how do I look?"

Ann stared wide-eyed, scanning every detail of me from head to toe.

Emma clasped her hands together, "You look beautiful!" She moved me in front of a full-length, free-standing mirror. "Here, see for yourself."

I looked in amazement. I truly did look beautiful. The dress was breathtaking—a pink full skirt swept apart in the front revealing a laced white underskirt. Each of the sides were pulled back and bunched at my hips. My hair, which Emma and Ann had meticulously styled, was twisted up in the back with several large curls left down on the sides.

I stared at someone who was me, but not me. The woman in the mirror was beautiful. She was confident and elegant. Delicate, but strong. Poised and composed.

Objects in the mirror may be closer than they appear. I smiled at the thought of modern-day words printed on rearview mirrors. "Not closer. Different," I whispered.

"Pardon?" Ann asked, standing behind me and looking at my reflection.

"Objects in the mirror appear different than they are," I mused.

She furrowed her eyebrow in confusion, but I just smiled.

I stared at my reflection. The woman staring back was doing a good job of holding it together. No one would have guessed all she'd been through . . . and was going through still.

Suddenly, a startling thought occurred to me. What if it wasn't me in the mirror at all? What if it *was* someone else? Someone *different*. What if—?

I reached out to touch the mirror.

"Are you ready?" Helen asked as she entered the room, pausing in stunned surprise when she saw me.

I pulled my hand back quickly and turned to Helen, flattening out my dress with the palms of my hands. "Well? What do you think?"

"My!" she said, coming toward me and grasping my hands in hers. "Aren't you quite a different lady than the one I picked up on the street this morning." She spoke teasingly with a deep drawl, as if she were a man who had picked me up for unmentionable reasons. "But I'm not sure," she whispered, leaning in close, "it's the dress alone that has changed since this morning." She winked, and I knew instantly she was referring to the visit from Lawson. But before I could object, she hooked her arm in mine and guided me toward the door.

Emma and Ann hooked arms, as well, following close behind.

"I know you've just arrived," Helen began rambling, "and this gala might prove a bit much after your long travels, but we've been waiting forever it seems—"

"And why did you not telegraph you would be coming?" Ann interrupted, as we reached the top of the stairs.

Why did I not telegraph? That seemed to be the question of the day, didn't it?

I opened my mouth to reply, but before I could form an answer, Emma chimed in. "Yes, and why did you not tell us you would be arriving separately?"

I froze.

Separately? Separately from who?

Ann and Emma ran into us, not expecting the sudden halt.

Helen turned and gave them a stern look. "Would you stop harassing her? It all worked out fine." She patted my arm. "There are some things we have no control over, right, Karla, dear?"

My heart raced, and I turned to Emma. "Why did I not tell you I would be arriving separately from *who*?"

She looked confused. She looked at Helen as if she didn't know the correct answer.

"*Who*?" I asked again. "Arriving separately from *who*?"

"From Isaac," she replied hesitantly.

My head spun! Did she really say Isaac? Where was he?! How come I hadn't seen him?

"Where is he?" I asked, making no attempt to hide the urgency in my voice.

"He traveled to Houma with Uncle for the day," Emma answered, still seeming uncertain of the conversation we were having. "I thought you knew."

I felt faint.

"I'm certain he would have stayed had he known you were arriving today," Ann injected.

I was reeling. I grabbed the staircase railing to keep from falling, and Helen grabbed me around the waist.

"Karla? What's wrong?"

I didn't answer. I couldn't.

"Karla?"

Another long pause.

"Perhaps tonight is not a good idea," she said with genuine concern in her voice. "You are so exhausted you can barely stand."

"NO!" I said, startling all three of them.

I took a deep breath and struggled desperately to gain composure. "No," I repeated, more softly. "It's just that—"

What could I say? Isaac was *here*! He was truly here! Just as I'd known he must be but was afraid to fully believe.

Helen and Ann exchanged glances. "We should get Grams," Ann said. "You don't look so well."

"Yes," Helen said. "Perhaps we should postpone tonight."

Their faces were full of concern, and I could tell they were mentally struggling with what to do.

I decided a little truth goes a long way, so I took each of their hands in mine and spoke softly. "I'm fine. Really. It's just . . . I've missed Isaac terribly. You can't *imagine* how much I've missed him! And I assumed I'd see him upon my arrival, and when I didn't—"

They were looking at me intently.

I took a breath. "It's been a whirlwind. Grams made me rest upon my arrival, and by the time I woke, Lawson had arrived—" I took another breath.

They looked somewhat comforted by my honest words.

Finally, Helen spoke. "If you feel for *one minute* you are overwhelmed," she said, pointing a finger at me sternly, "you will tell me."

It was not a question, but I nodded anyway. "I promise."

Emma clasped her hands together and jumped up and down. "Yay! We're having a gala!"

"Galas are intended for ladies!" Ann reprimanded, shaking her finger in front of Emma's face as Helen had done to me moments earlier, "and you'll do well to conduct yourself as such."

But they huddled together with a snicker, hinting they clearly had other intentions for the evening.

We started down the staircase. "What time do you expect Isaac will return?" I asked.

"Uncle told Grams she could expect them for supper," Helen answered. "Of course, they have no idea our supper has turned into such a grand affair and will be a bit earlier than usual."

"Oh, but won't Isaac be surprised!" Emma exclaimed. "He told us you would not be long behind him. But two days? You arrived much earlier than we expected. You must have caught the next boat out!"

Two days?! It had been longer than two days. It had been *weeks* since Isaac had disappeared from Crawley Antiques.

But then, he hadn't disappeared. He was here! I still could not believe it. I was so in awe of it that the time difference didn't bother me in the least. After all, I had accepted that Isaac and I had fallen through a mirror, so of what consequence was a difference in time? Besides, that meant Isaac had only had to go a couple of days without me, while I had been weeks without him, not knowing where he was or what had happened.

It was a blessing that time was different here. For Isaac, anyway.

"I'm so excited!" Helen remarked, as we stepped off the front porch and onto the lawn. "It has been forever and a season since we've had such a celebration in the garden."

We walked toward the garden Lawson and I had walked in earlier in the day, but rather than turn left onto the garden's pathway, we walked right past it.

"The gala is in the garden, is it not?" I questioned, glancing back at the pathway.

"Yes," Helen answered.

"But we just passed the garden," I stated, confused.

"Not *that* garden," she said, raising her eyebrows in amusement. "That garden would not hold all our guests. We are having the gala in the *East* Garden."

Two parlors! Two gardens! How grand this place was!! "How big is this property?" I inquired with genuine curiosity.

Emma was happy to answer. "This particular plantation is the biggest in Terrebonne Parish," she boasted, "with over one hundred thousand acres."

"I had no idea!"

"Yes," Helen said, "it is so large, we will likely never see much of it. I hear there are cane fields somewhere on this property I've yet to lay eyes on." She had a pinch of resentment in her tone.

Ann scrunched her nose. "And why would you desire to go to the cane fields?"

Helen answered with certainty. "I desire to go everywhere and to see everything." She looked at Ann as if she knew something Ann didn't. "And I am certain," she quipped, "there is more to see than that which is put within our limits."

I smiled, because I knew it to be true. I would never have believed such a place as Terrebonne Parish could exist, yet here I was—seeing with my own eyes what nobody would believe if they heard my lips tell of it.

Ann waved her off, finding it not worth speaking of anymore.

Helen whispered, "In fact, I owe you a great debt, Karla."

"Me?"

"Yes," Helen continued whispering. "The excitement of your arrival this morning seems to have distracted Grams from the fact I was in town in the first place, as I know I am not to be without an escort."

"Ahh," I nodded. "That would explain the lack of a carriage, I suppose—all that walking to get to Grams?"

Helen laughed, nodding her head, and I found myself laughing right along with her.

***

The gala had been going on for nearly an hour. A buffet of food was spread out—a once-fatly pig its centerpiece. Round tables with white tablecloths were spaced evenly along the grass with chairs seated around them. Between several of the tables were taller tables with no chairs draped with black tablecloths.

Lanterns dangled from tree branches and handmade posts with hooks so that not a single corner of the garden was unlit.

Lively music, courtesy of a small orchestra in the far corner of the lawn, filled the garden. Several couples were curtseying, dipping and twirling to the music in a section of the lawn intended just for such purpose.

Throughout the evening, people came to me. They hugged me and kissed each cheek and told me how wonderful I looked and how much they'd missed me. But I kept my eye on the main entrance where guests continued to flow in and out. I could hardly bear the anticipation of seeing Isaac's face.

"Excuse me, may I have this dance?" A short, chubby, and balding man stood gleaming beside me with one hand behind his back and the other held out, awaiting my acceptance.

"I'm sorry, I'm waiting for my son," I said, giving him my attention for a brief moment. "Maybe later in the evening?" I encouraged after seeing his look of disappointment.

The sound of children laughing stole my attention, and I looked in their direction hoping to see Isaac. A young boy, probably around eight years old, was chasing after a smiling young girl who appeared to be around the same age. She was holding an object in her hand high above her head as she ran. I watched as he chased her to a corner of the garden where he was able to wrestle the object from her before they both collapsed laughing on the grass. It was a long, tubular object, and he held it up to one of the lanterns and began turning the tube's end.

I smiled when I realized what it was. It was a kaleidoscope. I hadn't played with one for years, but in that moment, I recalled my excitement the first time I'd seen the colors and shapes morph with each turn of the kaleidoscope's end. I watched the same wonder come over the boy's face, and I was tempted to walk over and ask if I could take a peek.

"Karla!" More laughing, but this time it was Emma and Ann. Emma grabbed one of my arms and pulled me toward the dance area. They were visibly enjoying themselves. Strands of Emma's hair, which had earlier been neatly pulled back, now loosely fell across her face, and Ann's forehead was bejeweled with small beads of sweat.

Emma stopped pulling on my arm and tried unsuccessfully to tuck a few of her loose blonde curls back into her upswept bun.

Ann removed a handkerchief from the top of her bodice and dabbed at her damp forehead. "Oh, do come dance with us, Karla! It is so much fun!"

"I will—"

"Oh, goody," Emma clapped, having already given up on her hair.

"—after I see Isaac," I finished.

"Fuddy-duddy!" Ann pouted, tucking the handkerchief back into her bodice just as Thomas and Jackson walked up.

"Thomas! Jackson!" I exclaimed, surprised at my delight in seeing them.

"Ma'am," Jackson said, taking off his hat, revealing the same head of blond curls he'd introduced when we first met.

"Karla," I corrected.

"Karla," he said.

I looked around him to Thomas. "Thomas. It's good to see you again."

Thomas took off his hat and ran his fingers through his straight black hair nervously. "Miss Karla."

Jackson gestured to the crowd and lavishly-laid tables. "All this just for you? My apologies," he quipped, bowing slightly. "Had I known we'd encountered royalty this morning, I would have rolled out the red carpet myself."

"It's actually for me and my son, Isaac," I said, blushing. "We've . . . um . . . well . . . it seems we've been gone for a while, and—"

He held up his hand to interrupt. "No explanation necessary, your highness. I'm just happy to have an excuse to ask these lovely ladies to dance." He motioned to Ann and Emma. "Might I have this dance?" he asked Ann, holding out his elbow as an invite.

Ann took his arm with her chin high, demonstrating perfect etiquette.

"Shall we?" Thomas asked shyly. He held out his hand to Emma, and she daintily laid her hand in his and allowed him to escort her away.

By the time I thought to ask if Lawson had come with them, they were already curtsying and twirling with Emma and Ann on the dance floor.

Lawson had said he wasn't coming; but then, he probably hadn't expected that Thomas and Jackson would be here.

The thought that Lawson may be here occupied my thoughts for a second, but I quickly directed my attention back to the main entrance of the garden. I was concerned I might have missed Isaac's entrance due to the distraction of seeing Thomas and Jackson . . . but my concerns quickly disappeared when—just as staring at a stereogram painting will eventually produce a picture—Isaac was suddenly standing at the entrance.

I blinked, as if doing so could erase all the parts of the picture that were imaginary, leaving only that which was real. I blinked several times, but the picture didn't change.

Isaac was here!

CHAPTER 13

Nightmare

Isaac stood at the garden entrance, dressed in trousers and a waistcoat, fitting in perfectly with the other children who had sifted through the entrance throughout the evening. Even his longer hair, considered taboo at his former Christian school, was fashionable here. Only I would have known he didn't belong.

A thin, tall man wearing a black top hat escorted Isaac through the gate. He was wearing a black, long-tailed coat fastened low at the waist and matching black trousers. He stood by Isaac's side with one hand on his shoulder—not in a show of discipline, but in a show of support. He stood tall and proud, hooking his free hand on the lapel of his jacket.

Isaac looked around. His eyes were soaking in the gala—absorbing every detail—just as he'd absorbed the details of each antique store find. He didn't appear to be searching for anything or anyone particular, and I wondered if he'd been told I was here.

I fought back the urge to run to him. I wanted to bask in the moment that he was actually here. Alive. Standing in front of me.

I caught myself enjoying the fact he was enjoying himself. I watched his eyes—too far away to see their color today—as he scanned the extravagant scene. I watched him settle his attention on the long buffet table overflowing with various platters of food before glancing to the corner of the garden where the orchestra was playing.

Currently, the violinist was playing a lively polka tune that had couples swirling and ducking under each other's arms.

I watched a huge smile stretch across his face as he continued scanning the crowd. I watched as his eyes scanned closer and closer to where I was standing. Finally, his eyes met mine, but the connection was brief as he moved past me quickly to continue scanning the rest of the space.

I furrowed my brow. *Hadn't he seen me?*

But he hadn't. Or he had, and it hadn't sunk in yet, because just then, his eyes paused and the smile stretched even wider across his face. Slowly, his eyes came back my way. Our eyes met, and he instantly broke free from the gentleman and ran toward me.

The man startled, and a look of worry covered his face, but as soon as he saw who Isaac was running to, he crossed his arms over his chest and smiled approvingly.

"MOM!" Isaac yelled, and within seconds, he was in my arms!

I held him tightly, never wanting to let go, thinking he wouldn't want to let go either, but he pulled away after just a few moments and whispered, "Is this the coolest or what?!"

I had to remind myself it had only been a couple of days since he'd last seen me. He had no idea it had been weeks since I'd last seen him, not knowing where he was or what had happened to him.

"I knew you'd figure it out," he continued whispering. "I didn't have any doubt. Come on!" He pulled at my arm. "There's something I want to show you."

"Isaac, wait! We need to—" but before I could finish my sentence, the gentleman who had escorted Isaac into the garden was standing in front of us.

"Karla!" he said, his arms welcoming. "When did you arrive?"

I pulled Isaac to my side and held his hand tightly in mine. I was determined not to lose him again. "This morning," I answered, forcing a smile.

Isaac pranced from one foot to the other, impatiently.

I stood staring at the man. His face was kind, but indicated we had a lot to talk about—a lot of catching up to do—and I didn't have time for that. I needed to talk to Isaac in private.

I was trying to figure out a way to politely excuse myself

when Grams stepped up to the man's side and linked her arm in his. "Excuse my interrupting," she said, "but I do believe this is the gentleman the ladies have been inquiring of. Karla, dear, why don't you visit with Isaac. You and Uncle can catch up later."

The man tipped his hat and allowed Grams to steer him away, visibly delighted that he was in such demand.

"That's Charles," Isaac whispered, "but everyone calls him Uncle. I don't know why." He shrugged nonchalantly.

I pulled Isaac out of the garden and toward the house. He was rambling the whole time about all he'd been doing since he arrived—boating on the bayou, fishing, horseback riding. He was going on and on.

I directed him into the smaller garden I had walked in with Lawson. "Isaac," I began.

"Isn't this place fantastic!?" he exclaimed.

I put my hands on his shoulders. "Isaac, listen to me. Did you come through the mirror? Is that how you got here?"

"Of course," he said. "You found the nutcracker I left, didn't you? Isn't that how you knew how to find me?"

I smiled. I had to. He was so smart to have left me a clue. It wasn't his fault it took me three weeks to find it!

"Yes, I found it. But how did you know? I mean, what made you think you could go jumping into mirrors?"

"I tripped and grabbed the mirror to catch myself, but then I noticed it was shaking—the way that glass of water did in that dinosaur movie."

"And when you got here, where did you find yourself?" I asked.

Isaac looked confused.

"I was on a dirt road on the outskirts of town," I explained. "Is that where you were when you first arrived?"

He shook his head. "No, I was down by the boats. There was this one boat that had this big side wheel on it and another one that had—"

I rolled my hand impatiently in a hurry-up motion, encouraging him to skip the details.

Isaac indicated that he got the point with a brief huff before continuing. "Then, I heard this man yelling my name." His face twisted with puzzlement. "I don't know how he knew my name. It's so weird!"

"Yes, I know," I said, having had the same sensation when Helen first yelled out my name.

"Anyway," Isaac continued, "it was Uncle. He hugged me and asked me where *you* were. I didn't know what to say at first, so I just said what I knew to be true—that you would not be far behind me." Isaac smiled his signature smile and tossed his hair to the side.

He had known I'd come, just as I had known I'd find him. Neither of us had given up on the other.

"It took you longer than I thought, though," he chastised. "It's been two days already! *Two* days!" he said, holding up two fingers for emphasis.

I half-smiled at what two days had looked like for me, but I knew there was no need to tell him weeks had passed in our world. It just didn't seem important.

"Geeze!" he said, throwing his hands in the air. "You must have found a lot of things in that antique store worth looking at! What'd you do? Camp out there?"

I shook my head. "If you only knew," I said, taking him in my arms for another hug. I held him tight, and a brief sensation came over me that perhaps it hadn't been that long after all.

Isaac's face was buried against my dress. "Can we leave now?" he asked in a muffled voice.

"Oh, honey," I answered, placing my hands on the sides of his face so he could look up at me, "I'm afraid we can't."

Isaac pulled away. "Why not?"

How could I tell this sweet little boy I didn't know how to get us back home?

"Because—"

He was waiting patiently.

"Honey," I rubbed his hair. "I don't know how to get us back." There, I said it.

Isaac just stared at me.

"I wish I did, but I don't."

Isaac looked confused.

"But don't worry," I assured him. "I'm going to figure all this out. I promise. I'll find a way to get us home."

"Home?!" Isaac exclaimed. "Who cares about going home?! I meant can we go, so I can show you what I wanted to show you?"

Who cares about going home? I do. That's who! We don't belong here. We don't even know where 'here' is, or if we can trust anybody or anything we see 'here'.

But I didn't say any of that to Isaac. I didn't want to do anything to raise alarm or make him worry. He was okay—better than okay, actually. And for now, so was I.

"Alright." I threw my hands in the air, defeated. "Lead the way."

Isaac led me out of the garden and behind the house to a barn. "In here," he said.

The smell of fresh hay and manure flooded my nose as we walked to a stable at the very back.

"Here," Isaac said, placing his hand on the neck of a black stallion. "Meet Nightmare."

Nightmare? You've got to be kidding me! What kind of sick joke was this?!

"Nightmare," Isaac said, "meet my mom."

Nightmare stammered uncomfortably and twitched his pointed ears forward.

Isaac placed his hand on Nightmare's nose and rubbed him gently. "It's okay," he said.

Nightmare responded by bowing his head close to Isaac's.

I didn't know anything about horses—in fact, this was the first time I'd been this close to one—but he truly was magnificent to look at. Thick muscles twitched and flinched across his neck and legs with even the slightest movement, and I could literally *see* the blood pulsating through the thick veins that branched out all over his body. But it was his eyes that caught my attention. They stared at me calmly through short eyelashes, as if Isaac's touch had put him in a trance. He bent his head closer to Isaac's and rubbed his cheek to his.

"He's beautiful," I said, truly in awe.

"He's mine," Isaac beamed.

"What?!"

"Well, not *mine*, really. But Uncle says he's never seen Nightmare take to someone the way he's taken to me. I mean, I didn't know I liked horses," he continued, "but Uncle says I'm a natural-born rider—"

"Stop!"

Isaac turned to me with genuine confusion in his eyes. "Stop what?"

"Stop calling him Uncle. He's not your uncle." Isaac kept saying "uncle" like he'd been around him his entire life—like he was already emotionally attached to him, just as he had obviously already gotten attached to the horse. We were not going to stay in this place any longer than we had to, and I didn't want Isaac having to deal with loss again. He'd already had to deal with enough.

Isaac looked down. "Everybody calls him Uncle," he mumbled.

Nightmare nudged Isaac with his nose.

"I'm sorry," I said. "It's just . . . we're not staying here, so—"

He looked up at me with eyes that mirrored Nightmares—those chameleon eyes! Except, Isaac's brown eyes seemed to be pleading.

"We're NOT," I repeated, firmly.

"Why not?" he asked.

"Because we're not. This isn't our home."

"But it *could* be."

"But it's not," I said with as much sternness as I could muster. "And we're not going to talk about this right now."

"There you are!" A booming voice from behind made me

jump.

I gave Isaac a hushed look before turning around to look at who the voice had come from.

"I figured I'd find you here."

"Charles," I said, "How good to see you."

"Charles? Since when do you call me Charles?" He smiled and rested his elbow on Nightmare's stall.

I laughed nervously.

"I see you've met Nightmare," he said, patting his mane.

"Indeed. Isaac has taken quite a liking to him."

"Ahh. That's only half the truth. The entirety of it is that Nightmare has taken quite a liking to Isaac."

"So he's told me." I looked at Isaac, who was nuzzling his nose to Nightmare's. "Does that happen often?"

"I've seen all kinds of animals take to all kinds of people, but this . . ." he paused and looked at Isaac with Nightmare, "this is different."

"Different how?" I was interested.

Charles tilted his head. "I can't really say. Just—" He paused for a minute, then shrugged. "I've just never seen anything like it."

We watched Isaac with Nightmare for a little while longer.

"We should be getting back to the gala," Charles finally said. "People are going to start wondering where the guests of honor have run off to."

"Of course," I answered. "Isaac, shall we?"

Isaac patted Nightmare's neck and promised he'd be back tomorrow.

From the corner of my eye, I thought I saw Nightmare nod.

CHAPTER 14

Tomorrow

"Good morning, Miss Karla." Evelyn sat a tray of food on the end of the bed and pulled open the heavy drapes to let in the sun.

I raised my hand to block the light. Evelyn. Heavy drapes. Terrebonne Parish.

"Where's Isaac?" I sat up suddenly, a brief moment of panic overtaking me. What if last night had been a dream? What if *this* was a dream? Had I really found Isaac last night?

"Oh, I 'spect he's been up fer hours. He loves to run 'round dese properties doin' de stuff young boys likes doin'. I never see 'im 'til supper."

I flopped back on the pillow, exhausted from the sheer energy it took to momentarily panic.

Evelyn laid clothes out on the bed. "Come now, let's get you dressed."

I listlessly rolled out of bed, careful not to knock over the tray at the foot.

Evelyn helped me slip into another beautiful gown, tugging at the strings and using encouraging words to sway me into letting her pull the garments tighter than I would have liked. I huffed as she thread the last eyelet on the back of the dress.

"You never know who might come call'n. You must always look presentable. Now," she tied the strings and tucked them out of view, "hush up and eat yer breakfast." She gave firm orders, but did so with a gentle smile as she left the room.

I wasn't hungry, but I moved the food around on my plate just enough that Evelyn would think I'd eaten some of it, then I started to head downstairs. But I paused at the door and turned back to the bed where the tray was sitting. Was I supposed to take the tray down or leave it? I didn't know proper etiquette, and I didn't want to raise red flags with anyone that I didn't belong—at least not until I figured out how to get us out of here. I hastily grabbed the tray and headed out the door, down the hallway, and down the staircase.

I stood at the bottom of the stairs, awkwardly holding the tray, not knowing where to go next. Where was the kitchen?

"I'll take that." Evelyn popped out from behind the staircase, briefly startling me and catching the tray just before it dropped. She eyed the leftover food and gave me a knowing look. "Not hungry, Miss Karla?"

"I guess I'm just—" I sputtered.

"Yes, ma'am, I know you is tired. Travel'n such a distance, den have'n de big shindig last night. Dat's why I let you sleep in an' brings you breakfast. But tomorrow, you join the family fer breakfast. You hear me?" She tilted her head slightly, her chubby chin meeting her neck, and she raised her eyebrows to the point they nearly disappeared behind her headwrap.

"Yes, ma'am," I answered.

Evelyn left with the tray, disappearing behind the staircase.

I stood there, not knowing what to do next. Should I go to the ladies' parlor? Was there a living room or dining area where I would find Helen, Emma, and Ann? I didn't know what ladies did in the 1850s when they woke.

Just as I was deciding I should go back to my room, Helen came through the front door. "Oh good, you're up. *Finally!* You know," she said, wagging her finger at me, "I'll not allow you too many more mornings of rest, as I have missed you too much to let any time be wasted on sleep."

"You don't find sleep to be of importance?" I asked, as she looped her arm into mine and guided me out the door she'd just come in.

"A requirement, perhaps, but there are other things of far greater importance."

"Oh?" I asked.

Helen smiled. "Indeed."

"Such as?"

"Such as lots of things," she answered, matter-of-factly. "Family, for example."

"Speaking of which . . ." I glanced around. "Did you see where Isaac trailed off to this morning?"

"I believe he went to the barn, but he does so love wandering the property and taking off with Uncle, so I can't say for sure," she answered.

As we walked onto the front lawn, I again noticed the blue and orange flowers. I pointed to the blue ones. "What are those flowers?"

Helen's eyes followed to where I was pointing. "They're called Yesterday, Today, and Tomorrow."

I smiled. "They're beautiful."

"Yes, they're my favorite. Speaking of yesterday, did you run into Lawson last night?"

I looked at her curiously. I had indeed looked for him—I don't know why—but I hadn't found him. "Was he there?" I inquired.

Helen shrugged. "You tell me. I didn't see him; but then, I didn't see much of you either, so I thought—"

"Helen! Shame on you!"

"Well." She smiled. "You never know."

We walked across the lawn toward a blanket spread under a large shade tree. A book lay on the blanket, open and facedown so as to save the reader's place.

We sat on the blanket and I picked up the book. "What are you reading?"

"*The Scarlet Letter* by Hawthorne. Have you read it?"

"I have," I answered.

"I've been dying to read it," Helen beamed excitedly. "I hear the first printing sold out in ten days."

"So I heard, as well."

"I also hear it's very scandalous," she whispered, providing the real reason she was reading it.

New England critics *had* called the book scandalous, condemning Hawthorne for the subject matter of adultery. But the book wasn't about adultery. Any real lover of literature knew that. Yes, it was the story of a woman's sin of adultery and a man's secret and guilt, but there was so much more to the story.

"He's a great writer," I said, admiring the inked letters and the feel of the crisp pages between my fingers. The same book is likely sitting forgotten on a bookshelf in my world—tattered edges, yellowed pages, and torn cover. Or worse, it no longer exists. I brought the book to my nose, appreciating the fragrance of fresh ink and inhaling the aroma of the book's leather cover.

"And?" Helen asked.

"And what?"

"And did you like the book?" She looked down and plucked a blade of grass from the ground.

I flipped through the book's pages. "Some say it's a tale of sin and guilt," I answered, without really answering. "Others say it's a tale of love. Do you like it so far?"

Helen shrugged as she separated the blade of grass. "So far." She looked up at me. "But which do you think it is?"

I thought about it for a minute. "I suppose it depends on the reader," I said, again not answering her question.

Over the years, Hawthorne would come to insist that *The Scarlet Letter* was a romance novel, going as far as changing the subtitle on future prints to state such . . . but I always felt it was a tale of sorrow.

"Yes, but which do *you* think?" She stopped playing with her blade of grass and gave me her full attention, waiting for an answer she seemed desperately to need.

I took a deep breath and chose my words carefully. "I think Hawthorne must have been very close to his characters."

Helen raised her eyebrows. "Do tell?"

"I mean, he must have felt their anguish at being separated from one another. It's so evident in his writing." I felt the familiar twinge that separation from a loved one brings, and I didn't want to address my own anguish of separation from Mason—how painful that was—so I continued quickly. "And I think that people are judgmental when they ought not be." My voice rose. "Nobody is without sin, and sins should not be announced to the world, as we'd all be wearing scarlet letters in lieu of garments!" My words came out more forceful than I'd intended, and I felt just as taken aback as Helen looked.

She stared at me with big round eyes for what seemed like eternity. Then, she looked back down at her blade of grass. "So, you don't have any strong thoughts on it, then?"

We burst into laughter. That a book had gotten me so rattled was amusing—to both of us. When our laughter finally subsided, we lay on our backs, side-by-side, staring up through the tree branches at a bright blue sky.

"You can't help who you fall in love with," I mumbled.

Helen turned her head in my direction, but I kept my eyes upward—searching through the branches for what lay beyond the blue sky—and I aimed my next comment carefully. "And to be kept from the one you love is a cruel punishment."

I felt Helen still staring, so I turned my head to match her stare.

She smiled softly. "Are we still talking about the book?"

But she already knew the answer, so I took a deep breath and looked back up. This time, I refused to look at the heavens that had stolen Mason, and instead gave the tree my complete attention. For the first time, I noticed the branches were full of thousands of clusters of tiny green cones that spiraled out from heart-shaped leaves.

"It's a beautiful tree," I commented.

"It's called a Maidenhair tree." Helen rolled her head closer to mine. "It's a boy tree," she whispered, as if it was a naughty secret she took pleasure in sharing.

"What? How do you know?"

"Grams told me. See the tiny cones? Girl trees don't have those. In fact," she said, "girl trees smell like vomit!"

I burst out laughing. "You're lying, Helen! That's terrible!"

"I'm not!" Helen exclaimed, not the least bit offended. "The girls stink!! Pee-yew!" She clamped her thumb and finger over her nose for emphasis, and we both laughed hysterically.

We were still laughing when Isaac came running across the lawn. "Mom!"

I sat up and caught him in my arms just as he reached me. I pulled him into my lap and held him tightly, even though he was really too big for such affection.

"Good morning," I said as he squirmed to get free. "What have you been up to this morning?"

"I was in the barn with Nightmare. I'm going to go riding. Do you want to come watch?"

I glanced at Helen. "Shall we?"

"You go ahead." She picked up *The Scarlet Letter*. "I believe I have an opinion to form."

"Very well, then," I said, kissing her cheek before standing.

Why had I done that?

Because it felt right.

And it did. It felt perfectly right. I enjoyed those few moments with her, sitting in the shade on a blanket cushioned by soft grass. It gave me a strange feeling—one that was not familiar to me right away, but I embraced it as soon as I recognized it. It was happiness.

I walked around to the back of the house and toward the barn while Isaac ran on ahead.

Moments later, I stood behind a fence that surrounded a field connected to the barn, and waited.

Last night, when Isaac brought me to meet Nightmare, it was dark; but this morning, in the light of day, I could see the barn was old, but solid. It resembled the paintings of barns one often sees on the wall of their grandparents' home—a comforting scene of serenity. The ground inside the fenceline was dry dirt, marked with divots left behind by a horse's galloping hoofs. Outside the fence, the grass swayed green for as far as the eye could see.

I scanned more of the property, taking in its beauty, until I found myself staring back at the barn. My eyes settled on a piece of farm equipment sitting on the side of the barn just below the hay loft. It looked out of place compared to the rest of my surroundings, and it gave me an immediate uneasiness. It was a large medieval-looking piece of equipment with pointed iron barbs and sharp blades. It was obviously used for plowing, or some other sort of farming job, but the sight of it made me tense and instantly turned my stomach. I directed my attention to the barn doors at the front of the barn, trying to ignore the disturbing equipment's existence as I waited for Isaac to emerge.

Minutes later, Isaac and Nightmare appeared. Nightmare entered the riding ring at a walk with Isaac sitting tall on his back—Isaac's head, shoulders, and hips all perfectly aligned. Then, Nightmare went to a trot as they made a circle in the ring. Isaac tilted his hat and gave a little wink as he passed by. Then, with a simple "click, click" from Isaac, Nightmare transitioned into a canter, then a gallop.

I watched them in wonder. It was as if Nightmare and Isaac were connected. Isaac had never been on a horse before, but to watch him ride, you'd think he had an entire shelf full of equestrian trophies in lieu of football.

"He's great," a voice behind me said.

I turned to see Lawson, beaming.

"I've never seen a boy his age ride like that. How long has he been riding?"

I shook my head.

"That long, huh?"

I smiled.

"Mind if I watch?" He propped his foot against the bottom rail of the fence and rested his forearms over the top.

"Not at all," I answered. The muscles in his forearms twitched as he repositioned his arms on the fence, and I forced my eyes away before he saw me staring at them.

We watched Nightmare trot around the ring with Isaac for several minutes before I decided the silence had lasted long enough.

"Eh hem," I cleared my throat.

Lawson turned to me.

"I, um—I saw Thomas and Jackson at the gala last night."

Lawson looked back toward Isaac and didn't respond.

"You didn't come?"

"No, ma'am—" he began, turning back toward me as he shifted his foot on the bottom of the fence.

I gave him a stern look.

"I mean, Karla," he corrected.

"Might I ask why?"

"Because I told you I wouldn't be there, and I am a man of my word."

I looked at him, needing more of an explanation.

He sighed. "I only just got an invitation after our walk," he explained. "Mr. Darap was grateful for the help we offered upon your arrival, I suppose."

"Let us not discuss my arrival again, as I feel we are both a bit confused about it."

"Are you now?" He raised his eyebrows and turned to give me his full attention. "Now why would that be?"

I didn't answer. I didn't know how to. I needed someone to confide in, but I didn't know if Lawson was the right person. Funny though, it seemed *everyone* in Terrebonne Parish was "the right person."

Seeing I was not going to reply, Lawson spoke up. "Well, I for one am not confused. I have drawn a conclusion as to that day."

I looked at him curiously. "Have you now?"

"I have," he answered unequivocally.

"And what, pray tell, have you concluded?" I asked in a tone that even I found a bit flirty.

"See'n as only birds and angels fall from the sky, and as it is apparent you are not a bird . . ." He moved his hand from my head to my feet to illustrate, "that leads me to one conclusion."

I laughed. "So, if you find me in the early morning searching for breakfast on the lawn, I suppose you will be greatly disappointed?"

"I haven't been disappointed yet." His eyes held mine for a second longer than was comfortable. His skin was tan and rugged, and his dark hair layered across his forehead just to the tops of his thick eyebrows.

"Lawson—" I started.

"I am sorry for the loss of your husband," he said abruptly, not looking away when he spoke.

I began to feel uncomfortable. I didn't want to talk about Mason with anybody, especially not with a man who was obviously flirting with me, and who I also had some unexplainable feelings for. It felt wrong—like I was cheating.

Lawson continued. "I understand it was a time ago. I know it doesn't seem like it some days, but—"

"How could you know?" I made no effort to hide my annoyance. I was tired of people acting like they knew what I was going through. The pain was a constant sadness dulled only by the anger at being left behind.

"I know," Lawson answered, "because I lost a love, too."

I looked at him.

He was distant for a moment, and then he blinked and was with me again. "Her name was Albany. We were engaged." Lawson looked down.

It was obvious it hurt to talk about her. I knew that hurt, and I realized he knew mine.

"What happened?"

"Someone wanted her more than me." He looked up to the sky. "Someone you can't argue with."

"God," I answered, aware that with just that one word I had expressed so much contempt.

Lawson nodded.

"I'm sorry." How many times had someone said that to

me with empty emotion? I touched his arm and felt the fuzzy warmth under my palm. "I'm sorry," I said again, wanting him to feel my sincerity.

"Mom! Mom!" Isaac came riding up on Nightmare, and I was thankful for the interruption. It seemed there was so much that Lawson and I could talk about and share, but it also seemed like the wrong time and place.

"Mom, did you see me?" Isaac was grinning from ear to ear.

"Indeed!" I answered. "You were wonderful!"

Lawson chimed in, "That was quite a show. I think that horse really likes you."

Isaac reached down and patted Nightmare's neck. "That's what everybody says."

Charles walked up to the fence from inside the ring, catching Lawson's comment. He stroked Nightmare's side. "Before Isaac came, Nightmare wouldn't let anyone get too close to him. Not since his momma died, anyway." He looked up at Isaac. "Seems he knows you're not trying to take her place, though." He reached up and rubbed Nightmare's nose. "Just likes the company, I suppose." He glanced over at me and Lawson.

Lawson and I looked at each other, and I gave him a quick half smile.

"Come on," Charles said, giving Isaac's leg a soft pat. "Let's take him back to the barn and get him brushed down."

"See you later, mom!" Isaac and Nightmare trotted toward the barn with Charles following on foot.

"You reckon people are a little like horses?" Lawson asked.

"Most people I've met have been more like a horse's a—"

"Easy there," Lawson interrupted, offering his arm as we began walking. "Remember, you're a lady."

"I thought I was an angel?!" I argued, pretending to be offended.

"Neigh!" Lawson answered, shaking his dark mane, imitating the sound of a horse perfectly.

And once again, I found myself laughing.

***

I lay in bed that night with my mind racing. It had been a wonderful day. I enjoyed walking with Lawson, sitting with Helen, and watching Isaac with Nightmare. Everything in Terrebonne Parish was good—euphoric, almost. It felt like nothing bad could happen here, and I was beginning to think like Isaac: why go home?

Because you don't belong here.

I knew it was true. We didn't belong here, and we needed to find a way home. The idea of staying was not an option. It just wasn't.

But how would we get home? The mirror had brought us here, so it made sense that a mirror would get us home, but which mirror? Where was it?

I couldn't think about it. I was too tired. But a good tired. The kind of tired one feels after a long day of Fourth of July picnics or family reunions. The kind of tired that welcomes sleep as it wraps around you like a soft, warm blanket, signifying the end of a wonderful day and giving no threats of what tomorrow might bring. The kind of tired I hadn't known for a long time, but I welcomed it.

I would look into mirrors tomorrow. Tomorrow, I would find a way home.

"Tomorrow," I whispered, closing my eyes.

CHAPTER 15

Crickets

Chirp.

My eyes shot open.

Chirp, chirp.

I glanced around the dark room.

Chirp.

There it was again—a chirping so loud I could have sworn it was in the room with me. I glanced to the window, open in an attempt to cool the room of the July heat; but instead, it acted as a doormat for the sweltering night . . . and other things . . . to flood in.

Chirp.

My heart began to race. I knew that chirp. I'd heard it before. My heart beat in my chest so loudly it felt as if my heart had migrated to my ears; my eardrums vibrated achingly with each beat.

Another chirp!

No, no, no, no! No, not again!

But it was persistent. *Chirp, chirp.*

I sat up in bed and stared at the window, my heart still racing.

"Mason," I whispered, "is that you?"

I sat at Mason's grave like so many times before—my heart exceptionally heavy as I fought the urge to join him in his bed of grass.

I was lost, and I ached so badly for him! I leaned against his stone and ran my fingers across his face etched into the stone's front. My fingers trembled. "How am I supposed to go on when I don't want to? I struggle to get out of bed, and when I do crawl out of bed and through the day, I dread getting back into it. It's empty and cold, and it only brings another morning without you in it. Mason, please! I can't do this. I don't *want* to. *Please!*"

And then it occurred to me, I was pleading with the wrong person. It wasn't Mason who didn't want to be here with me, it was God who was keeping him from me.

I closed my eyes and bowed my head. "God, if you're listening, please let Mason come to me. I just need to see him. Just for a second. I just need to know he's okay. Send him to me in a vision, God. Let his auburn eyes be staring at me when I open mine. Or send him to me in a dream like you sent dreams to Abraham and Joseph and so many others. *Please, God*! I just need to talk to him one more time. Just *one more time!*" I sat rocking on my knees, my head in my hands on the damp ground. *"Please, God. Please, God. Please, God."*

Chirp.

I opened my eyes.

Another clear and audible, *Chirp.*

I looked around, honing my eyes and ears in on the sound until I found the source.

Chirp, chirp.

A cricket was perched in the grass at the foot of Mason's grave. He was staring right at me!

I tilted my head in wonder. Could God work through crickets? *Would* he?

I leaned forward. "Marco," I whispered, my voice quivering.

The cricket replied with two deliberate chirps! Two syllables—*po-lo!*

"Mason! Oh, thank you, God! Thank you!"

I listened to the cricket's repeated chirps. But what did it mean? How was I supposed to understand cricket chirps?

I listened patiently. It took me a few moments, but I finally realized the chirps produced a pattern.

Chirp, chirp. Pause. *Chirp, chirp, chirp.* Pause. *Chirp.* Pause. *Chirp.* Pause. *Chirp, chirp, chirp.* Pause.

It was Morse code!

Chirp, chirp, chirp. Pause. *Chirp, chirp.* Pause.

My hands shook as I fumbled in my pocket for my cell phone and pressed the voice record button. I wasn't familiar with Morse code, but I was determined to learn it.

"Okay, I'm listening," I whispered. "One more time."

I sat at Mason's grave recording the pattern of chirps until the pattern began to repeat itself, then I saved the recording under "Mason."

"Thank you, God!" I said, shoving the phone back into my pocket. "Oh, thank you!"

I rushed home and researched how to translate Morse code, anxious to decipher the message God had allowed Mason to send, thinking only briefly how a dream would have been much nicer than a chirping cricket.

I sat with a notebook and pen, listening to the phone recording and trying to decode Mason's message. I kept repeating the rules of translation to myself.

Each character or letter of Morse code is represented by a sequence of dots and dashes. Dashes are three times the duration of a dot. Each dot or dash is followed by a pause, which is equal to the dot duration. Letters of a word are separated by a space equal to three dots, and words are separated by a space equal to seven dots.

I sat for hours working on the encryption. Hours turned into days, and days turned into weeks. Every night, I lay alone in a bed made for two trying to make sense of it; but I was never able to translate a single word. Not *one*. The chirps were too short, the pauses too long.

After weeks of torture, I heard God laughing, and I realized he had been toying with me the entire time. It wasn't enough that he took Mason. Now, he was teasing me, enlisting crickets to help with his cruel joke, reminding me he had control of *everything*, even the smallest of creatures like a cricket.

I began to hate God. The hate boiled inside me as the reality of the situation became clear. God could talk to Mason, but he wouldn't let me! God could hold Mason, but he wouldn't let me! God was showing off—reminding me how much power he had.

Well, I wasn't going to be part of his sick games! I refused to let him toy with me. He and I were done!

Chirp, chirp.
The cricket chirped again outside my bedroom window.
"Oh, shut up!" I screamed, throwing a pillow at the window. "Shut up!"

CHAPTER 16

Broken

Evelyn pulled the drapes open, allowing the sun to intrude.

"Wake up, Mrs. Karla. It's church day."

Church?

I rolled away from the unwanted light. "I'm tired," I mumbled.

I felt Evelyn standing above me, and I pictured her round fists sitting on her chubby hips.

"Hmmph," she huffed. She hovered for a few seconds more, then shuffled out of the room.

I don't go to church. Not anymore.

I rolled over so my back would be to the door, diverting any unwelcome intruders that would surely follow Evelyn, insisting I go to church.

It wasn't long before I heard Grams. "Karla, dear?"

I pretended to be asleep.

She touched my shoulder. "Karla?"

"I'm tired," I mumbled.

"Everybody goes to church in this house," Grams stated firmly. "Unless you are ill."

"I'm ill," I said. I'd take whatever excuse was allowable.

"Karla?" Grams sighed deeply. "At least open your eyes and look at me, dear."

I rolled my head slowly toward her and opened my eyes, but I pulled the blankets up around my chin to tighten the hold the bed had on me.

"What is wrong?"

I knew Grams would only settle for the truth. There was no sense playing games. "I don't go to church anymore," I said flatly.

"Don't go to church?!" Her eyes widened. "But, why—"

I interrupted. I wanted this conversation over with quickly. It was *my* choice, and I didn't want to spend the entire morning explaining it. "I don't believe—"

"Don't believe?!" It was Grams' turn to interrupt. "Why, there's more historical documentation that God exists than there is that Julius Caesar or William Shakespeare ever existed. You believe in them, don't you?"

"You didn't let me finish." I rolled over so I could see her face easier, but I kept my grip on the blanket. "It's not that I don't believe in God. That would be easier—to not believe that he exists. It's just—" I took a deep breath. "I don't believe he's a wonderful, awesome, loving God like you do. Like all those people at church do."

There. I said it. Now she knew.

Compassion passed over Grams face. "Because of Mason?"

"No! Because of God! Because he *took* Mason. And then he took Isa—" I didn't finish. He took Isaac, but I found him just like I said I would, and Grams didn't know anything about that.

Grams straightened her dress, then laid her hands in her lap, placing one on top the other. She sighed deeply and stared forward as if staring back into a memory. "God does take things, it's true; but they're His to take in the first place. They belonged to Him long before He let us borrow them." She looked at me, as if checking to see that I was paying careful attention. "*Borrow,* Karla. That is all."

I furrowed my brow.

"God knows life will not be easy—that it will be full of struggles—so He gives us special people to help us through. He gives us husbands for strength and support." She looked forward again to the place her memories seemed to visit often. "And He gives us children." The word "children" made her smile as she continued her forward stare. "Children remind us to laugh. They remind us to stop and play every now and then."

She blinked quickly a few times, and then turned her gaze back to me. "It *is* sad when He takes them." She wiped a strand of hair from my forehead. "But how sad if He never gave them to us in the first place? 'Tis better to have loved and lost than never to have loved at all.'"

She was quoting Alfred Lord Tennyson. I knew his work. When Mason died, I began reading the bible obsessively—searching for answers to the hundreds of questions I had. Finding no answers in the good book for my immediate liking, I closed the bible and opened books of poetry. I found comfort knowing others had felt the same heartache as me and survived to write about it.

I'd mulled over some of Tennyson's writings and figured out quickly Tennyson wasn't for me. The Tennyson piece Grams referenced was titled, *In Memoriam A.H.H.* It was just as much about nature and biology as it was about sorrow and faith; yet, people often plucked those few lines from the entire work, as if they could bring comfort to the ill hearted.

> *I hold it true, whate'er befall;*
> *I feel it when I sorrow most;*
> *'Tis better to have loved and lost,*
> *than never to have loved at all.*

It was a joke that those words could bring comfort. It was a joke that they ever brought any comfort to Tennyson, even as he was writing them. After all, it took him seventeen years to write the entire poem. Seventeen years! He started writing it after the unexpected and sudden death of a dear friend and, seventeen years later, he finished it. It took him seventeen years to reaffirm his Christian faith. Seventeen years to turn doubt and despair into faith and hope. There was nothing in seventeen years of suffering I could find comfort in.

I did find comfort in other poets, though—those who'd been through the pain that follows loss—the ones who knew the pain was so great that it was better to have never loved in the first place. To that end, I favored Otomo no Yakamochi, and I quoted him for Grams to dispute her Tennyson.

Grams stood. "I will say you are sick. There are many types

of ailments; they need not know which you are afflicted with."
She turned to leave the room, but briefly paused at the door.
"Isaac will go with us," she said, turning to face me with a gentle
face, "if you've no objection."

I didn't answer. Isaac hadn't been back to church since Mason's death, either. But that was my doing, not his.

"Very well," Grams said, taking my silence as permission.
"We will see you when we return." She turned and left the room.

I repeated Yakamochi's words in my head. *Better never to
have met you in my dream than to wake and reach for hands that
are not there.*

His words dug deep into my heart, just as they had the first
time I buried them there. Too many times, I had awakened to
find Mason gone—stuck in a dream that would never again be
reality.

A hot tear rolled down my cheek, and I lay unmoving, listening for the house to grow quiet . . . and for the pounding in my
angry heart to subside.

Minutes passed, perhaps an hour. Finally, sure that everyone had gone, I crept out of bed and went to the armoire to search
for the simplest dress I could find—I couldn't be bothered with
corsets and strings today—but even the simple blue dress I chose
required a bodice, so I quickly buttoned the front and closed the
armoire door, coming face-to-face with my reflection.

The mirror on the front of the armoire dared me to touch it.

I took a few steps back. "Hello, mirror," I said aloud. *"Are
you a mirror? Or are you really a door? A portal?"*

I saw my reflection ask the question and wait for an answer.
Well, there's only one way to find out.

I took a step forward and readied my hand to push against
the glass. I paused. My hand was trembling. What was wrong
with me?! Didn't I *want* it to be the way home? I steadied my
hand and stretched my fingers forward slowly, allowing their
tips to gently touch the mirror.

Nothing happened. No movement under my touch. No morphing of my reflection. Nothing.

I pressed more firmly, but the mirror didn't give.

I let out a breath. "Yep, you're just a plain ol' mirror," I said, turning away. Then, feeling like I'd hurt its feelings, I turned back around and patted it gently. "That's a good thing. Trust me."

Talking to mirrors! I truly was losing it.

And so my morning went, making my way room to room, pressing against mirrors, partly relieved they were just mirrors and partly annoyed none of them were more than just mirrors. It was strange to want two things at the same time, each with the same level of desire.

Sometime around noon I found myself back in my room lying across the bed, taking a break from moving up and down the stairs and throughout the house. Sunlight cascaded through the large windows and onto my face as my eyelids began to flutter. Sleep was calling me, and I welcomed it.

I stood in the field—the fiery tree closer to me than it had been before, but still far in the distance. Again, I felt the warm sun and gentle breeze. Again, the breeze picked up as the wind grew wild and the leaves on the tree struggled to keep hold.

Again, I screamed, "Stop!"

But this time, I saw a calm in the midst of the storm. The calmness cocooned the figure under the tree, which was no longer raising their hand and screaming, "Peace. Be still." Instead, they were curled into a fetal position on their knees as the storm raged all about them—unable to touch them in their hunched and protected position on the ground.

A large cracking sound caused my attention to turn to the branch—always the same branch—flying through the air toward me. Again the branch slammed into my forehead, and everything went dark.

I woke from my Sunday nap to find everyone had returned from church. Nothing more was said about my lack of attendance, but Isaac surprised me at dinner by going on and on about how much he'd enjoyed the service. I let him talk without interrupting, sometimes stealing a glance at Grams' approving and smiling face.

I had never shared my rage and contempt for God with Isaac. It wasn't like I blew up in anger one day and Isaac witnessed it. We simply stopped going to church. It just happened. And Isaac never asked why, so there was no reason to explain it. Besides, I was glad not to talk about it. I didn't want Isaac to feel the same hatred I felt. I wouldn't wish it on anyone, especially Isaac, so I didn't say anything about God—good or bad. I simply stopped talking about him altogether.

I didn't think Isaac had noticed or given it much thought, but listening to him go on and on about church made me wonder if I was wrong. Maybe Isaac *had* felt the exemption of God in our lives. Perhaps I was too absorbed with my own disdain to notice.

"You really enjoyed it?" I asked.

He looked up from his dinner plate, his bangs brushing his eyelashes. "It reminded me of dad—of when we all used to go together." In that brief moment, just by mentioning his father, there was so much grief in his eyes. Just as his surroundings mixed and mingled together to create varying colors in his eyes, his emotions reflected in his eyes, as well. The grief was there—it was prominent—but there was also an essence of complete happiness from the memories he had of Mason. Talking about Mason was painful for him, but the memories themselves weren't painful at all. The memories brought him joy.

All this time I had avoided talking about Mason because it hurt too much, but how could I have not seen in Isaac's eyes what I was clearly seeing now? He missed his father, and he longed to be around anything that reminded him of him—anything that would keep those memories fresh in his young mind. While I was trying to avoid things that reminded me of Mason, Isaac needed them.

I got out of my chair and knelt beside him, hugging him tightly. "I know, honey. And you know what? Dad is with God now, so maybe—" I looked at Grams, who was eyeing me sweetly. "Maybe, being close to God is like being close to your dad because anywhere God is, there your dad is also."

Saying it out loud made it real. The words didn't just come out of my mouth for Isaac's benefit; they dripped from my lips and flowed to my heart. The knowledge didn't take away the hurt—or the anger at God—but it brought back a truth I'd known deep down all along.

"Well," Mr. Darap said, slamming the palm of his hands down on the table and breaking the silence that followed. "I think I'll have some of that apple pie I hear tell Evelyn baked up for dessert."

"Yes, sir!" Evelyn said, smiling a joyful smile as she waddled off to the kitchen.

Before the day ended, I decided I would go to church the following Sunday—not for me, but for Isaac. I didn't know if we'd be back in West Virginia by then listening to Pastor Dan, or if we'd be attending church service in 1850's Louisiana. Either would suit me fine; although, the latter was sounding more appealing the longer we stayed. Terrebonne Parish felt safe. Terrebonne Parish felt easy. Terrebonne Parish felt like home.

***

I'd hoped my night would be free of nightmares after having such a wonderful day, but there was no escaping them. That night, my head was muddled with flashbacks much worse than any nightmare had ever been. I couldn't push the memories away. To distract myself, I sang the words to Christmas carols silently in my head. I counted sheep. I even hoped desperately to hear the crickets I greatly despised. That was how badly I wanted to block the reality persistently creeping into my head.

"Oh, *please* crowd my head with memories of the taunting crickets at Mason's grave," I whispered with my eyes squeezed tightly shut, as if wishing hard enough would make it so. *"Please, please, please* give me that horrible memory instead of the one creeping in now."

But it was no use. The memory came as clear as the day it happened.

I had been sitting on the edge of Mason's hospital bed, holding his hand. My heart beat slower and slower in my chest, matching the slowing beeps of the machine. But I didn't need the machine to tell me his heart was slowing. I felt it. Our hearts had been synchronized from the moment we met. When his heart fluttered with joy, so did mine. When his heart thumped in excitement, so did mine. And when his heart slowed, so did mine.

I sat listening to our hearts tell me what I wasn't ready to accept. Mason had fought hard, but surely there was still some fight left in him.

Isaac had spent the entire afternoon with Mason the day before, sitting by his bed and talking to him, even though Mason didn't respond. I heard parts of Isaac's words. He was telling him about his day—a really good tackle he'd made at football practice. He told him about his teacher giving the class a pop quiz. But I couldn't hear everything Isaac said because sometimes Isaac leaned in close to his father and talked softly. He stayed with him well into the night.

I wasn't sure what time Isaac left Mason's side, but the next day, he refused to go to Mason's room. Instead, he sat downstairs in the hospital cafeteria. I begged him to join me, but he solemnly and unwaveringly shook his head no, so I left him to his own thoughts.

I sat on the edge of Mason's bed, drowning in my own thoughts, rubbing the top of his hand gently with my fingertips.

We had been sitting in silence for a long time. Mason hadn't spoken in days, despite my everyday ramblings peppered with questions like, "Don't you think?" and "Wouldn't you agree?"

But that day was different. It *felt* different. There was a heaviness in the room I'd never felt before.

"Swim." The words were soft and raspy, and they came from Mason.

I looked up eagerly. There *was* still some fight left in him!! I knew it! But his eyes were closed, and the thought crossed my mind that perhaps my foolish faith had manifested itself into imagined words.

I leaned in close, putting my cheek to his lips. "What, baby? What did you say?"

"Swim," he repeated. There was no mistaking it this time. He spoke that one word so clearly, and his fingers squeezed mine ever so slightly when he said it. I shot a confused glance at the nurse, who had been staying close the past few hours. I knew why.

"It's the medicine," she said. "It makes people say strange things. They don't know what they're saying."

But Mason knew. Maybe it sounded strange to the nurse, but Mason knew exactly what he was saying.

Swim.

It was the one fear I never tackled.

"You're such a strong woman," Mason would say, "are you really going to let a little water get the best of you?"

"It's not a little water," I'd argue. "It's an entire oceanful."

"Let me teach you."

"No," I'd reply.

"Come on. You can do this."

"Nope."

I stared at Mason's lips and willed them to say something else. But they didn't.

"Okay," I said. "Wake up and teach me to swim. I'll learn. I promise."

People who've watched a loved one suffer through a long illness often talk about the peace they find near the end. They talk about being ready to let go because they know their loved one will be better off . . . that they won't suffer anymore. But I never reached that stage. I always wanted Mason to get better. I always believed he would. Even in his last days of living, I didn't believe he was dying.

Swim.

It would be the last word Mason uttered. It would be the last time I felt the warmth of his hand in mine, his fingers squeezing mine ever so gently.

The next time I held his hand, he was lying in a wooden casket, and he did not return my squeeze, even though I begged him to. Even though I begged God to allow it.

Swim.

I lay in bed in Terrebonne Parish, tears streaming down my cheeks, unaware in the moment how that single word was a gift.

CHAPTER 17

Jeremiah

I stood on the porch. Breakfast had been a jovial time of laughter, warm biscuits, and hot coffee. And now, I stood full and content, staring out across the yard.

Not long ago, I dreaded mornings. The alarm clock would rudely wake me, and I'd force my legs over the edge of the bed. My legs, my torso, my heart—all heavy with anger and grief that was steadily weighing me down . . . and getting heavier every day.

But this morning, I felt good. It was a rarity that I could only assume was brought on by Terrebonne Parish.

Terrebonne Parish. It didn't make sense. A long walk was what I needed. I needed to clear my head and thoroughly analyze all that had happened over the past several weeks. I replayed the events over and over in my head.

Isaac had gone missing.

I found him in a place that couldn't really exist.

And Isaac needed God, even if I didn't.

I closed my eyes and stretched against the warmth of the day. I enjoyed it—I enjoyed that it was as far from the cold as one could get.

I hated the cold. The cold meant winter, and winter brought back too many memories. They weren't all bad. Not in the beginning. But in the end, they were too painful to bear.

The early winters were spent with a vibrant and healthy Mason, and they were beautiful. The white sparkling view from the upstairs window of the home we shared was picturesque. The sight of Isaac and Mason throwing snowballs in the back yard was blissful. And the sight of Mason wrapping a scarf around the snowman we built together was splendid.

Winter was Mason's favorite season. Mason—who hated the heat and would have preferred to live in Alaska. And so, because it was Mason's favorite, it became mine, as well. Anything that made Mason happy made me happy. Those were good memories—memories that preceded the nightmares. Those were the memories that were replaced, despite my not wanting them to be, with memories of Mason's pain and suffering.

It was cold the night Mason died, and it had been cold ever since.

In early December, the doctors told me he didn't have much time. They told me he wouldn't make it to Christmas, but I didn't believe them. I couldn't imagine a world without Mason in it. And despite how weak I could see him getting, I believed he would be home with me and Isaac come Christmas morning. I even wrapped gifts for him.

Mason was a great gift wrapper. He folded each crease perfectly and took time to carefully line up the patterns on the paper—unlike my wrapping technique, where I used as few pieces of tape as possible with the fewest folds. I always spent more time worrying about what to put in the packages than I did about how to make them pretty.

But that year, I carefully wrapped Mason's gifts. I made sure the cuts were straight, the folds were even, and the patterns matched up. I tied bows and ribbons around the finished packages and wrote clues on each of the name tags as to what was inside. Leaving clues on the name tags was something Mason had done the first year we were married, and it had been a ritual ever since. It made unwrapping the gifts a game and extended the excitement of gift opening a bit longer.

That year, I wrote, "You'll be RUNNING back to the gym before you know it!" on a pair of new running shoes I bought him. Mason was healthy. He worked out regularly, so I had no doubt he'd win against the persistent illness that clawed at his body.

I wrapped his gifts and placed them under the tree . . . where they stayed long after Christmas morning, long after his funeral, and long after everyone told me it was time to take the tree down.

But what do you do with gifts that were purchased and wrapped for someone specific? Take them back to the store? Give them away? Wrapping Mason's gifts was the last display of optimism I had been able to show. What would unwrapping them mean?

I never unwrapped them, and I don't know what happened to them. Cheryl came and took the tree down sometime after Valentine's Day. She didn't tell me what she did with the gifts, and I didn't ask. She had repeatedly asked what I wanted her to do with them, but I never answered because I didn't know what the correct answer was; so I let her handle it, and somehow that made it marginally easier.

Spring reared its sopping head. Then, summer edged in. The seasons morphed and warmed, but I stayed cold. Even in the heat of summer, I sat under a blanket on the couch staring out the patio door to the back yard. Through streams of sunlight, I swore I could see flickers of snowflakes, and Mason and Isaac chasing each other with hands full of snowballs. I couldn't get those images out of my head, just as I couldn't get the cold out of my heart.

Until now. Standing in the yard at Grams', I closed my eyes and raised my face to the sky, feeling the sun kiss it good morning. It was the first time I'd felt warm in a long time, and I realized how much I missed it.

I'd tried to hide those days in the cold from Isaac, and I'd conned myself into believing I'd been successful. Sure, he'd noticed the Christmas tree stayed longer than customary, but he had no idea how much pain I was really in.

Or did he? When I eventually went back to work, I continued the façade that I was okay—that I wasn't frozen inside. But I know now anyone who got close to me could feel the chill.

And what if Isaac not only felt the chill, but what if he had been frozen, too? He had lost his father, and then watched his mother become distant—no amount of climbing out of bed each morning and forcing a smile on my face could hide that.

Then, miracle of miracles, antique stores began calling—beckoning us through their doors—and we finally found ourselves smiling again. We weren't relishing life, but we were finding things we enjoyed—things that unexplainably felt familiar and brought us comfort.

And now, I knew why. Terrebonne Parish was why. Grams and Helen and Charles were why. It didn't make sense—Isaac and I falling through a mirror and finding this place—but it didn't have to make sense because it *felt* right.

Isaac and I were finally beginning to unthaw.

I stared across the yard and spotted Evelyn in the distance picking apples from one of the trees in the orchard. Someone was with her—a black man wearing khaki-colored pants and a white long-sleeved shirt with the sleeves rolled up to his elbows. He was standing on a ladder tossing apples down one-at-a-time to Evelyn, who was catching each apple in her apron before gently laying it in a wooden crate at her feet. They were methodical in their collecting and had a pretty good system going.

"Could you take Evelyn and Jeremiah some lemonade?" Grams asked.

I jumped at the sound of her voice, mystified at how she had walked up beside me without my noticing.

She stood holding two tall glasses of lemonade, each containing several slivers of lemon.

"Jeremiah?" I asked.

Grams nodded with a smile toward Evelyn and the man in the orchard.

"Oh. Of course. Certainly," I said, taking the drinks from Grams' hands. They were cold in my palms, despite having no ice.

"Thank you, dear," Grams smiled and gave a little wink.

I walked across the yard to the orchard, reaching them just as Jeremiah was coming down the ladder.

"Whew-ee," he said, "am I glad to see you! One a dem fer

me?" he asked, nodding at the drinks in my hands.

"Yes, sir," I replied, handing him one of the glasses. "Grams asked that I bring them."

"Sho is glad she did dat!" he said after taking a long drink. "Yes, ma'am. Sho is glad."

"Evelyn," I said, reaching the other glass out to her.

"Oh, no, ma'am." She picked up the crate of apples. "You sit down an' 'joy dat yerself, Miss Karla, an' I'll get dese apples to de house."

"But," I insisted, "I brought it for you."

"I know," Evelyn said, still holding the crate of apples and using a shoulder to wipe sweat from her brow. Apparently, the scarf she had wrapped around her head wasn't doing its job today. "An' I 'preciate it, but you sit wit' Jeremiah an' 'joys it. I'll get me a big ol' glass when I get dese apples to de cellar."

"But—" I began again, but she turned and hurried across the yard before I could protest further . . . and before I could ask her if she'd seen Isaac this morning.

I turned to Jeremiah. He was sitting on the ground with his back against one of the apple trees. His pitch-black, thick forearms were resting on his propped knees, and he held the half-empty glass of lemonade with his left hand, his fingertips loosely gripping the glass' top as his hand dangled between his legs.

He rested his head against the tree and closed his eyes. "Dat woman," he said of Evelyn with a smile. "So stubb'rn."

I stuck out my hand. "I'm Karla. Nice to make your acquaintance," I said. It sounded strange, even to me—too formal—but I didn't know what else to say.

Jeremiah opened his eyes and laughed. "Yes, ma'am, I know who you is." He stared at me, amused.

Instantly, I remembered Grams asking Evelyn to have Jeremiah help prepare the meal for the gala the night I'd arrived. Of course he knew who I was. I'd probably already been a thorn in his side.

"Of course," I conceded. "Thank you for my grand party the other night. I'm told you did a lot of preparing for it. It was wonderful."

"No need to thank me. I 'joys it. We's just glad to have you home, Miss Karla."

Again with the "having you home" thing, as if I'd been gone a while.

"May I?" I asked, nodding to a spot beside him on the ground.

"Oh, yes, ma'am," he said, using a corner of his shirt to wipe a bead of sweat from his hair line.

I sat down beside him with the lemonade in my hand.

He was an older man—probably in his mid fifties—but in very good shape. I don't know how I knew he was older. I just did. Maybe it was the way he held his shoulders, or the way he spoke; but it certainly wasn't detectable in his appearance. His shirt was thin, and the neck line was torn, displaying a sleek, dark chest that was muscular like that of a man in his twenties. The thick, curly hair atop his head was pitch black, showing no signs of gray. And even the few wrinkles around his eyes more closely resembled laugh lines than life lines.

As he wiped his forehead, I noticed his hands were the only thing that couldn't hide his age. They were wrinkled, calloused, and covered with scars.

"I work wit' my hands a lot," he said, catching me staring at them. "I use dem to take care of others, but don't take care of dem too good."

I diverted my eyes to the ground. "Sorry, I didn't mean to—"

"No!" he interrupted with a hearty chuckle. "Don't you 'pologize fer be'n curious." He held his right hand out and looked at it, still holding the lemonade with his left. "Dese hands testify to de work I do. Not dat I need dem to. Work itself is testimony 'nough. But de Lord gots a funny way of show'n de world things 'bout ourselves we think is private."

"The Lord has a funny way of doing a lot of things," I said.

"I know dat's right," Jeremiah replied, laughing.

We sat quietly for a few brief seconds, and then Jeremiah spoke again, as if he'd thought about my statement thoroughly. "Yes, ma'am. The Lord sho does have a funny way of do'n things."

I looked at him. He was staring at the open field ahead, but I continued to look at him, suspecting he had more to say. When he finally turned his face my direction, I raised my eyebrows, encouraging him to continue.

"Oh, sometimes you think it's de devil doin' somethin'," Jeremiah said, verifying my suspicion. "An' sometimes it is, and sometimes it ain't. But even when it's de devil," he nodded, "it's still de Lord."

I wrinkled my brow.

"Ain't that funny?" he chuckled.

"No," I answered. "It's confusing."

He continued smiling as he sat his glass of lemonade down on the ground between his legs, taking a second to carefully balance it to ensure it wouldn't tip over.

The lemonade was starting to turn my hand cold, so I followed suit.

"Let me see if I can 'xplain. See, my momma used to tell a story—an ol' story—I reckon been told many times by many folk, probably differn't each time, but likely 'bout de same." Jeremiah stared across the yard again, as if recalling how the story went.

"Once, there was an ol' woman who was very hungry, so she prayed fer God to provide her food. Fer two days she sat outside de king's castle an' cried out to God, prayerful she would receive some of de king's scraps.

"On de third day, de king, grow'n weary of hear'n de woman, sent his messenger to tell her dat her God would not answer an' she should go away.

"'He will answer,' de old woman replied. 'He is all powerful.'

"The messenger returned to de king an' tol' him what she said.

"'Her faith in her God is strong,' de king said, 'but how strong is it, really? If she is offered food from de devil, would she 'cept it, or would she continue to wait on her God?'

"The king got an idea. 'Take de old woman our fattest calf an' a basket of our ripest fruit. When she asks who is it from, tell her it is from de devil.'

"So the messenger did as he was tol' an' he returned without de items de king had sent because de woman gladly 'cepted dem.

"'See,' de king said, 'her faith is weak, an' her God is not all powerful. She did not wait on de Lord, but 'stead took de food sent from de devil.'

"'Not at all,' said the messenger. 'Her faith seemed stronger dan ever. She was overjoyed to have de food, an' when I tol' her it was from de devil, she began praising her God even more loudly.'

"The king was confused. 'Dat don't make no sense,' he said."

Jeremiah stopped talking and took another drink of his lemonade.

I stared at him, waiting for him to continue.

"And?" I asked.

"An' what?" He looked bewildered.

"And what happened next?"

"Well," Jeremiah said, "de woman ate fer days afterwards. She preserved de meat from de calf so it lasted many months, an' she used de seeds from de fruit to plant more fruit, so fer many years she had ample fruit to eat, an' de good Lord always took good care of her."

"I beg your pardon, but, in the words of the king, that don't make no sense."

Jeremiah laughed. "It makes sense." He put his finger to his temple. "You have to think 'bout it, but it makes sense."

He stood up, and I sat on the ground shaking my head in annoyance—partly because I couldn't figure out what the story was supposed to mean, and partly because Jeremiah didn't tell me.

"You'll figure it out," Jeremiah said. "An' if'n you don't, I'll tell you. I promise."

I smiled up at him. I couldn't help it; his big white teeth were smiling down at me.

He downed his last sip of lemonade. "Thanks fer de lemonade." He held the glass out. "An'," he winked, "fer de company."

"Thanks for the story," I said, taking the glass and sitting it on the ground with mine. "I think."

"I bes' be gett'n back to de house," he said, turning to leave. "There's always work to be done." As he started across the yard, he began whistling a tune. It sounded vaguely familiar, like an old church hymn, perhaps, but I couldn't place which one.

CHAPTER 18

Gone Fishing

It was morning three in Terrebonne Parish. I think. The days and nights meshed together until I wasn't sure how much time was passing, nor did I care. I had Isaac. We were safe. And we were happy. That was all that mattered.

I woke early and decided to take a walk before breakfast. As I walked across the large open field that stretched out between the house and parts of the property I'd yet to explore, I spotted Mr. Darap. He was standing in a paddock on the other side of the field holding something in his hand. Curious, I made my way toward him. As I reached the paddock, I opened the gate and maneuvered my way between piles of cow manure.

His eyes brightened when he saw me. "Good morning, Karla!"

"Good morning." I could see now that the item in his hand was a large axe, and he gave me a side hug, being careful to keep it at arm's length.

I nodded to the axe. "What are you doing?"

He was standing in front of a tall tree, and he patted its dark brown trunk. "Chopping down this old cherry tree." He sighed, as if the thought of it weighed heavy on his heart.

"It's a cherry tree?" I asked, looking at its dark green oval leaves—all of them barren.

He nodded.

"Where are the cherries?"

"It's late summer, so the birds have already gotten what Evelyn and the cattle haven't."

I rubbed the bark of the tree with my hand. "Why are you chopping it down?"

"See this branch?" Mr. Darap reached up and grabbed one

of the lower branches in his hand and pulled it down as low at it would allow.

I stretched on my tiptoes to get a closer look. "Uh huh."

"The cattle love to eat from it."

I frowned, baffled. "How can they reach it way up there?"

He picked up a twig from the ground and held it up. "They wait for it to fall to the ground like this one." He shook his head, as if the thought saddened him.

"Didn't you say they had eaten all the cherries—what the birds and Evelyn hadn't gotten to first?" I was confused, and I didn't mind letting him know as much. "Aren't they *allowed* to eat cherries?"

"Well, yes and no," he answered. "You see, they *used* to be allowed to eat the cherries. They could even eat the leaves if they wanted. But that was when the tree was living." He grasped the branch again and rubbed a leaf between his fingers. "But this tree is dying."

"It is?" I took a step closer and tiptoed again to get a better look.

Mr. Darap laid the axe at his feet and pulled a small knife from his pocket. He pushed the point of the knife into the branch, chipping out a portion of bark. "See? There's no green."

I carefully took the chip of wood from the blade and laid it in the palm of my hand. Yep. No green.

"That's a sure sign this tree's season of life has passed." He closed the knife and shoved it back into his pocket. "The problem is, the cattle don't know that."

"Well," I joked, "they don't have a pocket knife."

Mr. Darap smiled. He plucked one of the leaves from the branch and handed it to me. "See the wilted edges?"

I held it between my thumb and finger as its edges curled around my fingertips.

"Another, more obvious, sign that this tree is dying."

"They can't eat from a dead tree?" I let go of the leaf and watched it drift lifelessly to the ground.

"No, they can't," Mr. Darap answered firmly. "It was really good for them to eat of the tree while it was living. But now that it's dead—" He took my hand in his. "Once the tree dies, it becomes toxic—like a poison. If they keep trying to eat from it, it will kill them."

I'd never heard of such a thing, and it seemed outlandish to me, but I had no doubt Mr. Darap knew what he was talking about.

"You see," he explained, turning back toward the tree, "this tree is familiar to them, so they keep coming back to it. I suppose they've counted on it for so long, they don't know any better."

How sad, I thought, *that something they've come to trust and love is no longer good for them . . . that something they've relied on for nourishment can no longer supply it.*

Mr. Darap tenderly rubbed one of the leaves. "It's not healthy to look for nourishment in things that are dead."

Silence. A silence that seemed to last for several minutes but was probably only seconds.

"Karla," Mr. Darap finally said, still staring at the branch. "I know losing Mason has been very difficult—"

Annoyance bubbled inside and I struggled desperately to hide it. I knew he wasn't intending to hurt me with his words, but any dialogue regarding Mason was painful. It just was. He had to know that.

"I'm not one of your cattle," I mumbled with my chin to my chest, no longer interested in the tree and preferring to stare anywhere but at the tree *or* Mr. Darap.

"No. But like the cattle, you keep returning to the same place—looking for something that's not there anymore. You're looking for nourishment, but you're looking for it in the wrong place, Karla. It's not healthy."

"So now Mason is a cherry tree and I am a cow?" I made no attempt to hide the irritation in my voice. I was tired of everyone constantly diagnosing me. Still, the instant I said the words, I regretted them. I knew the anger I had inside was not toward those who were doing the diagnosing, but at the diagnosis itself . . . because part of me knew it was true; I *was* looking for something that was gone.

A cherry tree and a cow. A smile came across my face. Mason and me. Mason would have laughed at the idea—probably even "mooed" for me. I pictured him placing his fingers to his head like horns and mooing sarcastically.

And there I was again, imagining Mason still with me.

There I was again, eating from the same old branch.

"Memories are good," Mr. Darap said softly. He had been watching me intently. Did he know I was thinking of Mason as if he were still alive and in this very moment? "They're *very* good," he continued. "But they're not memories if you can't leave them in the past. If you keep holding onto them, imagining they are your present and your future, they'll prevent you from making new memories."

There was no reason to argue with him. I knew he was telling the truth. I just wasn't ready to hear it.

"Fair enough." I wrapped both my arms around his neck and hugged him tightly. "Thank you for the botany lesson," I whispered in his ear.

"Dendrology."

"What?" I asked, pulling away.

"Botany is the study of plants." He smiled slyly. "Dendrology is the study of trees." But he winked, because he and I both knew we weren't talking about the study of either one.

I turned as my skirt swept across the grass and I walked out of the paddock, making sure to carefully latch the gate behind me. I walked through the field and toward the house. A gentle breeze started across the field. I watched it make its way toward me as it caught each blade of grass. I watched the same way one watches a rainstorm make its way across the sky. Then, I closed my eyes and held my arms out wide in anticipation of the warm breeze. When it reached me, it encompassed every inch of my body, sweeping over and around me gently before traveling on to its next destination.

I kept my eyes closed long after the breeze blew through, and I took calming breaths with each step as I moved blindly across the open field. I knew from my walk over that there was nothing for me to run into or trip over; and the peace I had knowing I could walk the path ahead of me with my eyes closed was indescribable.

In the distance, I heard the faint thud of an axe as it made contact with a dead cherry tree.

I stretched my arms further, welcoming the warm summer air and enjoying the serene peace that had unexpectedly come.

But then, a scream.

I startled as my eyes shot open. Where had the scream come from? I looked around but was temporarily distracted by how far I'd come across the field. I couldn't believe it. I'd nearly walked all the way back to the house with my eyes closed!

Another scream stole my attention, and I looked up to find Emma and Ann in the side yard between the field and the house. Ann was walking backwards from Emma, and she was screaming as Emma edged closer to her. Emma was holding a rolled-up newspaper high above her head, and she looked as though she were trying to hit Ann with it. As I got closer, I noticed they were both blindfolded.

"Are you there, you cheating Moriarty?!" Emma cried out blindly.

"Yes, sir, I am here!" Ann replied, moving further away from the sound of Emma's voice.

"Cheater!" Emma squealed. "You're off your knees!"

"Likewise!" Ann bellowed back.

Emma yanked the blindfold from her eyes. "As if you gave me a choice," she huffed, letting her previously raised hand rest at her side.

Suddenly, realizing Ann was still blindfolded and standing just a few steps in front of her, a huge smile stretched across Emma's face. She walked right up to Ann and wacked her on the arm with the newspaper.

"Oww!" Ann yelled, rubbing her arm with one hand and pulling the blindfold from her eyes with the other. "Hey!" she yelled. "You cheated!"

"As did you," Emma said, smiling smugly. "Now, you're it."

"Ohhh," Ann growled, grabbing the newspaper as Emma ran away screaming.

"Karla!" Helen came around the corner of the house from the front yard. "Chuckaboo! I've been searching for you all morning. You've had breakfast, yes?"

I hadn't had breakfast, but I wasn't hungry. "I'm fine," I answered. "Did you call me a Chuckaboo?"

"Not *a* Chuckaboo. *My* Chuckaboo," she said, hooking her arm in mine as we walked.

I raised my brow in confusion.

"It means you're my dearest friend. I swear, Karla, you do like to keep me guessing."

Me keep *her* guessing?

"What shall we do today?" She smiled slyly, indicating she already had a few ideas of her own.

"I don't care. Whatever you like." And I meant it. This morning, I just felt good. Like, *really* good. I felt refreshed. Re-energized. And even though I didn't feel like my heart was healing from the pain of losing Mason, or like I was drawing any closer to God, I felt . . . alive. This was Terrebonne Parish. This was the 1800s. And for whatever reason, nothing bad could happen here. It was a place of solitude—a place for healing. This was a *good* place.

Helen and I made our way behind the house and were starting toward the barn when I heard Isaac call out gleefully. "Hey! Up here!!"

I looked to find Isaac standing in the hayloft of the barn about one hundred yards ahead of us, waving his hand to get our attention.

I smiled and waved back.

He picked up a handful of hay and tossed it to the ground below, but just as he released the hay, his foot slipped. He struggled briefly to keep his balance, but fell face forward from the loft and disappeared from my view behind a row of tall bushes surrounding the fence around the barn.

I froze in horror. I didn't see him land, but I knew what was sitting on the ground below the hay loft—a large piece of spiked farm equipment with pointed barbs jutting out from all directions. I recalled seeing it the first time I watched Isaac ride Nightmare. I had tried not to think of it then, but now it was *all* I could think about. There's no way he could have avoided it in the fall!

Everything went silent. The silence was so loud I could *hear* it; it was like an ominous roar echoing the horror of what was to come.

The world stood *still*. It didn't just slow down the way people sometimes describe things happening in dreams. It completely stopped. Nothing moved around me—not the blades of grass, not the leaves on the trees . . . not even Helen.

In the silence that followed, I listened. I didn't hear Isaac screaming. I *wanted* to. I wanted to hear him calling for help, but I didn't. I didn't hear anything. And I knew why. Nobody could survive a fall like that. Not only did the hideous equipment have spikes coming from all directions, it had blades. No matter how he landed, something would have killed him—a spike to the heart or a major organ, a blade to the neck.

I screamed—a blood curdling scream that broke the silence and caused everything to start moving again.

Helen startled backwards. She looked at my face in horror. "What?" she asked, looking back and forth from my line of vision to my face.

She hadn't seen Isaac fall!

"What?" she asked again, alarm flooding her face as she reached for me.

I realized I was the only thing still frozen. I jolted and broke free from Helen, bolting forward, running as fast as I could toward the barn . . . toward Isaac.

Helen chased after me. "Karla! Wait! What happened?"

My dress and layers of petticoats prevented me from running as fast as I wanted, and it took what seemed forever to run the hundred yards or so to the barn.

As I approached, my stomach churned, fearing what I would see, yet not being able to reach Isaac fast enough. As soon as I got a clear view of the murderous farm equipment sitting at the base of the barn, I froze—not at what I saw, but at what I didn't see.

I didn't see Isaac! I'd prepared myself to see him impaled on the spikes or laying injured on the ground, but he wasn't there! Either he'd fallen further into the equipment than I'd expected, or he'd miraculously cleared it completely and was lying behind it. I hoped for the latter as I edged closer.

"Isaac!" I screamed. "Isaac!!"

Helen finally caught up and came running to my side. She stopped and placed her hand on her chest, trying to catch her breath. "Are you mad?" she asked between breaths.

"Isaac! He was here!" I said, pointing at the farm equipment as I got closer. "I mean, he was there," I pointed up at the loft. "Then, he fell. You didn't see him?"

She shook her head, still breathing heavily.

"Isaac!" I screamed, circling the piece of equipment and looking behind it.

"Karla?" Charles came out of the barn, covered in wood chips and saw dust. "Karla? What's wrong?"

"Isaac fell." I didn't understand what was happening. I saw Isaac. I *saw* him! I knew I did. He waved at me. I waved back. Then, he fell. I *saw* him fall. It didn't make any sense.

Charles gave Helen a glance, and she shrugged her confusion.

"He's fine," Charles said, wrapping one arm around me and pulling me to his chest.

"But where is he?" I looked up at his face and tried to pull away, but he kept his arm firm around my shoulders.

Charles returned Helen's look of confusion with a discerning glance, and she raised her eyebrows and nodded.

I attempted to pull away again, but Charles held me tighter, wrapping his other arm around me in a full hug. Soft flecks of saw dust buried into my cheek.

"He's fine," he repeated. "He's gone fishing."

I pulled away, abruptly and successfully this time. "What? But when? I just saw him—"

I looked around again. There was no sign of him anywhere, but I knew he *had* been there just moments earlier. "Isaac!" I yelled out.

Charles looked at me sympathetically. "He's not here," he said, wrapping his arm around me again. "I told you, he's gone fishing."

Helen and Charles shared that same look again, and then Helen wrapped her arm around my shoulder and moved me from Charles' arms into hers.

"I swear, Karla," she said lightheartedly, "this heat must be getting to you. Or else, you're just plain mad." She laughed.

"You didn't see Isaac? Up in the hay loft? You didn't see him fall?"

Helen looked at me. "No." The sincerity in her eyes told me she really hadn't seen him. At least that much was true.

Was I really just bonkers? And then, another thought . . .

"But wait," I said, taking Helen's arm off my shoulder to turn back toward Charles. "When did he—"

But he'd already gone back into the barn—back to work on whatever wood project he was working on.

I debated going into the barn and grilling him with all the questions I had, but Helen's gentle hand on my shoulder as she turned me away changed my mind. She directed me away from the barn and across the yard toward the house, moving her hand from my shoulder and hooking one of her arms in mine.

But I kept thinking about Isaac and all the questions I should have ran back to the barn to ask. When had he gone fishing? And without asking me? And with whom had he gone?

"He's fine, I'm sure," Helen kept reassuring me. "I didn't see him. I swear you must have imagined it. It's the heat. It must be."

Seeing that I wasn't so easily convinced, she gave up trying to sway me and said instead, "Let's go see what Evelyn is doing, shall we?"

We walked toward the back porch where Evelyn sat in a rocking chair, rocking back and forth and peeling peaches.

"Good morning, Evelyn," Helen said, smiling.

"What you girls been up to?" Evelyn asked, not looking up from her task.

Helen unhooked from my arm, bounded onto the porch, and swung twice around the porch post before planting herself on one of the steps. "Well, Karla here went mad as hops moments ago," she said, giving me a playful look. "But other than that—"

"Very funny," I said to Helen. "Have you seen Isaac?" I asked Evelyn. "Uncle said he's gone fishing, but I swear I saw him in the hay loft."

"He's fishing," Helen said quickly, turning to look at Evelyn.

Evelyn looked up from peeling peaches long enough to catch Helen's eye, then looked back down at the peach in her hand. "Dat boy disappears fer hours at a time do'n whatever it is boys his age does. I told ya, I never knows where he is."

I watched as she turned a peach in her right hand across a motionless blade in her left, removing the entire peel from the peach in one long strip. She placed the peel in a large bowl and the peach in a different bowl, then pulled another peach out of her apron. "He fine," she said, turning the new peach across the blade. "You worries too much Karla. It ain't healthy."

"It ain't healthy," I repeated, softly. "That's what everyone keeps telling me."

But I was going to find Isaac. I couldn't just sit here all morning wondering if I was crazy. I had to go look for him.

Suddenly a terrifying thought crossed my mind. *What if I didn't find him*? The thought left as quickly as it came—either by sheer force of will or because, for whatever reason, Terrebonne Parish still felt safe to me. It was hard to explain, except that the same feeling I'd felt earlier was still there—that secure sensation that nothing bad could happen here. Yes, something wasn't right about seeing Isaac fall from the hayloft and disappear before hitting the ground, but it didn't cause the same panic I'd felt when Isaac went missing from the antique store. In my heart, I knew Isaac was okay. But I also knew Charles and Helen—and probably even Evelyn—knew more than they were telling.

***

Mr. Darap was propped in a chair in the men's parlor. I couldn't see his face because he had a newspaper in front of it, but I knew it was him by his trousers and shoes. It's funny how quickly something—or someone—becomes familiar.

I'd searched for Isaac all afternoon, yelling across the fields and through the woods behind the house. I'd even returned to the barn several times to look for him—partly because I *knew* I had seen him there, and partly because, if he *had* gone fishing, the barn would be the first place he'd return to . . . to check on Nightmare, of course.

But I never found him before it got too dark to continue the search.

I'd missed dinner and supper on my quest for Isaac and was heading through the house toward the stairs, hungry and tired, when I noticed Mr. Darap sitting in the parlor. I entered quietly.

"Karla," Mr. Darap acknowledged without removing the newspaper from in front of his face.

Surely he hadn't *heard* me; I was careful not to make a sound when I came in. I'd planned on patiently waiting until he was done reading before speaking with him.

"Where's Isaac?" he asked, the paper still in front of his face.

"I was going to ask you the same thing."

"Oh?" Mr. Darap lowered the newspaper and gave me his

full attention.

"I'm told he's gone fishing," I said, watching intently for his reaction.

"Oh." And there it was, that same knowing look I'd seen on Helen and Charles' face earlier, and later on Evelyn's. But he recouped quickly. "I suppose that explains why Isaac wasn't at supper, but it doesn't explain your absence."

"I was looking for him," I answered.

"Isaac?"

"Yes."

"The same Isaac who's gone fishing?"

"Yes."

"I see."

We stared at each other in silence before I finally looked away, realizing that was the extent of the conversation we'd have regarding Isaac's whereabouts.

I took a deep breath, begrudgingly changing the subject. "I suppose you got the cherry tree taken care of?"

"All cut down and hauled away," he said, raising the paper back to his face.

"I suppose the cattle will have to find something else for nourishment now?"

"That is correct," he said plainly.

"But what if they don't?"

"They will," he said, not sounding concerned in the least.

"But what if they don't?"

He lowered a corner of his newspaper. "They'll be just fine," he said with a wink.

CHAPTER 19

Perfectly Imperfect

I woke the following morning and ran to Isaac's room, still in my night clothes, only to find his bed had not been slept in.

How long did these fishing trips last, exactly? Was it not just a day trip?

I sullenly returned to my room and sat on the edge of the bed, angry that I had lost him again and baffled at how it had happened. He was there, and then he wasn't. Of course, that's not how everyone else told it. Everyone else said he had simply "gone fishing."

Maybe they would share more today. Maybe, after a good night's sleep, they had decided to let me in on their little secret, whatever it might be. I was prepared for anything they might tell me—any strange tale they might choose to share. At this point, nothing would surprise me. Not after everything I'd already witnessed. Not after Mr. Darap's newspaper gave evidence of what I already knew to be true—Isaac and I were in Terrebonne Parish, living in a world that only existed in 1856. I'd glanced at the date on Mr. Darap's newspaper as he held it up the night before in the parlor, and I was not the least bit stunned . . . nor scared.

I dressed quickly, assuming everyone was already downstairs having breakfast. I expected answers this morning, and I wasn't going to be still until I got some. At the very least, they could tell me when they expected Isaac to return.

I hurried down the stairs, then circled behind them to the dining room only to find it empty.

Was it too early? What time was it? I hadn't even bothered to check.

I went to the kitchen where I found it empty, as well. I listened to the house. It was quiet. There were no voices. No shuffling of feet across floors. No opening and closing of doors. Nothing.

Where was everybody?

I went out the kitchen door onto the back porch. The sun was up, and the day was already warming.

The barn. If Isaac was back, he'd be at the barn with Nightmare.

I walked to the far corner of the yard and across the field. I hesitated at the barn door, casting all my thoughts on a vision of Isaac standing at Nightmare's side—a vision I desperately hoped to see when I opened the doors. But of course, I didn't. I swung open the doors to find Nightmare, all alone, poking his head out from his stall. I made my way down the hay-peppered aisle to him, and he stomped his foot and whinnied with his head low in greeting.

"Good morning." I rubbed his nose and stared into his dark brown eyes. They were like bottomless mud puddles after a hard rain. I stared at my own reflection in them. "You miss Isaac, too, huh?"

A full day and night had passed since Isaac had mysteriously—between falling from the hayloft and falling into the farm equipment—disappeared to "go fishing." The fact that I—and perhaps Nightmare—were the only ones concerned about Isaac's absence alleviated some of my concern. Funny how peace amongst those around you can extinguish anxiety so quickly. In another world—literally—I would have been panicking beyond any control, just as I had in Crawley. But despite my hurt and confusion, I didn't have the sense of urgency I'd had when Isaac went missing then. I absolutely hated that he was gone, and I had a natural mother's impulse to worry, but I also felt an unexplainable calm that everything would be okay. I just had to wait patiently.

"Karla!"

I jumped. So did Nightmare, who threw his head back and whinnied loudly.

"Oh, Nightmare, did I startle you?" Helen asked sympathetically as she walked up beside us. She patted Nightmare's neck to quiet him, then she reached into her dress gathered in front of her like a basket and pulled out an apple. "Here. I'm sorry." She stretched her palm out flat and put the apple to Nightmare's mouth.

Nightmare bent his head and gently took the apple, his large lips kissing her hand as he pinched the apple from her palm with his sizeable teeth.

"Startled *Nightmare*?!" I asked. "What about *me*?!"

"I'm sorry, Chuckaboo." She wiped her hand on her dress and pulled another apple from her dress-basket. "Here, I've one for you, as well." She held out the apple, smiling.

I was starving, but my stubbornness took over. "No thank you," I said, crossing my arms.

She shrugged as she polished the apple on her chest and dropped the hold she had on her dress-basket, allowing the final two apples to fall into Nightmare's stall. "Saves more for us, doesn't it boy?" she said, giving Nightmare a final rubdown. I instantly regretted declining the apple as she took a bite and juice ran down her chin. She wiped it with the back of her hand. "Isn't he gorgeous?" She motioned to Nightmare. "I mean, those eyes!"

"Where were you?" I asked, annoyed.

"Picking apples." She beamed, holding up the apple in her hand. "See? Apples."

I rolled my eyes. I was obviously questioning where she had been when I walked through a quiet house and empty yard moments earlier. Where was *anybody*? And what time was it? Was it earlier in the morning than I'd suspected, or later? Had I missed breakfast? I was seriously considering scooping up the last apple from Nightmare's stall before he could get to it.

"Were you looking for me, Chuckaboo?" Helen batted her eyes, feigning flattery.

"I was looking for Isaac, actually."

She displayed an expression of temporary hurt, then pulled

me by my arm. "Come on."

I stood my ground. "Where are we going?"

"To take your mind off Isaac," she answered, taking another bite of her apple.

I stood staring at her, firm in my stance. I didn't want to take my mind off Isaac. I wanted answers.

Helen sighed and gave up pulling on my arm. "You just want to talk, then?"

"Yes," I said. *Finally!*

"Okay," Helen took another bite of her apple and chewed it quickly. "Let's talk about Mason. We've not the chance to meet, you know. Tell me all about him."

My mouth dropped open. *Not the chance to meet?* She said it as if she *would* one day meet him; she just hadn't *yet*. The thought was disturbing.

I forced myself to let the implication go for two reasons. First, nineteenth century dialect was strange to me, so perhaps she meant something other than what she said. And second, because if she *meant* what she said, I didn't want to talk about that either.

And I definitely didn't want to talk about Mason. I didn't talk about him with anyone except Isaac. And even then, the mention of him was brief. Sometimes, but not often, Isaac or I would bring up a shared memory we had of Mason, or we'd discuss how Mason might have handled a situation, but we quickly changed the subject to prevent one of us from tearing up. It was a defense mechanism that helped keep the pain away.

Or maybe it didn't. No matter how much I kept Mason's name off my lips, I couldn't keep his memory from my heart. There was a gaping hole there that could only ever be filled with memories of Mason.

His name alone brought back memories. Not all of them good, but I strangely liked that. It reminded me that our life was genuine—not an unrealistic fantasy of knights in shining armor and fairytale princesses. Although, the "happily ever after" part would have been nice.

"So?" Helen was persisting. "You and Mason. Perfect couple?" She put her hands under her chin dreamily.

No, Mason and I weren't the perfect couple. We argued sometimes, but even those memories were comforting. I couldn't explain it, but sometimes Mason felt so distant, I wondered if he had existed at all—our life together was such a wonderful, fulfilling one that it seemed impossible anyone could really live it. But who would incorporate things like arguments when they're dreaming up an imaginary past? So, it was those memories—the ones of the fights we had, or of the miniscule things he did that had annoyed me—that got me through the days when it felt like Mason had been too good to be true. That he had been a dream come and gone too quickly.

I turned my wedding band on my finger. Sometimes, I purposely thought about the petty disagreements just to remember how real he was—how real our life had been. I thought back to one particular fight in which we didn't speak for two full days afterwards. It was so trivial—I don't even recall what started it—but it ended with each of us accusing the other of being selfish.

We made up slowly. I kicked it off by fixing him a cup of coffee one morning. I sat the cup on his side of the bathroom sink while he was in the shower so he would see it when he got out.

Later, when I took my shower and the room filled with steam, the words "I love you" appeared on the bathroom mirror accompanied by a big heart.

Neither one of us ever said we were sorry. We didn't need to.

"Karla?"

"Hmmm?"

"Life with Mason," Helen repeated. "Was it perfect?"

"Yes," I said. Because it was.

"You never disagreed?!" Helen raised her eyebrows and looked at me intently, her green eyes displaying a deep desire for the answer.

"Of course we did, but that's what made it perfect."

"Beg your pardon?" Helen crinkled her forehead.

"We were two different people with two different thought processes, so we didn't always agree on *everything*. But we loved each other, you know?"

Helen continued staring at me blankly.

"Despite having differences, we just . . . we loved each other. No matter what. So, in that way, it was perfect."

"Sounds perfectly *im*perfect," Helen groaned.

I thought about it and smiled. "Okay, so we were perfectly *im*perfect. But you know what that made us?"

"Perfect." Helen answered, rolling her eyes as if the sappy thought was tiring.

I smiled even bigger.

"Well," Helen said, throwing the apple core into Nightmare's stall. "I have a *perrrr-fectly* good idea." She raised and lowered her eyebrows several times.

"Oh no. What is it?" I asked apprehensively.

"Not telling," she said, slyly.

I perked up. "Is it going on a scavenger hunt for Isaac?"

Helen tilted her head to the side with a look that told me I already knew the answer to that question. The look also reflected her boredom at my still harping on the subject.

I released an exasperated sigh. There really wasn't anything I could do about Isaac at the moment. I knew that. I just had to wait for him to show back up, and something deep inside me was okay with that. Not happy about it, but okay.

"Well?" Helen was now looking at me with eyes full of anticipation. "What do you say, my lady?"

She certainly did have a way with me, and I wondered if she had a way with everyone. I guessed she did. Her mischievous, yet charming, ways were easy to get sucked into.

"Sure." I shrugged. Why not?

Helen kept smiling. She had a crazy happy look in her eye.

"Well?" I nudged. "What is it?"

"Not now." She leaned in and whispered covertly. "Tonight."

"Tonight?"

"Tonight."

"*Now* you're scaring me."

"Uh, uh, uh," she said, wagging her finger. "You already said yes. You can't change your mind now."

"Grams says a lady has a right to change her mind," I argued.

"Since when are *you* a lady?" she asked, playfully tugging at my hair, and then running away before I could return the favor.

I chased after her, already feeling somewhat better. Helen had a way of instantly improving my mood. Her carefree ways and playful nature were exactly what I needed. She was the kind of person I never imagined being friends with and yet, here she was. My only true friend.

Of course, Cheryl was my friend, but she was my sister, so that didn't count. Besides, Cheryl was nothing like Helen. Cheryl was tender and loving—and even funny—but she was not spontaneous like Helen. Cheryl was responsible and mature. I needed Cheryl. But I needed Helen, too.

I gave up the chase about halfway across the field and I stood watching Helen run. I loved her already. There was no denying that. Helen was going to get me through Isaac's absence until he returned . . . or she was going to drive me plumb crazy. Whichever came first.

CHAPTER 20

Helen's Secret

"Psst."

My eyes shot open.

"Psst!"

The moon light flitted through the window of my bedroom, providing plenty of light. I rolled over in bed to find Helen leaning over me, her brown hair hanging loosely on top of her shoulders as she stared at me with wide, excited emerald eyes.

"Psst!"

"Okay. Psst. I heard you," I said, swiping her away from my face.

"Get up," she whispered.

"For what?" I rubbed my eyes sleepily.

"You'll see." She pulled the covers away, and I instinctively pulled them back over my nightgowned body.

"Get up!" she whispered loudly, pulling the covers away again and pulling my legs to the side of the bed.

I reluctantly sat up and allowed my legs to dangle.

"Ssshh." Helen put her finger to her lips. "Tiptoe."

I sat on the edge of the bed with my eyes closed, still more asleep than awake.

Helen snapped her fingers in front of my face. "Hey! Wake up. Come on."

"Come on where?" I asked, too loudly for Helen's liking.

"Sssshhhh!" She put her hand over my mouth and looked over her shoulder as if expecting someone to enter. "Be quiet!" she whispered anxiously. "Someone might hear."

I removed her hand from my mouth and put my finger to my lips to indicate I understood. I tiptoed quietly toward the changing hutch, but I only got halfway across the floor before

Helen grabbed my wrist to stop me.

"What are you doing?" she whispered.

"Getting dressed," I whispered back, noticing for the first time she was still in her nightgown.

"You don't need to. You're fine the way you are. Let's go."

"We're not going outside?"

Helen smiled. The moonlight captured her expression fully—one I'd seen a couple of times already and knew meant trouble.

"Helen?"

"Ssshhhh." She pulled me by the arm, toward the bedroom door.

"At least let me put shoes on," I begged.

"You don't need them," she insisted. "Come on."

We tiptoed through the bedroom door and into the hallway. Devoid of the moonlight that so generously lit my bedroom, I held Helen's hand with one hand and used my free hand to skim the wall as I walked. Every now and then, Helen steered me around a creaky board. She knew exactly where they were; clearly she'd snuck around in the middle of the night many times before.

We reached the top of the stairs and my nerves started to get the best of me. I paused and pulled back on Helen's arm.

She stopped and cuddled close to me. "What?" she whispered, her large eyes looking around. "Did you hear something? Is someone coming?"

"No, but where are we going?"

A look of relief flooded her face. "You'll see," she whispered, pulling on my arm.

I refused to budge.

"I swear, Karla," she huffed, "don't be such a fuddy-duddy. You act like always knowing what's about to happen is a good thing. I mean, goodness Karla, don't you like surprises?"

"No," I said, flatly. "Not really."

"Well, that's too bad because I'm not telling and you're not *not* coming. Now, come on!" She tugged on me firmly and started down the stairs, pulling me reluctantly behind her.

The marble slab steps didn't give way to creaking the way the floor boards had, and I found myself taking them two at a time to keep up with Helen. When we got to the bottom, she let go of my arm and circled behind the staircase toward the kitchen, making a beeline for the back door.

"Ssssh," she reminded, holding the door open for me.

I stepped onto the back porch, and Helen came out immediately behind me. She caught the screen door with her right hand to prevent it from slamming and used her left hand to close the main door quietly. Then, she carefully and quietly closed the screen door.

I was about to ask her "What now?" but before I could say anything, she bolted down the porch stairs and across the lawn without a word.

"Helen!" I whispered loudly, impulsively running after her.

The full glow of the moon lit the entire yard with an iridescent light one only sees in their dreams. Helen ran ahead of me, barefoot, her white gown flowing and her loosed hair tousling behind her. Her form floating across the lawn was ghost-like, but not eerie. It was magical.

She ran the full distance of the yard but stopped at the tree line where the canopy of trees blocked the moonlight from lighting anymore of our apparent pathway. She turned and waited for me to catch up.

"Helen!" I panted, reaching her side, not hiding my impatience. "Are you going to tell me where we're going or not?"

"Not," she answered, taking my hand and running into the darkened woods.

I ran, hand-in-outstretched-hand, behind her. Slivers of moonlight occasionally flickered through the canopy above, but not enough to see where one was going, unless they were familiar with the woods themselves.

Helen proved very familiar. "Jump," she instructed each time we came across a fallen tree or large rock. It was her lack of surprise at the obstacles that told me she'd traveled the path many times, not the barely-noticeable-wear-pattern my eyes eventually picked up on.

After running together for a few hundred yards or so, the path became so narrow we could no longer hold hands.

Helen navigated through the tangles of vines and tightly cramped trees more swiftly than I, and I looked up to find she was no longer in sight.

"Helen! Wait up!"

"Just keep straight," she yelled out.

I could tell by the distance of her voice she wasn't too far ahead and, if I looked closely, I could still see the barely-noticeable wear-pattern on the forest floor like an arrow pointing me in the direction I should go.

I ducked under tree limbs and stepped over fallen branches. Every now and then, I'd catch a glimpse of her white gown as she appeared, then disappeared, in front of me.

I was starting to get tired, and I wondered how much deeper she planned on taking us into the woods. I paused to wipe perspiration from my forehead, wondering briefly how much time I had to catch my breath without her getting too far ahead. It'd been a while since I'd last seen her white gown flicker between the trees ahead.

"Marco!" I yelled from habit.

"Polo!"

I stood frozen. Only Mason and Isaac knew about the Marco Polo game!

"Polo!" she answered again, a little more loudly.

Her "Polo" came further ahead than I was comfortable with, overshadowing the fact that she'd even replied with a "Polo" in the first place, and I started through the woods again. Picking up my pace. Worried she'd get too far ahead, and I'd be lost.

"Keep coming this way, Chuckaboo!" Helen encouraged after a few minutes. "We're almost there."

Helen's voice was close again, providing permission to slow

my pace once more.

The ground under my bare feet felt unusually cool compared to the hot July air. A refreshing surprise considering I'd already broken a sweat from the night's humidity.

As I walked, I noticed the path under my feet changed considerably with each step. Some of my steps landed on a soft, damp surface that felt moss-like, while other steps landed on sharp slivers of pine needles. The combination of pine needle shards and the midnight heat forced me to slow my pace even more.

"Helen!" I cried, as I pulled a sticky strand of hair away from my moist cheek and paused to pull a pine needle from the heel of my foot. The hike had been getting more difficult, and I looked behind me to realize why. For the last hundred yards or so, we had been trekking uphill.

I wasn't a geography expert, but I couldn't recall Louisiana being known for having mountainous terrain. I looked down at my bare feet and night gown and thought about all the other things that hadn't been logical since arriving to Terrebonne Parish—all the things that seemed impossible but were possible. I shook the confusion about the mountainous terrain away. Why should anything surprise me anymore?

"Marco!" I called out again.

"Polo!" Her voice was even closer this time, indicating she had slowed down quite a bit. Or she had finally stopped moving altogether.

I desperately hoped for the latter as beads of sweat trickled down my temples. I lifted my hair as I walked, hoping my moist neck might find the slightest hint of a passing breeze. But I felt nothing.

My night gown was now entirely soaked with perspiration, clinging to my thighs with each step.

I paused to catch my breath, still holding my hair off my neck with both hands. "Helen!" I whined. "It's so hot! I'm exhausted. Where are you?"

"You're almost here. Keep coming straight." Her voice was close, verifying what I'd hoped; she'd finally stopped moving. "It'll be worth it. I promise," she yelled out.

I didn't see how anything could be worth this. I was sweaty. I was tired. I was barefoot in the middle of the night in my night clothes.

I was determined to let Helen know just how annoyed I was once I caught up to her, but I wasn't prepared for what I saw when I rounded the bend.

As I made the final turn, the path opened up to a large clearing with a rock foundation. Light from the moon cascaded across the tops of trees far below the clearing's ledge, verifying what I'd suspected—that we'd climbed much higher than seemed possible.

And then, a bigger shock. Helen was standing in front of me completely naked. Moonlight spilled across her body, spotlighting every curve.

I stood with my mouth open in utter shock. I blinked several times, unable to speak.

Helen curtsied—as best as one can without a dress.

I blinked again, moving my lips to speak, but before I could utter a word, Helen turned, sprinted the few feet to the cliff's edge, and jumped.

"No!" I ran toward her and threw myself down on the cliff's ledge. Stretching out my hand in desperation. As if I had any chance of grabbing her before she fell the distance to her death.

"Helen!!" I slammed my fist to the ground. "No! No! No!"

CHAPTER 21

Jump

A noise below. Could Helen have survived?

I looked down, expecting to find Helen a mangled mess on the rocks below, but instead, I saw her splashing in a pool of water. She splashed water over her head and motioned for me to join her.

"Jump!" she yelled.

I breathed a sigh of relief, followed by one of frustration. She was going to give me a heart attack. Seriously. Hanging out with her could not be healthy for me.

"Come on!" She waved. "The water is perfect!" She flipped to her back, allowing her naked body to float to the top, casually backstroking across the water's surface.

But I couldn't jump. I couldn't swim. And even if I could, a jump that far would kill me. I was sure of it. I was still in awe of how Helen had done it so effortlessly.

"Come on," Helen yelled up.

"No!" I yelled back.

"Are you afraid?" she yelled jokingly.

I didn't answer.

"You're afraid," she said, realizing it wasn't a joke at all. "There's nothing to be afraid of. Just decide to do it, then do it!"

I noticed a well-worn path leading from the water below to the top of the cliff. It was evidently used to climb up and jump, over and over again, but I used it to climb down instead. I carefully scooted my bare feet on the loose ground, tiny granules of sand rolling with each step, until I made my way to the bottom. A large area of soft, moss-like grass ran along the water's edge. I enjoyed the way it felt on my bare feet. I walked around in circles, allowing the moss to smoosh up between my toes.

Helen swam over to the bank. "Fuddy-duddy," she pouted, crossing her arms on a rock ledge and resting her chin on her arms.

The ledge she clung to was near several flat, layered rocks that formed a staircase out of the water. Or into it. The rocks so perfectly formed stairs that I wondered if they were formed by nature or hand-chiseled.

The water was crystal clear with small rocks of various grays, turquoises, and oranges settled around the water's edge. Toward the middle, where Helen had jumped in, the water was dark, indicating the depth was perfect for diving and swimming.

"You're not a swimmer, huh?" Helen asked, looking up at me with sopping wet hair as she wiped water from her eyes.

"No," I said apologetically. "And I'm definitely not a jumper." I sat down on the plush grass and crossed my legs. I looked up at the cliff Helen had jumped from. "That's quite a jump."

"Eh," she replied, shrugging. "We're lucky to find a cliff for jumping at all. We're not known for cliffs, you know."

"I was wondering about that."

"Don't wonder too much. It'll only make your head swim."

I laughed. "Pun intended?"

Helen raised her eyebrows and smiled. She dipped her cupped hand in the water and splashed a handful onto my legs. It wasn't as cold as I'd expected it to be. Still, it was wet and refreshing against my hot, sticky skin, and I fought the impulse to dive in despite the possibility of drowning.

Swim. That's what Mason had last said to me.

I shook my head. "Not now," I whispered.

"What, Chuckaboo?" Helen asked.

"Nothing."

She didn't take my 'nothing' for an answer, and she tilted her head, waiting.

"It's just . . . Mason told me I needed to learn to swim."

"Mason is right."

I looked at her. "*Was,*" I corrected with a cautious tone.

"What?"

"Mason *was* right. Not *is* right. Mason's—"

"Of course," she said, with no apparent sympathy—as if she was right the first way she said it, but was correcting herself to appease me.

It was not the first time her use of past and present tense threw me. She'd done the same thing in the barn when she said she'd not "yet" met Mason.

I stared at her blankly.

"I mean," she explained. "He *was* right, but he still *is*. You definitely need to learn to swim." She was sly enough that I couldn't tell if her first statement using present tense was another slip up, or her second statement of explanation made perfect sense.

"I know," I conceded. "And I will."

"I know." She smiled.

"Just not tonight," I said with a warning tone. I didn't want her getting any ideas.

She looked at me lovingly. "Not tonight," she agreed. She pulled herself up onto the rock to sit beside me and dangled her legs into the water.

I leaned over and splashed water on my legs and arms, then cupped a handful to my face and the back of my neck.

"Would you care to know what I do here?" Helen asked, ringing out her hair.

"Swim." I smiled smartly.

Helen smiled back, seemingly amused by my quick wit. "And?"

"Run around naked?"

"It's good for the skin," she beamed, not offended in the least. She hopped to her feet and fanned her bare body with both hands. "You should try it sometime."

I pointed a reprimanding finger at her. "We're not doing that tonight, either."

"Suit yourself." She walked over to one of the rock walls surrounding the pool. Water spouted from a gap between two large boulders so forcefully the splashing on the rock floor sounded as if someone were showering. I'd been so focused on the cushioned mossy carpet that skirted the pool when I first made my way down from the ledge, I'd paid no attention to the torrent waterfalls spouting here and there along the walls that towered around us.

Helen cupped her hands and took a drink.

I joined her, suddenly realizing how thirsty I was. The water was ice cold in my palms as I raised it to my lips—so cold it hurt my teeth as it splashed over them with each refreshing drink. It was a baffling contrast to the lukewarm temperature of the water in Helen's swimming pool, but I again shook the oddity away as soon as it entered my thoughts. It was no good attempting to make sense of things that made no sense.

Helen walked over to a fatly tree along the back side of the mossy rug. It stood tall in front of an entire tree line, as if the tree were a sergeant, and the other trees were a platoon of soldiers guarding the entrance to an entirely new area of the forest—one less traveled.

I took a final sip of water and started toward her as she pulled a towel out from behind the tree and haphazardly dried off with it. Then, she pulled her nightgown over her head, which had been lying on the ground where she'd apparently tossed it before making the plunge, and it fell loosely over her body, sticking to places on her skin that were still wet.

She leaned behind the tree again and pulled out a pale blue patchwork blanket. She slung it over an arm as she reached behind the tree a third time.

"What in the—? What is that? A bottomless pit?" I asked, circling the tree.

The base of the tree's trunk was hollowed out, serving as perfect storage for Helen's possessions.

She reached in and pulled out a small, red paper-bound book with gold lettering on the cover. "Isn't it wonderful? It's like an armoire. It keeps everything dry," she cooed. "And hidden," she added with a wink.

She slid the book under her armpit and started unfolding the quilt. I grabbed an end and helped her spread it across the soft ground, and we sprawled out on it comfortably.

"Okay," I said, reaching for the book. "Let us see what great writer lures you into the dark of night, shall we? Let us see who entices you to hike miles and miles, then strip down *completely naked* just to absorb their enchanting words."

She pulled the book from my reach and laid it dramatically to her chest. "Aaah, but, my love! There is none alone who can charm my soul. It takes an army!"

I rolled my eyes, and she handed the book back to me, grinning. But she was right. The book wasn't by one single author. It was a collection of poetry by several different authors. So . . . it really did take an army to woo her!

"Read to me?" she asked with doe-like eyes.

I opened the book, and Helen snuggled up next to me. The sultry heat had already dried her skin, but her hair was still soaked. It dampened my nightgown as she curled in close.

I held the book at an angle so the moonlight shone across the pages like the soft glow of a lamp lit for just the occasion. I flipped through a few pages, then stopped on a random page and began to read, "I am the daughter of Earth and Water, and the nursling of the Sky, I pass through the pores of the ocean and shores—"

"I change, but I cannot die," Helen whispered softly.

I followed the words on the page as she said them. "That's right," I said, knowing she couldn't see the words from where she was laying. "You memorized this poem?"

She drew circles with her fingertips gently across my abdomen. "I've memorized a lot of them I suppose, but that one is one of my favorites."

"Why?" I had no idea what message the author was trying to convey. It sounded like pure gibberish to me.

"Because it's the truth," she said simply. She stopped making circles and took the book from my hands before I could protest. "My turn!" She flipped to her back to use my stomach for a pillow.

First, I'm a chalkboard. Now, I'm a pillow. Her wet hair soaked through my gown, but I didn't mind. On any of the accounts.

She flipped to a new page and began reading. "Tis the last rose of summer, left blooming alone; all her lovely companions are faded and gone . . ."

Helen's voice faded away as I stared upward into the night sky. A few dark clouds shifted slowly. They were separate, but they moved as one, and I was acutely aware that they never drifted to block the moon. As if they knew better. As if they'd been given orders not to mask its glow.

". . . When true hearts lie wither'd, and fond ones are flown. Oh, who would inhabit this bleak world alone?"

"Not I," I mumbled.

Helen closed the book and turned her head toward me. "Not you what?"

"I don't want to inhabit this bleak world alone." My lip quivered.

Bleak. Alone.

But I *was* alone. Mason was gone. Isaac was gone . . . again.

I didn't like it. Life isn't worth living if you're living alone.

"You're not alone," Helen whispered, reaching up and placing her warm palm on my cheek. "You have me."

But Helen wasn't real. She couldn't be. None of this could be real.

Maybe it was a dream. Maybe I'd gone mad in the real world—forced there by the loss of the two most important people in my life—and this was a world I'd created in my mind.

Maybe this is what insanity feels like.

Then I'd just stay insane. Curled up inside my wrinkled brain where I'd be safe from any more pain.

Chirp!

I sat up, causing Helen to topple off my stomach.

They followed me here!?

Couldn't I ever escape their mocking and teasing—their constant reminders of my loss?

Chirp!

But then, a thought occurred to me. If I had imagined a world to break away from reality, I certainly wouldn't have allowed the taunting crickets to be part of it.

No, this world had to be real. The cruel chirping of the crickets was evidence of that.

"Let's get back," I told Helen, jumping to my feet quickly.

"Chuckaboo!" she exclaimed. She hadn't yet recovered from my first sudden jolt, and now I had toppled her over completely in my rush to stand. She rubbed her elbow and gave it a once over, scowling. "What's the hurry?"

"Now." I said, turning toward the sound of the crickets. Several more were beginning to chime in. A chorus of hecklers. "I'm ready to go *now!*"

"Okay. Okay. Here," she said, standing to her feet and handing me an end of the blanket. "Help me fold this."

I hurriedly helped shove everything back into Helen's secret armoire, and we climbed the path back up the cliff and started through the woods.

I couldn't get in bed fast enough. At least in my bed I could shut the window and block out the crickets' taunts.

Helen and I only spoke once on the way back to Grams' house. Actually, only Helen spoke. "You know," she said, stopping on the path and turning to face me. "That being alone thing?"

I looked down, hoping she'd take it as a sign that I didn't want to discuss it further.

She leaned in and put her lips close to my ear. "There's not just me—" she whispered. I looked up at her with questioning eyes, and she moved from my ear so that we were face-to-face. The moon light caught every feature of her round face, and I saw her eyebrows raise up and down several times. "There's Lawson!" she spat out quickly. As she said his name, she smacked me on the behind, then took off running.

"Oooh, you!" I yelled, chasing after her.

We were halfway back to Grams' before I realized I was already laughing again.

CHAPTER 22

Robin

Isaac had been gone for four days. My heart raced each morning as I got out of bed and ran to his room, still in my nightclothes, to see if he had returned. Each time, his bed was untouched, confirming my fears.

This morning was no exception. Isaac was still gone.

I sat on his bed. Isaac's room was just as big as mine and laid out in a similar fashion. There was a fireplace on the wall adjacent the foot of his bed, and in front of the fireplace was a red armchair with a small oak table beside it. An armoire stood flush against one wall. The only obvious difference in our rooms was that my room had a mirrored vanity and Isaac's didn't.

I lay back on Isaac's bed and curled up on my side. The heart-racing anticipation I felt each morning of possibly finding Isaac in his room was replaced each time with disappointment. Every morning felt like a new loss.

I stared at the heavy red drapes hanging from his window. They were not pulled shut, and I realized it was still dark outside. Maybe it wasn't morning, after all.

I stared out the window at the darkness until the darkness morphed into a dream.

Bright colors—reds and oranges—flashed through the air. I was standing in the field as leaves swirled around me.

The wind was thrashing at my face and body. The force was so strong it felt as though it was piercing my skin and pounding directly onto my heart.

"Stop!" I screamed.

"Peace. Be still!" The figure below the tree was screaming.

"Stop!" I screamed again.

"Peace. Be still!" The voice echoed all around me.

"STOP!" I fell to my knees to protect myself from the debris the wind mercilessly threw my way, vaguely aware this part of the dream was different from the other times.

This was the first time I'd fallen to the ground.

This was the first time a branch hadn't barreled at me full force as I stood fighting against the wind.

Even in a dream state, I was aware that this time, balled up on the ground, the tree limb that always woke me with a thud to the forehead couldn't. This time, I would be able to avoid it.

I squinted to find the figure under the tree balled up on the ground, as well . . . hunched in the same protective cocoon I'd left them in in my last dream.

"Stop!" I screamed into the wind. "Stop!"

"Peace! Be still!" the balled-up figure yelled. Over and over again. "Peace! Be still!"

I joined in. "Peace! Be Still!"

But the wind relentlessly raged around me. The leaves continued to break away and disintegrate.

A large cracking sound—the branch—broke through the squalling of the wind, and I tucked my head in tight under my arms and screamed.

I jerked, uncurling from my cocoon and sitting bolt upright in Isaac's bed—a bed that now looked as though it had been ransacked. I'd fallen asleep and dreamed the same dream I'd been dreaming since my first night in Terrebonne Parish. The same nightmare.

Light streamed through the bedroom window, verifying it was finally morning.

I straightened Isaac's bed and returned to my room. I sat at the vanity, staring into its mirror. It was one of few I'd yet to press against—to test if it was some kind of portal. It was just so small that it seemed impossible, but now, sitting in front of it and desperately missing Isaac, I began to wonder. Could such a little thing be something much bigger? Could it have swallowed up Isaac to another world just like the one in the antique store had swallowed us up and brought us here? And if so, did it return him home, or take him to another world?

What if it took him to a world not as nice as this? The idea was unbearable, and I plunged my hand into the mirror without thinking. "Ow!" I yelled as my fingers jammed at the knuckles on impact.

But the glass didn't shatter. Neither did it move. No portal. It was simply a mirror, just as it seemed.

And Isaac was simply fishing, just as everyone said.

I had to believe that. If I didn't, I was going to go crazy.

I pinned my hair up. I found keeping it off my neck helped compensate for the layers of corset and petticoats that smothered the skin from breathing in the heat of the day.

"Gone fishing," I mumbled, staring into the mirror. It had to be true, because I was the only one worried about him. Everyone else—Charles, Helen, Evelyn, and even Grams—kept telling me he'd gone fishing and there was nothing to worry about.

Apparently, men in the 1800s are "gone fishing" often, evidently staying gone for days at a time. I supposed it was normal for Terrebonne Parish, but it wasn't normal for the world we came from, so it was difficult for me to believe that Isaac would just take off and not tell me.

It was also strange to be uneasy and at ease at the same time, especially after seeing him fall from the hayloft.

That was the most difficult part. I had *seen* him fall. And no amount of mental reconstruction could make me believe I'd imagined it.

But I *had* to have imagined it; otherwise, he would have been mangled in the farm equipment below the loft, and he wasn't.

But something felt off. I didn't necessarily feel he was in danger—the initial scare of watching him fall had subsided due to everyone else's lack of worry—but there were still things about the situation that troubled me. For example, when I first arrived, Isaac wasn't here because he'd been off fishing with Charles; but, this time, Charles was in the barn when Isaac "disappeared," so who was he off fishing *with*?

Charles hadn't given me an opportunity to ask, and Helen didn't know. Later, when Grams also confirmed Isaac had gone fishing, I asked her. She'd been sitting in an arm chair crocheting and, without looking up from her task, said she believed he'd gone with Thomas and Jackson. The explanation didn't make any sense because I hadn't seen the two young men since the day of my arrival. It seemed odd that they would show up just to take Isaac fishing.

"Up early again, are we, Miss Karla?" I was putting on the final layer of clothing when Evelyn entered the room. She stood behind me and began lacing up the strings on the back of my dress.

"I thought Isaac might be back."

"Mos' times, worry keeps folks in bed. Gets you right up, don't it?"

"Not always." I recalled all the days I lay in bed after Mason died, unable to get up, even if my heart had willed my body to.

But then, it wasn't worry that kept me in bed those days. It was grief.

"Grief keep you in bed," Evelyn said, as if she'd read my mind, which seemed to happen a lot around here. "Now, worry," she said, finishing up with the strings. "Yes, ma'am! Dat get ya up an' mov'n."

She turned toward the door and said under her breath, "Mov'n 'nto an early grave, dat's what."

I struggled to keep a smile from my face. She'd murmured, but not so quietly that I couldn't hear. Perhaps that was her intention.

She started across the floor. "Now, you head on down when

you's ready. Breakfast be served dreckly."

Yay, breakfast! Not another morning of everyone mysteriously being gone and my wondering if I'd missed the meal.

Evelyn started to leave, but she paused and turned to me once more. "And Miss Karla."

"Yes?" I raised my eyebrows.

"Don't worry so much. Laws, chil'! You gonna make yerself sick!"

I smiled. It was the most worked up I'd seen Evelyn since my arrival, and I kind of liked this feisty side of her. "Yes, ma'am."

She swatted her hand like she was swatting away nonsense, then she shuffled from the room.

I stood at the window and looked out onto the expansive lawn that butted up against the thick tree line. The trees seemed to go on forever. Of course, I knew, after my midnight escapade with Helen, that they didn't go on forever. The thick forest of trees led to a cliff where Helen found pure pleasure in living on the edge. Literally. I shook my head at the memory of her completely naked as she jumped into nothingness.

A robin flew from one of the tree branches and landed on the lawn, pecking the grass for grubs. I thought of Lawson and the conversation in which he claimed I either had to be a bird or an angel.

So, if you find me in the early morning searching for breakfast on the lawn, I suppose you will be greatly disappointed? I'd joked.

I haven't been disappointed yet, he'd responded. His brown eyes were genuine. His skin, tan. His smile, perfect.

I shook the conversation—and Lawson's face—from my mind. Lawson was a distraction. I couldn't think about him. I needed to focus all my attention on Isaac. On finding him.

Today would be the day. I felt it. He couldn't stay away much longer.

The robin pulled a thick worm from the ground and laid it briefly on the grass before getting a better grip. She jerked her head in several directions before looking up and catching my stare, with her breakfast squirming helplessly in her beak.

"Good idea," I said through the glass. "I'm a bit hungry myself."

As if she heard my words and feared her meal was in jeopardy of being stolen, she spread her wings and flew away.

CHAPTER 23

The Prodigal Son

Everyone was together for breakfast. Everyone, except Isaac.

The oblong dining table of dark oak had a detailed design of vines and leaves trailing along its edges. Ten high-back wooden chairs with soft, flower-printed cushions sat around the table—four on each side, and one at each end. The walls of the dining room were wallpapered with a pattern of overlapping and various-sized diamonds over a yellow background. A beautiful gasolier hung over the table.

Mr. Darap sat at one end of the table with his back to a large lattice-paned window that looked out into the side yard. To Mr. Darap's left sat Emma and Ann, giggling at their own whispers. To his right, Charles, shoveling forkfuls of scrambled eggs and potatoes into his mouth.

Grams sat at the other end of the table, adjacent to Mr. Darap. She neatly spread apple butter on a biscuit and took a small bite.

Mr. Darap sat tall and straight, observing the scene. He was smiling proudly, the way any head of a household who is happy to have their family together for a meal would.

I sat to Grams' right, and Helen sat on her left, placing Helen and I directly across from each other.

Evelyn stood in the doorway leading from the dining room to the kitchen, ready to fetch anything from the kitchen at anyone's request. She stood with her arms folded in front of her in a simple brown dress, a white apron tied around her waist.

"Evelyn," Grams said, motioning to two empty seats between Helen and Charles. "Do get Jeremiah and have a seat, won't you?"

I looked up, surprised at Grams' suggestion. *Was it normal for servants to eat with the family?* I had been uncomfortable with Evelyn and Jeremiah waiting hand-and-foot on the family from the moment I arrived, but I hesitated to address it. First, it was because I was too focused on finding Isaac. Then, when I found Isaac, I didn't address it for fear it might give away the fact that Isaac and I didn't belong here.

And now, here Grams was, inviting Evelyn to sit.

"No, ma'am," Evelyn said. "We is gonna wait 'til everyone's had dey fill. Not oft'n you get a chance to all be together with family fer breakfast."

"You are family, as well," Grams replied, looking at Evelyn sternly, indicating she'd have no arguing about the matter.

"I thank you, ma'am." Evelyn smiled. "But I sho am jes enjoy'n de sight from here."

"Very well," Grams said, picking up her fork and shaking her head slightly.

I felt a sharp-toed shoe kick my shin under the table, and I flinched in temporary pain. I scowled at Helen, and she raised her eyebrows up and down several times while tilting her head toward Mr. Darap.

I rubbed my shin and gave her a questioning glare.

She nodded her head again in the direction of Mr. Darap.

I looked and realized immediately it wasn't Mr. Darap she was nodding to. Through the picture window behind Mr. Darap, I saw Lawson atop his horse, trotting across the lawn.

I felt a smile start across my lips, so I buried my chin into my chest, pretending to look at my plate, hoping Helen hadn't seen.

A few minutes later, a knock at the door took Evelyn down the hall, and seconds later, she returned with a beaming Lawson at her side.

"I beg your pardon." He removed his hat. "I didn't mean to interrupt breakfast."

Mr. Darap and Charles both stood to shake Lawson's hand.

"Not a problem." Mr. Darap motioned to one of the empty seats. "Join us, won't you?"

"No, I couldn't—"

"Don't be silly. There's plenty," Mr. Darap said. "Evelyn? Do you mind bringing a plate for Lawson?"

Evelyn lowered her head and left the room.

"I guess I'm early," Lawson said, as he pulled out a chair and sat down beside Charles. He placed his hat in the empty chair between him and Helen.

I still had my face buried, and I felt Helen's eyes boring a hole right through me.

"Good morning, Miss Karla," Lawson said.

I looked up and caught his confident stare. "Lawson." I nodded, maintaining my composure. "It's good to see you this morning."

"You, as well." He looked around the table. "Ladies," he said, grouping a hello for everyone else.

"Lawson," Helen responded in greeting, while Ann and Emma just snickered.

"Girls!" Grams reprimanded. "If you are done eating, you may be excused."

They got up quickly and laid their napkins on the table before curtseying a goodbye and heading out the door.

Grams was not amused, but Mr. Darap attempted to stifle a smile. He raised his napkin to his lips. When he brought it down again, the smile was gone, as if the napkin had magically erased it before he too could be reprimanded by Grams for ill table manners.

"Ahem," he said, clearing his throat, making an obvious attempt to get on with business. "Lawson is going to help clear some fields today. Isn't that wonderful?"

"It's my pleasure. Really. There's not much to do on our property for the time being, so I'm happy to lend a hand around here."

Helen sat watching me across the table, a widening grin across her face.

I intentionally avoided her stare and instead looked to Lawson. "Do you have much property? You and your family?" I was making conversation. Anything to avoid Helen.

"Nowhere near what Mr. Darap has here, but we have seven hundred acres."

I raised my brows. "That's quite impressive. How do you manage it all?"

"With lots of help," Charles answered for Lawson, taking a bite of scrambled eggs. "Which is why your help is greatly appreciated." He gave Lawson a wink.

Evelyn brought a plate of eggs, two strips of bacon, and a biscuit over Lawson's head and laid it on the table in front of him.

Charles stood up, laying his napkin on the table. "Excuse me. I should go ahead and get started."

Lawson started to stand without taking a bite of his food, but Charles put a hand on his shoulder to keep him seated. "You eat first. Jeremiah can bring you to join me when you're finished. Besides," he said with a smile, "you won't be no good to me working on an empty stomach."

Lawson conceded, picking up his fork. "I won't be long."

"Again," Charles said, "we're just grateful for the help."

Charles left the room and Lawson bowed his head in silent prayer for the meal. He had missed Mr. Darap's lengthy breakfast prayer, thanking the Lord for each one of us. By name.

I focused my attention back on my plate to give him privacy.

The prayer was brief. After whispering an "amen," he scooped a forkful of eggs into his mouth. "Where's Isaac off to this morning?" he asked after swallowing the bite.

I jerked my head up. If Isaac was with Lawson's brother, Thomas, wouldn't Lawson have known? My heart began pounding out its familiar rhythm of panic.

"He's not yet returned from fishing with Thomas and Jackson," Grams answered quickly.

Lawson swallowed another bite of food and looked at Grams. "Is that where they've taken off to? I was wondering where they've been."

"They didn't tell you?" I asked.

"No." He wiped his mouth with his napkin.

"Don't feel bad," I scowled at Grams. "Nobody told me, either."

"Oh, I'm not mad they didn't tell me. I'm mad they didn't invite me!" He laughed heartily, and I couldn't help but join him.

Mr. Darap and Grams laughed, as well. I realized it was the first time I'd actually heard Grams chuckle, even though I'd seen her smile often.

The only one in the room not laughing was Helen. She was too engrossed in watching my every expression . . . and I was sure she'd have plenty to say about it later.

"Well," Mr. Darap said, taking a final sip of coffee before standing. "Are you ready to earn your breakfast?" he joked.

"Yes, sir!" Lawson sounded off, shoving a final bite of bacon in his mouth. He stood and bowed slightly to Grams. "Ma'am. Thank you for the wonderful meal."

"Thank Evelyn." Grams nodded to the door where Evelyn was still standing. "It was all her doing."

Lawson walked over to Evelyn and took her hand in his. "It was delicious, my lady."

If Evelyn's dark skin would have allowed it, she may have blushed. Instead, she swiped at him with her free hand. "Git on outta here. You jes put in an honest days work, an' we'll calls it even."

"Yes, ma'am!" He circled back around the table to pick up his hat. "Ladies." He nodded, putting his hat on his head. "Have a great day."

"You, as well," Helen answered, still staring at me.

"Karla. Helen," Grams instructed after all the men had left the room. "Why don't you help Evelyn clear the table."

"Oh no!" Evelyn quickly began picking up dishes. "On a day as nice as 'dis? No, ma'am. Dey need to git outside an' 'joys demselves. Go on, now!"

Again, Grams shook her head. "Very well, then. Girls, shall

we go outside?" She picked up her cup and saucer and took it with her.

Helen and I followed her through the house to the front porch, but as soon as we stepped through the door, Helen darted down the steps and started running across the lawn. "We will discuss breakfast later, Chuckaboo!" she yelled.

Grams shook her head with a smile. "That girl. She has great difficulty sitting in one place for any length of time."

"Yes," I agreed. "And I've no doubt she has much to say about breakfast."

Grams eyed me sweetly. "I've no doubt you're right. I do apologize for her lack of couth at times."

"I like it," I said honestly.

"Come." Grams started across the porch. "Sit with me a spell."

There were six white wooden chairs with flower-print cushions sitting in pairs on the far end of the front porch. Small glass-top tables sat between several of the chairs, and we sat down in two of the chairs with a table between us.

"Grams?"

"Hmmm?" Grams asked, sipping her tea with one hand and holding the saucer with the other.

I was afraid I was about to say something wrong, but I had to ask. "Is it customary for servants to eat with the family?"

"Servants?" She raised the cup to her lips again.

"Yes. You asked Evelyn to join us for breakfast—"

Grams nearly dropped her cup. "Evelyn isn't a servant!"

"She's not?"

"Of course not!" Grams said, bringing her tea cup down and resting it on the saucer. She didn't sound angry, only surprised that I'd thought such a thing. Then, her face softened. "Although, the possibility exists that she doesn't know how *not* to be."

"I don't understand."

"Neither do I," Grams said. "But still, it could be so."

I looked at her, needing more of an explanation.

Grams sighed, making an attempt to explain something she herself didn't seem to understand. "I think Evelyn *was* a servant, at some point in her life, but she's not now. It seems Evelyn doesn't know how to stop being something she was."

"She's comfortable?" It was a question, but one Grams had already answered. Sort of.

Grams leaned back in her chair. "Or it's familiar," she suggested. "It's hard to say with certainty."

"And Jeremiah?"

"Same. That, and he just likes finding an excuse to be around Evelyn." Grams gave me a wink.

I smiled.

"It'll take some time, but Evelyn will come around." Grams closed her eyes, and a rare breeze blew through the length of the porch. "Things happen in the Lord's time, not ours."

I stared at Grams. Her face was old, yet young. There were wrinkles around her eyes and mouth, but the skin between each set of wrinkles was smooth and fresh. She was the perfect combination of youth and wisdom. She knew a lot about a lot of things, and I wondered if she knew anything about my dream—if she could help me make sense of it.

"Grams?"

"Yes, dear." Grams opened her eyes and took another sip of tea.

"I've been having this dream."

Grams didn't look surprised, and despite her not asking questions about what the dream was, I continued, volunteering information she hadn't asked for.

"I'm standing in a field. The wind is horrendous, and it's whirling twigs and leaves everywhere. I can barely see anything because of all the debris. But I do see someone—a figure—standing under a tree on a hill. I can't tell who it is, but they look familiar."

Grams nodded. Not in a curious way, but in a knowing way. As if she'd heard this story before.

I continued. "The person is yelling, 'Peace. Be still.'"

Grams was still looking at me, encouraging me with her eyes to continue.

"Peace. Be still." I repeated. "The same way Jesus said it in the bible when the disciples were on a boat with him, and a storm came—"

"A storm so powerful the waves began to cover the boat," Grams interjected, verifying she knew the story very well. "The disciples were frantic, but Jesus was sleeping soundly through the storm."

"Yes."

"And what did the disciples do?" Grams asked.

I knew she knew the answer, but I *had* asked her for help with the dream, so I played along. "They went and woke him," I answered.

Grams raised her eyebrows, feigning surprise. "So, they called out to Jesus?" she asked.

"I suppose. They went and woke him," I repeated.

"And what did Jesus do?" she asked curiously.

"He asked them, 'Why are you fearful, oh ye of little faith?' And then he calmed the sea by saying, 'Peace. Be still.'"

Grams stared at me as if I had just answered my own question.

"But in my dream," I explained, "the storm doesn't cease when the person yells, 'Peace. Be still.' The storm continues to rage, and even seems to get angrier, so the person in my dream isn't Jesus."

"No," Grams said, "but maybe they think they are."

I caught her eye.

"Or maybe they're trying to be," she suggested.

I thought about it for a minute. "But then, who is it?"

"You said they seemed familiar?" Grams asked.

"Yes, and they sounded—" I stopped midsentence.

Grams laid her cup and saucer on the glass table between our chairs and placed a hand on my knee.

"They sounded like *me*," I finished, surprised at my own revelation.

She patted my leg.

I looked at her, confused.

"You were trying to calm the storm all by yourself, then?"

I looked away . . . not to avoid the question, but to really think about it. Was it true? Had it been me yelling, "Peace. Be still?"

"Karla?"

I blinked several times, not understanding how I couldn't have recognized myself in the dream immediately.

"In your dream, does the storm ever cease?" she asked.

I nodded my head. "Yes, the person on the hill—I," I shook my head, still baffled by it. "I fall to my knees, and I'm immediately cocooned in a . . . protective . . . like, bubble."

"But does the storm *cease*?" she asked again.

I tried to remember that part of the dream clearly. The storm, throwing leaves and twigs in all directions. "No. No. The storm doesn't cease. The storm rages on, but I'm protected from it."

"When you fall to your knees, you say?"

"Yes," I answered.

Grams smiled.

"Yes," I repeated, in case she hadn't heard me. "When I fall to my—"

Grams continued smiling, waiting patiently for me to understand my own statement.

"Oh!" I said as soon as it hit me. Then, "Oh," more softly. I was only protected when I fell to my knees—when I fell down to God in reverence of his power.

Anger boiled inside me. The dream is God's way of once again mocking me—of showing me yet again that he is more powerful than me!

Because I'd refused to allow him to taunt me during my waking hours, he had invaded my dreams just to remind me how much control he has.

"So, God wants to make sure I know *he's* in charge, not me," I said.

"No!" Grams pulled away. She didn't hide her frustration, and it was the first time I'd seen her even somewhat upset since my arrival. "He's trying to show you He's the only one who can protect you. Protect you from the storm. Protect you from turmoil. Protect you from *yourself*."

She made an obvious attempt to calm herself as she picked up her tea cup. She held it in front of her as she spoke. "You're not in charge, it's true; but that's not what God's trying to tell you. He's trying to tell you there will always be storms in your life, but if you'll let Him, He can bring you peace despite the storm."

I looked up from my lap where I'd been staring like a disciplined child ever since she'd pulled away.

"Storms do rage on, Karla. They rage on around us and *within* us, and none of us are strong enough to stop them."

I didn't reply, and I found myself staring back into my lap, so she continued.

"You say the storm only ceases around you—that you're only protected from it—when you fall to your knees?" she asked again.

"Yes," I said, sighing with the answer's repetitious weight.

"When you fall to your knees." She mused.

"Yes," I said again.

"Well, then. Perhaps *that's* where you should begin."

I looked up, ready to concede that maybe she was right about the dream, even if I wasn't yet ready to give in to the idea that bowing down to God was the only place for reckoning; but before I could say a word, my eyes grew big and my heart raced.

"Isaac!" I screamed.

Grams startled in her chair and followed my gaze.

Isaac was casually trotting across the lawn with a huge smile across his face.

I bolted out of my chair, nearly knocking it over, and ran

down the stairs two at a time. I met him halfway across the lawn and caught him in my arms, hugging him tightly as I kissed the top of his head.

He returned the hug quickly, and then squirmed to get free. "Mom! Geeze!"

"Don't ever just take off like that again, do you understand?" I shook my finger firmly in his upturned face.

"Thomas and Jackson asked if I wanted to go fishing. I couldn't find you. What was I supposed to do?"

"You were supposed to not go."

"But I like to go," he said, pouting just enough that my frustration with him was replaced with sympathy. I recognized that pout. It was the same one that appeared any time he mentioned things he missed doing with his dad. He and Mason used to fish together all the time, but Isaac and I had never been. I'd forgotten how much Isaac enjoyed it, and I instantly felt bad that I'd never taken him.

"You could have called—" I began.

"On the cell phone?" he asked smartly.

"Funny," I smirked. "Next time, just ask me. Okay?"

"But—"

"But nothing," I interrupted. "You ask, or you don't go."

Isaac rolled his eyes but nodded he understood. "How's Nightmare?" he asked, abruptly changing the subject.

Nightmare? I was trying to keep from going sick with worry, and he was concerned whether Nightmare had been okay while he was gone?

Of course, I'd known that would be the case. That's why I'd checked Nightmare's stall ten or more times a day searching for Isaac.

But still, it hurt that Nightmare was the first person—or thing—he wanted to see upon his return.

"I'm going to go check on him," he said before I could reply. "Love you!" And off he ran, behind the house toward the stables.

I fought the urge to go with him—to stay by his side 24/7—

but it wouldn't do any good. I knew that. I had to trust that things were as they seemed—that Terrebonne Parish was safe for me and Isaac.

I walked across the lawn and back onto the porch, resuming my spot beside Grams.

She reached over, patted my hand and smiled. "Feel better?"

"That kid," I said, shaking my head. "He's going to be the death of me."

"Yes, well, children are like that."

CHAPTER 24

Picnic

"So, the prodigal son returns?" Lawson walked up as I stood leaning on the fence watching Isaac ride Nightmare around the paddock.

I beamed.

"That's the biggest smile I've seen on your face since your arrival."

I blushed. I knew it was ridiculous for a mother to be so in love with her son, but not all mothers had been through what I'd been through.

"You should have seen me plucking worms from the front lawn earlier today. Now, *that* was a smile," I joked, hoping to take the attention away from the strong affection I had for Isaac. I didn't need my love for him analyzed.

"Worms, huh? Well, there goes my angel theory I suppose."

"I told you you'd be disappointed," I reminded him.

He shook his head. "No. Still not."

I stared at him, so much sincerity in his eyes.

He'd appeared quite dapper all the times I'd seen him before, and even now, covered in dirt from a hard day's work in the field, he was still very dashing.

He removed his hat and used the back of his gloved hand to wipe sweat from his forehead, leaving a smear of dirt.

I instinctually reached up to wipe it away. I meant only to wipe it away quickly, but I stood with my thumb to his forehead, mesmerized by his mahogany brown eyes staring down at me. A few moments passed before I was able to regain voice and movement.

"Got it," I said, pulling my hand away abruptly.

"All clean?" he asked. His dark, wavy locks were curlier than usual, soaked with sweat.

"I wouldn't go that far," I laughed, swiping dirt from the front of his shirt. "You're quite a mess. What have you been doing to get so dirty?"

"Clearing the fields." He shrugged, catching my eye again. "I suppose I should wash up." He said the words but made no attempt to go.

"Woo, chil', look at you!" Evelyn exclaimed, catching sight of Lawson. She had come around the barn carrying a small covered basket, but neither Lawson nor I had paid her any mind. We were still staring at each other, lost in a moment that felt strange and familiar at the same time.

Evelyn walked up beside us. "You bes' jes go on down to de creek an' wash up," she ordered Lawson, looking him up and down. "Good hot day like today . . . take you a swim an' get cleaned up at de same time."

"Yes, ma'am," Lawson said, without meeting her eye.

I saw Evelyn in my peripheral vision, finally beginning to snap out of the spell I'd been under staring into Lawson's eyes. She shifted her weight and wiped her neck with a handkerchief. Then she placed her hand on her hip and continued staring at Lawson, resolute.

Lawson smiled slyly and held my gaze a second longer. Finally, he turned to Evelyn. "I'm sorry, did you say something?"

I lowered my head to conceal a laugh.

"Chil'!" Evelyn said, swatting him with her handkerchief. "Go on, now. You go get cleaned up, an' me an' Karla will have some lunch ready fer you when you return. Karla, you come on wit' me."

"Yes, ma'am," I answered, still smiling.

"Yes, ma'am," Lawson echoed before starting across the yard.

I got Isaac's attention and motioned that I was going inside. He waved in acknowledgement before he and Nightmare transitioned from a walk to a trot.

I walked into the kitchen with Evelyn, who carefully took eggs from the basket she was carrying and laid them on the counter of a small cupboard in the corner of the kitchen. Then, she set about making sandwiches and putting them inside the basket she'd been carrying the eggs in. She left the kitchen, instructing me to wait, then returned with a small, quilted blanket in her arms.

"Here, you spread dis out an' eat outside. I don't want Lawson bring'n his sopp'n self back in here 'til he dries." She spoke with authority.

"Yes, ma'am," I took the basket from Evelyn and kissed her cheek softly. "Thank you." I held up the basket. "Would you like to join us?"

"Laws, no!" she answered. "I 'as plen'y of work to do. Plen'y!"

"I can—" I started.

"Don't you even think it," she interrupted. "Now go," she turned me around and swatted me on the behind playfully. "Dere's a hungry man out dere need'n fed."

I dutifully went outside and found a spot under a shade tree at the edge of the woods to spread the quilt. I hadn't been to the creek, so I didn't know where it was or how far away, but I figured if I sat along the tree line, I'd see Lawson come out somewhere. And I did. I had just finished spreading the sandwiches and a bowl of homemade applesauce onto the blanket when he popped out of the woods, shaking his tussle of black curls.

"Over here!" I waved.

He waved that he saw me and began walking in my direction.

I watched, and as he got closer, I wondered if he'd jumped into the creek clothes and all or gone skinny dipping like Helen had done. I felt my cheeks grow warm at the thought.

"Clothes and all," he said when he reached me, holding his arms out wide.

I looked up in brief panic. *Had I spoken my curiosity out loud?* No, surely I hadn't.

"I hope that's okay. It defeats the purpose of washing if I'm just going to put dirty clothes back on, don't you think?"

"Oh, I quite agree," I said.

"Except, being that I'm soaking wet, perhaps you'd not prefer my company."

I motioned for him to sit. "I think it's Evelyn who doesn't prefer your company. She booted us from the house."

"Did she?" He laughed as he sat down on the quilt. "It looks good."

"Yes. Evelyn must have just made the bread. I watched her cut the first slices when she made our sandwiches, and they're still warm."

"Shall we fight over the heel, then?"

"No, sir. You may have it. After all, you worked today, and all I've done is . . . well . . . all I've done is relax."

"You sure?" he asked, smiling the same charming smile he delivered every time we met.

"Oh, yes. Now, it's your turn to relax."

We sat and talked for what seemed forever. Lawson was easy to talk to. He didn't mention his love, Albany, and I made no mention of Mason. We didn't need to. We had mentioned them once, and in so doing, we knew we shared a pain no one else could understand.

Lawson talked about his family and their farm. He talked about his love for the water, and how he preferred fishing off a boat rather than on land. And, of course, he told convincing tales of fish that got away.

While I couldn't really talk about my job—the type of technology we provided at Maximum Capacity hadn't been invented yet—I found plenty to share with Lawson. We talked about all our favorite things, including our favorite authors. I had to be careful not to mention authors who hadn't been published prior to 1856, which was difficult.

"Are you going to eat the rest of that?" Isaac asked, looking desperately at my sandwich. He'd stabled Nightmare and come to join us.

I handed him my sandwich. "It's all yours."

"Thanks!" he said, taking a big bite and eyeballing Lawson's.

"Uh uh, you're not getting mine," Lawson said, guarding it with his hands, and all three of us laughed.

***

That night, I had a restful sleep. The recurring nightmare of leaf-damaging wind and broken branches ceased.

I basked in the quiet of the night while it lasted. I'd learned once too often there is always another nightmare just around the corner.

CHAPTER 25

And Then, Rain

I woke to the sound of rain falling.

"Oh, good! You're awake!" Grams said, entering my bedroom.

I sat up, rubbing my eyes. I was confused by the rain. It felt out of place with the happiness I'd found.

"Why is it raining?" I asked Grams.

"Why?" She seemed amused by the question.

"Yes, why? I thought—" I stopped.

"You thought what?" Grams urged.

"Well . . ." I hesitated. "Everything has been so great since Isaac and I arrived. I didn't think anything bad could happen." *Yes, Isaac had taken off and gone fishing for a few days, but he had returned safe and happy.*

"Bad?" Grams looked baffled. "Rain is bad?"

"Well, isn't it?"

"No, just the opposite." She sat on the side of the bed. "How could anything grow without a little rain? What would the animals drink? How would we cook?"

"It's just that . . ." I started. "Well, I just—"

"Besides," Grams chimed in, "if not for the occasional rain, we might not change our usual routines. Rain forces us to deviate from our plans, which is exactly what it has done today. You get dressed and meet me in the parlor. We've not much time, dear. Hurry up."

Grams stood up and left the room with a smile on her face.

What kind of things could one do in the rain? Or *because* of the rain?

I threw my head back down on the pillow and brought the covers over my head.

"Nothing good about rain," I mumbled.

But I smiled as my thoughts wandered back to a rainy day Mason and I had spent together. We'd planned on hiking one of our favorite trails, but the threat of rain kept us on the couch—Mason reading a newspaper, and I reading a Paul Young book. The promised rain had arrived and had been pouring down all morning. Finally, around noon, a beam of sunlight streamed through the living room blinds to where we were sitting. I raised my book to block the sun from my eyes. Mason did the same with his newspaper, but only for a split second. In the next second, he was laying his paper to his lap and blurting out, "Let's go rainbow hunting!"

"What?" I looked at him, expecting to see a sign he was joking, but instead I saw a look of resolve. "You can't be serious."

"Haven't you ever gone hunting for rainbows?"

"Yes, *when I was a child.*"

"Well, then," he said, jumping to his feet. "Let's go."

"Seriously?"

"It's raining," he said. "And the sun is out. Isn't that the right formula for rainbows?"

"Okay," I said, playing along. I stood up as he grabbed his car keys. "But what are we gonna do with it when we find it?"

"We'll just play it by ear," he said, opening the living room door for me to exit first.

As we made our way to the vehicle, the sun once again hid itself behind dark clouds, and we quickly dove into the car just as the clouds gave way to a downpour.

"Just in time," Mason said. "We almost got pulverized by water BB's!"

"Water BB's?"

"You ever get hit by drops of water that big?! Feels just like getting peppered with a BB gun!"

"You've been peppered with a BB gun before? Not sure I want to ride around with you if people often shoot at you," I joked.

"Too late. You're stuck with me."

We drove around for about twenty minutes before the rain shifted from a downpour to a soft drizzle. The gray clouds parted, and the sun once again poked through the clouds.

"There it is!" Mason pointed east of the road. A pale rainbow arched above the treetops. Its hues of red and purple were faint at first, but they quickly grew bright and prominent right before our eyes.

"Told ya!" he said, playfully smacking my arm with the back of his hand.

It was beautiful. The brightest one I'd ever seen.

"Well, you were right. We found it. Now, what'll we do with it?"

He acted like he was thinking deeply, then blurted out, "Chase it!" as he stepped slightly on the gas for dramatic effect. "You know there's a pot of gold at the end of it, right?"

"Is there?" I mused. "I've never heard that."

"Good thing I'm here, then," he said, giving me a wink. "And there's trolls who guard the gold, so we'll need to come up with a master plan before we get there."

"You mean Leprechauns," I corrected.

"A-ha!" Mason said with a finger in the air. "So you *do* know a little something about the gold."

I smiled. "Maybe I've heard rumors."

"That's good. With your knowledge and my speed, we're going to be rich!"

While he drove, we talked about all the glorious things we were going to do with the money—the gold—once we found it. I was going to give it all to the poor, and Mason was going to build me the castle "her highness deserves."

He frequently glanced at the rainbow as he drove, turning in the appropriate direction at each intersection to keep the rainbow directly in front of us. At some point it occurred to me that, while we should have been closer, it was somehow getting farther away.

"Tricky little thing, ain't it?" Mason said, making the same observation.

I looked at him and quickly lost fascination with the rainbow, instead becoming absorbed with him. If not for his chiseled chin and morning shadow, he'd have looked like a young boy gearing up for his first football game—the excitement of the moment was written all over his face. I was captivated that such a simple moment could bring him so much happiness. I could have stared at him all day. Longer than I could have stared at some stupid rainbow.

"Karla!" Grams' voice startled me. I'd been so lost in memories of Mason that I hadn't gotten out of bed yet. Now, Grams was standing in the doorway of my room. "You're not up yet?!"

I threw back the covers and swung my feet over the edge. "I'm working on it."

"Well, let's go." She clapped her hands thigh level as if to say "chop, chop."

"Isaac?" By this time, all I had to do was say his name to imply it was a question of his whereabouts. If I hadn't been through all I'd been through, I'd have thought myself an overprotective mother. But I *had* been through everything I'd been through, causing me to constantly question his whereabouts and worry about his safety.

And yet, I reminded myself, he'd come back to me each time. Safe. Thanks to whatever magic Terrebonne Parish created . . . or whatever magic had created Terrebonne Parish. Because of that, my worries were covered with a blanket of security that could potentially be dangerous, heightening the worry with the same peace of mind that comforted it. It was a strange sensation.

"Isaac is in the barn with Nightmare," Grams answered. "Where else would you find him on a day such as today?"

"Oh, I don't know," I answered sarcastically. "Off fishing somewhere?"

"In the rain?" Grams raised her eyebrows as if the idea was impossible. Then she smiled. "Hurry up, now. You never know what the day holds. Maybe—" She paused. "Maybe . . . we'll even see a rainbow." She winked, then turned and left the room quickly.

My eyes widened and my heart thumped in my chest. *Why would she say that?* She couldn't possibly know what I had been thinking about—what memories the rain had brought. Could she?

No, she didn't know. If she knew, she wouldn't have said it. She would have known that reminding me of the good times only reminded me that there would be no more of them. It was a coincidence that she mentioned a rainbow.

I told myself that, then told myself to believe it.

I stood and stretched, listening to the heavy rain on the tin roof. I quickly got dressed into the clothes Evelyn had laid out for me—a blue day dress with simple full sleeves gathered into cuffs at the wrists, and a plain bodice that opened in the front. It was the simplest and least lavish dress I had put on since my arrival, and I worried what wearing such ordinary clothes meant for the day ahead.

I found Grams waiting for me at the foot of the stairs. "Shall we?" She handed me an apron.

Confused, I didn't immediately reach for it.

Grams gently shoved it closer to me. "It's an apron, dear. Put it on."

I took the apron, allowing the look of confusion to remain on my face, hoping it would prompt answers. Instead, Grams looked down at my shoes and said, "You won't be needing those, dear."

"Shoes?" I asked, looking down, more confused than ever. The last time I was told I didn't need shoes I ended up trekking several miles in the heat of the night with Helen. I wasn't about to make any such trek in a downpour.

"Yes, dear, the shoes. You don't need them. Take them off. Quickly now," she said, snapping her fingers.

I sat down on the stairs to take them off. "Mind if I ask why?"

"Not at all," she said. "As long as you don't mind if I don't answer." She smiled a big smile—one that told me whatever we were about to do, she was excited about it.

"So, you're not going to tell me what we're doing and why I don't need shoes for it?"

"No, I'm not going to tell you—" she started.

I placed my shoes to the side of the staircase, noticing for the first time that Grams was barefoot, as well.

"But I'll *show* you," she finished. "Ready?" She reached out her hand.

"I suppose." I put my hand in hers and stood to my feet.

She escorted me through the kitchen and out the back door.

The smell of dead worms met my nose, and I scrunched my face at the stench.

"The worms?" Helen asked.

She was sitting in a chair on the covered porch, Emma and Ann in chairs as well.

I nodded.

"It's not the most pleasant smell, perhaps," Grams agreed. "But isn't it nice how God urged them to the surface to make the birds' jobs a little easier this morning?"

"Nice for the birds, but not so much the worms," I mumbled.

Helen, Emma, and Ann were in plain clothes and barefoot just like Grams and I. They each had an easel in front of them. Emma and Ann had paintbrushes in hand and were already at work painting, but Helen sat with an elbow on her knee and her chin in her hand.

"Helen," Grams said. "You haven't even started?"

"Neither has Karla," Helen argued, deflecting the attention from herself, which she noticeably did quite often. "Besides, I'm thinking."

"*This* is what we're doing?" I asked. "Painting?"

"Yes," Grams answered, taking a seat in front of one of the easels and instructing me to do the same.

"And we're doing this because it's raining?"

"Yes," Grams answered again.

I sat down beside Grams. "And we *wouldn't* be doing this if it *wasn't* raining?"

"That is correct," she said assuredly.

I was confused. "We can only paint when it rains??" I huffed, the idea ridiculous to me.

Emma and Ann snickered.

"Of course not, but there's more fun to be had when it rains." Grams clamped a piece of white paper to the top of her easel, then handed me one to do likewise.

I looked at Helen, who nodded in agreement as a huge smile stretched across her face.

"Okay. So, what are we painting?"

"Whatever you want, dear," Grams said. She reached for a wooden box sitting on the glass table between our two chairs and opened its lid by turning a small brass key that was in a keyhole on the front.

Inside the box were blocks of color—at least forty of them—in all different shades and hues, each in their own little divider. Some of the blocks had names pressed in them like "Ashton and Browning" or "Devoe, F.W.," while others had been used so often the names were no longer legible. In the bottom right corner of the box was a small glass bowl.

"Hold this under the rain until it fills with water," Grams instructed, handing me the bowl.

"It's easier to catch the water on the corner where the rain drips down," Ann volunteered. She and Emma had a small glass bowl of water sitting on a table between them near a paint box just like the one Grams and I had. But the water in their bowl had already turned dark from rinsing their brushes repeatedly.

I held the bowl under the dripping eave until it filled. "Here," I said, setting it on the table between Grams and me and taking a seat again.

Grams pulled a small metal pin from the top edge of the box. The pin appeared to run through the box's front and down to a slim drawer below. After removing the pin, she opened the drawer to reveal several paintbrushes. She handed one to me. She also handed me a small porcelain cup, then placed a similar one on her side of the table.

I looked at her, baffled.

"For mixing your colors, dear."

"Oh!" I nodded.

I looked at Helen, who had begun painting. I presumed she had finally found inspiration, because she was now working quickly, as if she couldn't get her idea on the paper fast enough.

Grams immediately got to work, dipping her paintbrush in water and dabbing at various blocks of paint, being careful to rinse her brush between colors. She put two or three different colors in the porcelain bowl and stirred them until they formed a beautiful sky blue.

"Well, go on." She motioned with her brush for me to get started. "We've not much time, I'm afraid. It appears the rain is already tapering off."

"I still don't see what the rain has to do with painting," I said, dipping my paintbrush in water in a show of obedience nonetheless.

Emma and Ann snickered again.

"I mean, am I supposed to be painting the rain?"

"It really doesn't matter what you paint," Helen answered, working even more feverishly on her art. "Trust me."

"It's true," Emma chimed in.

"Just start painting, and the picture will present itself," Grams encouraged as she rinsed her brush again and started for a new color.

I dipped my paintbrush in the water and smeared it in a dark brown. I didn't bother blending it with another color or trying anything fancy. I had no idea what I was doing, and it apparently didn't matter. I figured I'd just do my best to paint a landscape of some sort.

I swiped the dark brown paint onto the paper at the bottom, and then layered other hues of browns and yellows over it.

To my surprise, it began to look somewhat like a wheat field. I leaned back in my chair to admire my work.

"Hurry, dear." Grams tapped my leg with the back of her hand. "You can admire your work later. When it's done. You need to finish your part before the rain stops."

Finish my part? I sighed. "I'm afraid I still don't understand."

"Paint, dear."

I dutifully swiped my brush in deep green and touched it to my easel. "So, it's like a race? We have to finish painting before the rain stops?"

"Not a race, Chuckaboo, but we do want to finish before it stops raining."

"So, finish while it's pouring rain. Got it!"

"Well," Helen answered, still at work, "not *pouring* rain. But sprinkling, at least."

"Yes," Ann clarified. "There's a perfect moment during a rainstorm. If you miss it, well, then . . . you miss it."

"Paint, dear," Grams said, nudging me gently with her elbow.

I wet my paintbrush and rubbed it in one of the dark blues, swirling it across the top of the paper for the sky. Then I dipped my brush into another shade of blue before adding white for the clouds. The white paint layered over the blue sky turned the clouds a light gray. I liked it. It was beginning to look like the rainy sky overhead, and I hadn't even planned for it.

I looked down at the box of paints. The previously-neat blocks were looking terribly sloppy now.

Grams saw me staring at them. "Normally, we'd work more orderly. We'd shave pieces of the blocks into our dishes and mix them properly, but—" She motioned to the sky. "Time waits for no man."

"Nor woman, apparently," Helen said, laying her paintbrush down. "Done!"

Emma and Ann did the same. "Done!" they said simultaneously.

Grams laid her paintbrush down and looked at my picture. "Oh!" she exclaimed. "You did splendidly! Just splendidly! You're done?"

I was going to work with the colors some more, but seeing that everyone else was done, I supposed I could be done as well. I laid my brush down. "All done."

The rain had finally stopped its constant drizzle and the clouds were now gently peppering soft drops of water onto the lawn.

"Perfect," Grams said, observing the light sprinkle. "Ladies? Shall we?"

Emma and Ann unclipped their pictures from their easels and ran off the porch with their pictures in hand. Helen did likewise, followed closely by Grams.

I sat for a startled moment watching them run around the yard barefoot as they twisted and twirled with their pictures.

"Come on, Chuckaboo!" Helen yelled.

I obediently unclipped my picture and followed suit. I jumped off the porch and felt the wet grass and mud squeeze between my toes, not bothered by it in the least.

"Tilt your picture so that it catches the rain," Emma was saying.

"But not directly," Ann instructed.

"The trick is to allow the rain to add to your artwork, not erase it," Grams explained.

Helen was holding her picture out in front of her with both hands, dipping and turning as if she were dancing with a suitor. "If you swing your picture, it creates some really unique effects. This way, the raindrops don't hit it much at all."

I looked at my artwork and noticed a few large drops of water had already hit it. I tilted the picture out of the direct rain and turned in circles. The rain was refreshing on my arms and face. I lifted my head to the sky. Strands of wet hair, which had not been put up properly for the day, stuck to my cheeks and forehead. I swiped away at one of the strands with my shoulder, being careful to keep my picture tilted.

Emma and Ann were laughing hysterically. I looked to find they had discovered a mud puddle and were taking turns jumping in it.

Helen was still dancing with her picture, her eyes closed; and Grams was walking slowly through the grass, carefully moving her picture from side to side.

I laid my picture on the covered porch and went over to Helen. The rain had stopped for the most part. "Might I have this dance?" I asked, taking the picture from her hands and reaching it out for Ann to take.

Helen opened her eyes, curtseyed like a lady, and put one of her hands in mine. She put the other on my shoulder.

Emma and Ann ran the pictures over to the porch, then returned to their mud puddle.

Helen began humming a waltz, and we danced at arms-length as if we were at a formal ball. "Da, da, da, da, da. Da. Da. Da. Da."

I interrupted. "Excuse me, but have you any suitors I should be wary of?" I joked, playing the full role of a gentleman.

"Oh." She batted her eyes. "I have many! My dance card is full, you know. It's just luck that you happened upon an opening."

"Well, the paper you were dancing with didn't put up much of a fight."

We weren't paying attention to where we were dancing and got too close to Ann just as she jumped into the mud puddle. A warm splash of muddy water landed on our legs, breaking up the dance. Normally, Helen would have huffed at Ann and scolded her carelessness, but having already been soaked, Helen instead gave me a shrug and jumped into the puddle herself.

I joined her, and before we knew it, the four of us were covered in mud, laughing uncontrollably.

"Oh, no, you ain't!" Evelyn's voice rang out across the lawn. I looked up to find her standing on the porch with her fists on her hips. "You ain't bring'n dat mess in dis house!"

Grams stood beside her with her arms crossed, beaming. I don't know how long she'd been watching us, but she had switched from the role of rain-dancing artist to disciplinarian as she joined Evelyn. "Girls," she instructed, "go around to the side of the house and wash off quickly. You can sit on the porch until you dry."

I noticed her bare feet had already been rinsed clean, again making me wonder how long she'd been standing on the porch watching us dance in the rain and splash in mud puddles.

I looked down at my muddy clothes.

"Come on." Helen pulled at my dress sleeve.

"Race you!" Ann said to Emma as they took off running to the side of the house.

I walked beside Helen and held my hand out to catch any stray drops of rain that may still fall.

We walked to the side of the house where a large wooden barrel full of water sat under one of the eaves, still catching a trickle of water as it dripped from the roof above. Emma and Ann were already splashing handfuls of water onto their legs and feet when Helen and I reached them.

We washed as best we could, helping get the backs of each other's legs. By the time we finished up, it had completely stopped raining, and the sun was shining.

We walked back to the porch to dry.

"There it is," Grams said when we returned. She was sitting in one of the chairs staring at the sky.

I followed her gaze to find a stunning, vivid rainbow cascading across the now-blue sky.

"Oh, it's beautiful!" Ann exclaimed, sitting on the porch steps and putting her chin in her hands to admire the sight.

I stole a glance at Grams, who glanced at me. "There it is," she repeated softly.

I sighed deeply and turned to admire the rainbow while it lasted. I knew all too well it would soon fade.

And I was right. The brilliant shades of purples and reds

lasted for only a few minutes before beginning to dull, then fade. Once it started fading, it faded quickly. Within minutes it had grown so faint that, unless you knew it was there, you couldn't see it at all.

Then, it was gone completely.

I watched the entire sequence and thought about how fleeting the moment had been—how brief the best moments in life seemed to be.

"Oh, Karla!" Helen said, causing me to jump. "It's exquisite!"

She was holding one of the paintings, and I walked over to find it was mine she was fawning over. I hadn't paid it any mind when I laid it on the porch earlier. I was too wrapped up in the moment—too consumed with the exhilarating sensation that dancing in the rain had brought. But now, I looked down at the work I'd created and gasped in surprise.

It truly was impressive! The rain drops had caught parts of the artwork in such a way it appeared the sky was raining paint. Even the large drops of water I had accidently let hit the "dirt" of the painting seemed purposeful. They looked eerily similar to the mud puddles we had just played in.

"Oh my!" Emma and Ann said simultaneously, standing behind Helen and looking at the painting over Helen's shoulders.

"Have you done this before?" Ann asked.

I shook my head, still staring at the painting, unable to believe that I *had* done it.

"Well," Grams said, coming up beside Helen and taking the painting in her hands. "She did have some help."

I looked up, prepared to defend my work, but Grams continued. "God did some of the work with the rain He provided," she explained, admiring the work, as well.

There was no arguing with that, I suppose. It certainly didn't look that impressive before it got rained on. In fact, one would have thought it'd been done by a small child before the rain. But now—

"We can work really hard to make things just so," Grams

said, handing me the picture. "We can carefully paint the perfect picture. But only when God puts His hand on it can we see its true beauty."

Grams wasn't talking about my painting anymore. She was never talking about what she was talking about. I knew that by now.

"It wasn't a perfect picture before it got rained on," I mumbled, taking the picture.

"But it was yours. Something you created."

"It was a bit of a mess, really," I said, looking at Grams.

"Yes." She smiled. "But if we let Him, God can take a bit of a mess and turn into a masterpiece."

Evelyn clapped her hands together as she came out onto the porch, interrupting the profound exchange of words taking place. "Now, dat's more like it! Much better." She nodded her approval. "Now, you sit an' get dry, an' I'll bring you som'n to drink."

"I'll help," Grams said. Evelyn opened her mouth to protest, but Grams insisted. "And you'll not argue with me," she asserted, pointing a finger at Evelyn.

Evelyn swiped her hand in the air, acknowledging defeat, before turning to go inside.

Grams followed with a triumphant nod.

We sat on the porch, passing each other's artwork around for each to look at. Emma had painted a woman's face.

"I was hoping to put it in the rain and have her look as though she were crying," she explained.

"She looks like she's sweating profusely!" Helen laughed.

"Or like she's a waxed doll who's been left in the heat," Ann said, taking the artwork from Helen.

Emma shook her head. "Not my best, that's for sure."

Ann had painted what appeared to be a tablecloth spread across a lawn with grapes and cheeses. "It rained on my picnic," she pouted.

Evelyn stepped out onto the porch with a tray. "Well, I can't fix yer picnic, but how 'bout some iced tea, Miss Ann?"

"Yes, ma'am." Ann readily took a glass, and Evelyn laid the tray on one of the empty tables.

"Laws! Ya'll made a mess!" she said, staring at the splattered paints on the other two tables. She pulled a cloth from her apron and began wiping.

"We'll get that," I said, standing up.

Evelyn stopped cleaning and put her hands on her hips sternly. "If you clean up, what that leave me to do?"

I stood dumbfounded.

"This is my job. You'ns job right now is to drink dat tea."

I looked at Helen, who just shrugged and picked up a glass.

I picked up a glass, as well, just as Isaac came running across the wet lawn.

He bounded onto the porch. "You gonna drink that?"

I hadn't even got it to my lips, but I handed it to him, smiling.

"Thanks!" He took a big drink before handing it back to me. He looked around at the paints. "You gonna paint?"

"We already did." I handed him my painting.

"Not bad," he said, giving it a brief glance before handing it back to me. "Looks like it got wet."

We all laughed.

"See mine?" Helen said to Isaac, handing him her painting.

I hadn't gotten a chance to look at it before Evelyn brought the drinks out.

Isaac looked at it with a confused face. "What is it supposed to be?"

I glanced over his shoulder to take a peek.

"Two love—"

"Helen!" I interrupted, seeing it was a man and a woman embracing.

"Two lovely people, um, kissing," she finished.

"Ewww!" Isaac exclaimed as he tossed the painting on the table. His disgust caused Ann to spit out her tea in laughter.

I shook my head at Helen, who smiled innocently.

"Did you see the rainbow?" I asked Isaac.

He turned expectedly to the sky.

"It's gone already," I explained. "You didn't see it then?"

"No, I didn't see it. I was—"

"Let me guess," I interrupted. "In the barn with Nightmare."

He smiled. He took the glass from my hand and took another drink before handing it back and starting inside.

"Uh uh," Evelyn said, gently grabbing his shirt sleeve and pointing to his feet. "Take off dose muddy shoes 'fore you go in dere."

Isaac chucked his shoes off obediently and left them at the door as he headed inside.

"I love you!" I shouted to an Isaac who was no longer in earshot.

***

After the morning rain, the sun remained, quickly drying the landscape. At supper, we sat around the table talking about our day.

I had gone on a quick stroll around the property, exploring nooks and crannies I hadn't yet been to.

Ann and Emma had started working on new dresses with Evelyn, who was teaching them to sew.

Isaac and Charles had cleaned out the barn and fixed a fence post that had come loose in the rain.

Mr. Darap had checked on some of the fields along the property and tended to the cattle.

Grams had gone into town with Jeremiah as her escort.

Helen didn't say what she had done, probably because whatever it was would have been frowned upon.

After supper, everyone went their separate ways. Helen went in the parlor to read, while Emma and Ann traipsed off upstairs.

Mr. Darap took Isaac to the gentlemen's parlor where he'd

promised he'd teach him how to play The Mansion of Happiness. According to Mr. Darap's description of the game at dinner, it was a board game in which players go on a path of virtue and vices in order to reach the Mansion of Happiness, also known as Heaven. It was the second board game they'd played since my arrival. The first, which I'd watched them play one evening after dinner, was The Game of Pope or Pagan, which, like The Mansion of Happiness, tested the player's moral compass.

Grams and Charles were still sipping tea when I excused myself. I went through the kitchen and opened the screen door to the back porch where Evelyn sat rocking in a wooden rocking chair with her head resting against its back and her eyes closed.

I sat down beside her and stared into the dark night. The stars shone bright overhead; if the moon was out, it was hiding on the other side of the house out of sight.

"How was yer day, Mrs. Karla?" Evelyn asked without opening her eyes or stopping her rocking.

"Good—" I began, then paused. "*Very* good, actually," I corrected, realizing how honest my answer was.

"Good," she said. "Dat's good."

"What are you doing out here?"

"Lis'nen."

"Listening to what?" I asked, looking around.

"Close yer eyes."

I laid my head on the back of the rocking chair and closed my eyes. I kept them closed as I rocked back and forth, mimicking Evelyn.

"Jes lis'n," she whispered.

I heard the soft creak of the chairs as we rocked on the porch.

"What am I listening for?" I whispered back.

"Sshh," Evelyn said, hushing me.

I rocked quietly, listening. A rustle of leaves nearby welcomed a rare summer breeze. A frog croaked from a good distance away. A hoot owl.

Chirp!

I opened my eyes and sat straight up in the chair. Evelyn's hand instantly went to my arm, but she didn't open her eyes or stop rocking.

"Lay back, chil' an' lis'n."

Something in her voice—maybe in her touch—made me obey. I closed my eyes and lay my head back again.

Chirp, chirp, chirp.

"Ain't dat beautiful?" Evelyn asked.

I listened, habitually counting the seconds between chirps, decoding what letter it might translate to.

"Don't try to hear de words." Evelyn caressed my hand. "Just lis'n to de music."

Chirp, chirp.

I listened as Evelyn sighed a sweet breath.

Chirp, chirp, chirp.

We listened in silence for several minutes.

"Som'times," Evelyn said after a while, "when yer look'n fer som'n you want, you become blind to what you been given."

"Why do people say that?" I sat up in my chair, annoyed by such euphemisms, the pleasant moment interrupted.

"Maybe 'cause you need to hear it."

"I already know it."

"And yet, you still blind."

"I beg your pardon?" I directed my stare at her, very much offended.

Evelyn kept rocking with her eyes closed. "You want what you don't have, an' you don't 'preciate e'erything you do have . . . 'cept maybe you 'preciate have'n Isaac." She finally stopped rocking and looked at me. "God could take 'im, too," she said looking me squarely in the eye.

He had already tried to take him, and I didn't let him!

"An' He will." Evelyn continued. "Take 'im, dat is." She raised her eyebrows in a knowing manner. "Which of you He'll take first is what we don't know." Her tone was not threatening or stern. She was simply reminding me of what I already knew. "Maybe it be you first, maybe it be Isaac. You got no control over dat."

In my heart, I knew if God had truly wanted to take Isaac from me, he would have. I knew that if it was God's will, I wouldn't have found him.

But I wasn't going to give God the satisfaction of knowing I knew that.

"How many times you ask God to bring Mason back?" Evelyn asked suddenly.

I flinched. How did she know anything about Mason? How did she know what I'd been through?

But then, it didn't matter, did it? Not in a world where nothing made sense anyway. Where everyone seemed to know me better than I knew myself.

"Too many to count," I answered honestly, looking down at the ring on my finger, twisting it numbly.

"An' how many times He answer'd you?"

"None."

"You sho 'bout dat?"

I furrowed my brow.

"You believe Mason is in heav'n?" Evelyn asked.

"What?" I turned to her, trying to read her face. Where was she going with this?

"Do you believe Mason is in heav'n?" she repeated, more pointedly.

"Yes, I *know* he's in heaven." *What did that have to do with anything? Just because I know he's in heaven doesn't mean I have to like it.*

"You *know* dat?"

"Yes. Of course." I insisted.

"An' you believe heav'n is a place of eternal happ'ness? A place where d'ere is no sadness?" she continued.

"Yes."

"You believe Mason is pain-free now?"

"Yes." I imagined him hanging out with God, or Peter. Or perhaps John. And I smiled. "He's probably off fishing on some crystal-clear river, hooking the biggest bass he's ever seen."

"An' do you *want* 'im to be happy?"

"Of course I want him to be happy," I said defensively. "More than anything in this world."

"More than anything in 'dis world," she repeated. "So 'den, why you want 'im to leave heav'n?"

"Because I miss him!" I cried, tears quickly finding their way down my cheeks.

Evelyn's voice softened. "So, you want 'im back fer yourself? Makes no diff'rence dat he's feel'n better dan he has ev'r felt before? Or dat he's patiently wait'n fer de day you reunite wid 'im? Makes no diff'rence dat *he's* okay wid God's plan?"

I heard what she was saying, but Mason had been happy with me and Isaac, too. Why did one happiness trump the other?

"Som'times, God don't give you what you want 'cause it's not what's bes' fer ever'one involved, so He gives you a song instead." Evelyn closed her eyes again. "A song fer comfort. Fer heal'n." She resumed her rocking. "You so busy lis'n fer de answer you want, you miss'n de answer God gave you."

"The answer he gave me?" I scowled.

"Yes." Evelyn smiled serenely. "You miss'n de song, chile'."

"I didn't ask for a song," I mumbled.

Evelyn chuckled. "An' God didn't ask fer a stubb'rn child either, but He sho did get one."

***

That night, I couldn't sleep. The conversation with Evelyn kept me awake. I kept going over everything she said, trying to figure out if she was right or not. Mason loved me and Isaac. He would have chosen staying with us if he'd had a choice.

Wouldn't he?

CHAPTER 26

The Law of Lawson

Despite my happiness, I still felt the need to test any mirror that had not yet resisted my palm. I didn't desperately want to go home—not anymore—but my curiosity continued to get the best of me, so I left every mirror smudged with my handprint, each time sighing with both relief and frustration when it didn't budge.

"Good afternoon."

I jumped at the sound of Lawson's voice. He'd walked quietly up behind me just as I'd finished pressing on the window that looked into the women's parlor from the porch. While it wasn't a mirror, it did cast a reflection, and I'd run out of mirrors to test.

"I'm sorry." He smiled. "I didn't mean to startle you."

"You didn't," I lied, straightening my shoulders and attempting to sound believable.

Lawson raised his eyebrows but didn't comment further. He was a gentleman, allowing me to regain my composure with dignity. "I hear you'll be joining us for church Sunday," he said, changing the subject.

"I suppose," I answered, shrugging. "I promised Isaac."

"I think you're supposed to go for God."

I couldn't tell if he was joking or being serious.

"I think it just matters that you go," I remarked.

Lawson shook his head. "I used to think that, too, but it's not true."

I looked at him defensively, feeling like a child being scolded. But when I saw his gentle face, I relaxed a bit.

"You go to worship God." He nodded resolutely.

I was confused. How could he have so much adoration for a God who took his love away? For a God who always took everything from everyone—and always the thing they cared about most. How could he love a God who did that?

"You still worship God?" I asked, not attempting to hide my surprise.

"Don't have a choice, really—" he paused, shrugging, "if you think about it."

"Of course you have a choice. Everyone has a choice. I believe they call it free will. It means you don't have to do everything God says." I heard the disdain in my voice, so I knew it hadn't gone unnoticed by Lawson.

"You're correct. We don't have to do everything God says, that's true. But we *do* all have to follow *something* or *someone*."

I shuffled my feet and looked away.

"You don't believe me?" he asked. He offered his arm. "Shall we?"

I hooked my arm in his and we strolled down the stairs and across the lawn.

"So, by that argument, we're all followers," I argued. "None of us are leaders?"

"Oh, some of us *think* we're leaders—and maybe there are moments we *feel* like leaders—but we're always acting on something. Orders we've been given by a superior. Our intuitions. Our impulses. *Something*."

I turned the side of my mouth up questioningly, but I wasn't about to argue the point further. I was enjoying the morning too much to allow anything to ruin it.

He caught my look. "You're not convinced?"

"Let's just say I disagree."

"What comes after Autumn?"

"Beg your pardon?" First, scolded like a child. Now, quizzed like a student.

"Summer. Spring. Autumn. Then what?"

I looked at Lawson a little frustrated. But then, I couldn't stay frustrated long. I liked him. He was kind. He knew hurt. So, if he had discovered some way past all the hurt and anger, I'd gladly take part.

Lawson waited patiently for my response.

Fine. I would play along. "Winter," I huffed.

"What comes after the night?"

"The morning." I rolled my eyes. It was a bit ridiculous, though.

"And on and on," he said, rolling his hand in the air. "Winter follows Autumn. Day follows night. *Everything* follows *something*."

I considered if what he was saying was true. Was there any scenario where something didn't follow something?

I looked up at a momma bird sitting on the branch of a sycamore tree. Her babies were squawking loudly from their nest, and she turned her head in their direction. Then, she spread her wings and glided to the ground. She swiftly plucked a worm from the grass and, in response to her babies' hungry chirps, carried the worm to them.

A squirrel plucked an acorn from a nearby tree and scuttled away, leaving the branch to sway in the aftermath. As a result, several more acorns toppled to the ground below.

My heart rate picked up at the truth before my eyes, and I became fully aware of the blood coursing through my limbs—each blood cell chasing after the other.

Of course. Action. Reaction. But did that prove everything followed something? And if so . . .

"Why God?" I asked.

Lawson didn't look at me. He was watching the momma bird, now perched on the side of her nest, as she dropped worm sections into the mouths of her eager young.

"Lawson?"

He gave me his attention.

"Why God?" I asked again.

He dropped my arm and began walking. I joined him, easily matching his idle steps.

"There's an old proverb," he began. "It says, 'He who knows

not, and knows not that he knows not, is a fool. Shun him. He who knows not, and knows that he knows not, is a child. Teach him. He who knows, and knows not that he knows, is asleep. Wake him. But he who knows, and knows that he knows, is wise. Follow him.'" Lawson shrugged. "God is the only one who fits into that last category. So really, He's the only one I can confidently follow."

I watched his face as he spoke. There was no doubt quivering along his chin line. No confusion across his brow. He was sure of what he was saying, as if he'd thought about it long and hard, and repeatedly came to the same conclusion.

He looked down at his hands and began pushing back the cuticle on his left thumb with his right thumbnail. "And He's the only one who promises that *something* follows death—that death isn't the end." When he looked up again, his mahogany-brown eyes were brimming with liquid sorrow. "Death follows illness," he said. "Death follows tragedy. You and I both know that."

I could have drowned in those eyes, and I would have been okay with that.

"But life follows death." A smile found its way to his face. "At least there's that. I *know* there is that."

It was true. Even in my anger with God, I never doubted that there was life after death. How could I? If I believed otherwise, it meant I'd never see Mason, or any of my family, ever again. I couldn't bear the thought of that. Throughout my pain—throughout my anger—the one thing I knew for sure was that Mason was in heaven, waiting for me.

"Everything follows something," I conceded, echoing his words softly.

I looked down, thinking but not speaking; partly happy there is life after death, and partly irritated that God had say over even that.

So, I believed it was true—that everything followed something—and maybe the most logical to follow out of all my options was God. He knew all, controlled all, and gave all. I suppose it made sense . . . but I still wasn't ready to succumb to a God who continued to take more than he gave. At least, in my eyes.

But I was getting there.

CHAPTER 27

The Chapel

When Sunday morning rolled around, I found myself getting dressed for church. I needed answers. I hadn't found them with Pastor Dan. I hadn't found them in my bible. But perhaps I'd find them in Terrebonne Parish. Terrebonne Parish had done so much good already, and Isaac had enjoyed church. In fact, he seemed to finally be healing, so I figured it was time for me to give it another try, too.

Two carriages arrived to take us to church. The ladies rode in one and the men in the other, including Isaac. The church was just on the outskirts of town where I'd run into Helen just after my arrival. Surely we'd passed it on our walk back to Grams, but I'd been so overwhelmed, I hadn't noticed it.

Now, as the carriage came to a stop, there was no way *not* to notice it. Its soaring steeple stood in grandeur against all the other buildings around it. Its arched windows and intricate wood and stone design were magnificent.

I walked through the large and ornate wooden doors in awe as I entered the sanctuary. The inside was even more splendid! I stared at the raised arches that ran across the ceiling to the chancel. At the front of the church, which seemed countless footsteps away, was a pulpit. To the right of the pulpit was a lectern, holding a large bible. A communion table sat between them. The entire chapel was stunning—a beautiful structure with light-embracing windows and grand curvatures.

The last time I walked through the doors of a church, I was trailing behind a casket that imprisoned my husband and best friend. That day, I swore I'd never step inside a church again.

Yet, here I was.

I was here because I'd promised Isaac.

I was here because this was my last hope at finding answers to questions I desperately needed answers to.

I kept reminding myself of all the reasons I was here to stave off the urge to turn and run.

We settled into a pew about three rows from the front, and I got the impression it was the pew the Darap family regularly sat in because Grams and Mr. Darap went straight to it without hesitation, while the rest of us followed behind.

The sermon was long, and the church was humid. Fans waved desperately in every pew—ladies trying in vain to cool themselves gracefully.

The preacher spoke about the covenant God made with Abraham. I listened attentively while he talked about how God split the animals, which he explained was the way in Abraham's day that two individuals sealed a covenant, and how God walked between the two parts of the animals alone rather than with Abraham. The preacher said God had done so to show Abraham that the covenant was a gift from God, not a contract by which Abraham had to do something in return. He said it was a symbol of God's commitment to his promise, and nothing Abraham did, good or bad, would cause God to ever take away those promises—those gifts.

I tried to listen without judgment, but I couldn't help feel that, although God hadn't halved animals to make a covenant with me, he *had* made me promises he hadn't kept. He promised me Mason, then took him away.

When the preaching was over, I was sorely disappointed that the sermon hadn't delivered a message specifically for me as I'd hoped . . . and even expected. I stood up, disheartened that I wasn't departing with some new and life-changing insight or inspiration that would help me make peace with the God I'd been at odds with for the past several years.

I moved methodically with the others through the aisles toward the door. Churchgoers nodded acknowledgement to one another, seemingly waiting until they reached the somewhat-cooler outside air to hold any at-length conversations.

I, too, was anxious to feel even the slightest breeze on my dampened face, so I planned to quickly show my hand to the priest at the door and escape, ever-so-ladylike, into the fresh air. But the priest had other ideas.

"Karla!" he said as I held out my hand, nodding slightly and bowing appropriately. He clasped my hand in one of his and wrapped his arm around my shoulders.

"I spotted you early in the service," he continued, steering me away from the door leading outside and toward a door that led to the far-left side of the sanctuary.

I glanced back at the door desperately, only to find it getting farther away.

"As if I had needed to spot you to know you were here." He gave my shoulders a little squeeze. "The whole of Terrebonne is talking." He continued escorting me down the aisle as I made one final futile glance over my shoulder, feeling the fresh air grow distant. "Come into my study. I'd like to talk with you." He motioned me into a room. "After you."

I hesitated for only a brief moment. *This was what I came for, wasn't it? Hadn't I hoped to be able to drill the priest as I had so many others? Wasn't I still desperately seeking answers?*

I took a deep breath and walked into the study. Shelves on both my left and right stretched from floor to ceiling and were filled with books—resources and guides to the bible. Directly adjacent to the entrance was a large and magnificent stained-glass window, which took up nearly the entire wall. Hues of blue, red, and orange were perfectly blown or pieced together to form an archangel with blond hair wearing a flowing gown. My eyes locked onto the angel's eyes, which seemed to be staring right at me. The glass maker had done an excellent job at conveying peace in the angel's face. But those eyes . . . was that sympathy I saw in them?

"Karla, have a seat, won't you? How have you been?"

I forced my eyes to look away from the stained glass as I sat down in a simple chair with scrolled arm rests. "Since I arrived, you mean?"

I noticed the name plate of his desk read *Father Jacobs*.

He motioned into the air with both hands in a circular motion. "Since everything."

I looked at him expressionless, but inside I was churning. Did he know how I came to be here?

He continued. "Since Mason."

"Ah." I dropped my head and fingered the gloves I had been holding since the start of the service. I opened my mouth to speak but closed it quickly. I wasn't going to lie to a priest—not even to a priest who may or may not be in a world that may or may not exist.

"I've been a lot of things, father. But mostly, I've been angry." I looked up at him. *There! I said it. What did he think about that?*

But he didn't look surprised. He simply nodded.

"Where was he?" I asked.

"God, you mean." It wasn't a question. He was prepared for this conversation. He knew my questions, probably heard the same ones hundreds of times from other lost and broken souls.

"Yes. God. Where was he?"

"He was there," he answered without hesitation—with so much assuredness. "You think you're the first person who feels that God abandoned them?"

I didn't answer. I laid my gloves in my lap and fingered the gold ring on my left finger.

"Everything He does is for a greater purpose—an ultimate outcome."

"Like Job?" I mumbled, softly but sarcastically.

Father Jacobs leaned in closer. "What?"

I shifted in my chair and straightened my shoulders. "No, I don't think I'm the first person he abandoned. He abandoned Job, too." I looked him square in the eye.

He nodded. "Ah, the story of Job."

"Yes, the story of Job. Where was he when Satan did all

those terrible things to Job?" I raised my brows. "Job's family was killed. His home was burned. His body made ill. Where was God then?" My voice raised with each word.

The priest didn't hesitate. "He was proving that He is God."

I rolled my eyes. Unladylike, I'm sure, but it was impulse.

Father Jacobs continued. "You see, Satan was convinced that people are only loving and faithful to God when they have good things in their lives. God allowed Satan to test Job to prove that Job loved Him, not because Job was wealthy and strong, but because he genuinely loved Him."

"Much good it did him," I scoffed.

"It seems that way at first, I know. But Job never turned from God during the time Satan was torturing him, despite the torment and pain. I won't lie to you. He cried out many times in anguish, but he kept his faith in God. In this way, God proved to Satan what true love really is." Father Jacobs smiled. "And if you recall, Job was rewarded for his faithfulness. His health and fortune were restored even greater than before, and he lived a long and prosperous life."

Job *had* been rewarded for his faithfulness. He was even given another wife and ten more children. Not that it made up for the loss of his firsts.

Of course, God probably thought it did. He always thinks he knows what's best for everyone. He never bothers to ask. He just barks orders and expects you to go along with everything. I pictured him barking orders at Noah building the ark before the great flood.

"What about Noah?" I asked. "Where was God when Noah was building the ark, besides spitting out orders and telling Noah what to do and how to do it?" There was no hiding the annoyance in my voice. "Some God! Did he ever pick up a hammer or saw and offer to help? No! He was standing back watching. Just watching! Making sure Noah did exactly *what* he said *when* he said."

"You're right," Father Jacobs said patiently. "He was standing back watching, but not for the reason you think.

"In the beginning, He was watching His people with sadness, hoping to find one man worthy of the gift of life He had given. The gift of life that *He* had given." He paused, as if letting that statement sink in. "He didn't have to do that, Karla. But He did. He gave us what we don't deserve. And as He was watching the self-destructive nature of mankind, He was hoping to find one good soul who would remind Him of why He made mankind in the first place. He found it in Noah.

"So, He told Noah His plan to flood the Earth. He told Noah that he and his family would be spared if he built an ark. Then, He stood back and watched to see if Noah trusted Him. In building the ark, Noah proved his devotion to God.

"And lastly, while Noah worked on the ark, God watched the people around Noah who mocked and looked to destroy both Noah and the ark. He was guarding—keeping Noah safe so he could accomplish the task given to him."

I considered Father Jacob's answer. There was no part of it I could argue with, even though I wanted to. Yes, God could have built the ark for Noah, or drove a few nails in at the least, but he also could have chosen not to spare Noah and his family at all. What I viewed as God displaying his power could also be interpreted as God showing mercy.

But I wasn't done with Father Jacobs yet. "And Adam?"

He frowned and tilted his head to one side. "What about Adam?"

"Where was he when Adam ate the forbidden fruit? Was he standing back then, too? Just watching? Watching Adam commit the sin that would destroy the world? So now we all must die?!"

Mason!

If not for Adam . . . and God allowing bad things to happen . . . nobody would have to die, and Mason would still be here.

"Yes," Father Jacobs replied. "But He wasn't just watching. He was also giving."

"Giving what?! Giving himself a power trip?" I realized how

angry my words were, but they were true, and I was tired of hiding it—of pretending sorrow was the only emotion I felt, because more than sorrow, I felt pure betrayal at what had happened to Mason.

"No." Father Jacobs remained calm. "He was giving Adam what He gives to us all—the gift of choice." He paused and took a deep breath before continuing, obviously trying to find the right words to help me understand. "There are those who argue that because God made us, and He already knows what our future holds, that we're like puppets. That we have no say in our lives because our lives are predestined. But God proved that is not true when He placed the first souls on Earth. He proved that we *do* have a choice because He allowed Adam and Eve to choose."

I didn't look at him. I'd heard those words my entire church life. Father Jacobs was talking about free will, and as angry as I was, the simple fact was that it *was* true. Adam had a choice. I couldn't deny that. Nobody *forced* him to eat that fruit. Yes, maybe Eve, with her womanly ways, seduced him, but Adam made the final decision. Adam alone bent his elbow and brought that deliciously sour fruit to his lips.

We could go at this for hours, and I knew what each answer from Father Jacobs would be.

Where was he when Samson's hair was cut?

Strengthening Samson for battle.

Where was he when Joseph was in jail?

Preparing him to one day rule over Egypt.

Where was he when Jonah was in the belly of the beast?

Giving Jonah much-needed time.

Where was he when the twin towers fell?

"The same place He was when He hung on the cross," Father Jacobs answered.

I looked up, stunned. Had I asked that last question aloud? It was 1856. 9/11 hadn't happened yet.

Father Jacobs looked at me and repeated, "He's the same place He's always been. Enduring pain for the purity of others.

He's the same place He was when Adam was in the Garden of Eden, and when Joseph was in jail, and when Sampson was held captive. He's teaching. Watching. Giving. *Loving.*"

It was all true. I knew it was. But he hadn't answered the question I really had—the one that kept me from church. The one that kept me from God.

I took a deep breath and calmly asked the question that just weeks earlier I had screamed at Pastor Dan. "How does he know my pain? He was never without his son. He's never experienced being separated from someone he loves." I looked him directly in the eye. "He doesn't know loss."

Father Jacobs came around from his desk and sat in a chair next to me. He held my cheek in one of his hands, cupping it with so much warmth and tenderness I thought my cheek would melt in his palm. "God doesn't know loss? Child, He knew loss *first.*"

I creased my brow.

"Lucifer was once one of God's favored angels," he said. "And he was lost to God long before the world was ever created."

I pulled away. "Lucifer? That's your answer? That's supposed to make me feel better?"

"I told you God knew loss *first*—"

I didn't respond.

"—but He's also known loss the *most.*"

I turned my wedding ring on my finger numbly.

"Every man, woman, and child on Earth is a child of God's," Father Jacobs asserted. "And when a child turns from God, refusing Him admittance into their heart. Or when a child dies without asking Him in—" Father Jacobs' face expressed deep sadness. "They're lost to Him forever, Karla. And that kind of separation is eternal. That excruciating pain is ceaseless."

He leaned back in his chair and took a deep breath before he spoke again.

"God doesn't know? God experiences more loss in one of our days than you and I will experience in our entire lives." Father Jacobs leaned toward me again and continued in a soft voice.

"He knows, Karla. He does. He knows how it feels when you can't hold onto someone you love. But that's why He sent His Son to die on the cross—so there could be life after death. So that *your* separation from Mason is only *temporary*, unlike the permanent separation He faces every day as His children turn their backs on Him. *Your pain* is fleeting—not like the incessant agony He suffers daily and will suffer forever."

He took my hands in his. "You *will* see Mason again because God *does* know your pain, and He loves you too much to allow it to last forever."

Tears were streaming down my cheeks. For the first time, I understood. My chest grew warm. After years of feeling empty, I realized my heart was still there. Still pumping. The sound of it beating inside my chest was like that of a tribal drum pounding out a warrior's homecoming. The heat from each racing heartbeat radiated out into my entire body—my arms, my stomach, my legs. A hollowness I hadn't known was so deep filled with a warmth I'd never known before. Love for the God who made me—who knew me and loved me—filled my whole being, and the emptiness that had been inside was replaced with compassion for my Father.

And as I thought about all God had been through, compassion morphed into pure sorrow. How much pain God must feel daily! My heart, which was beating with new life, was simultaneously breaking. It ached with the same pain I knew God felt. I felt His agony and knew, finally, He felt mine.

Father Jacobs brought me to his chest, and I cried. I cried silently and deeply. I cried for my loss, and for all of God's losses. I cried for the pain I'd caused Him. I cried for the pain I was still in and knew wouldn't go away easily.

But I also cried tears of relief. The weight that had held me down for so long had finally been lifted. The hole in my chest had been filled. I could live fully until death came for me. And then I would depart from death and live again! There was no expression of joy that could explain how it felt to realize, without any doubt, that I would one day see Mason again.

Because God loved me.

Because God cared about my pain and made it so it wouldn't last forever.

Because God knew what forever felt like, and because of that, my separation from Mason was just temporary.

Just temporary.

CHAPTER 28

Stay

Every day after my meeting with Father Jacobs was different. Each day new. Days passed like leaves skimming the surface of a gentle stream, effortlessly and slowly. I can't be sure how many days passed, but they were filled with picnics and horseback riding, walks in the garden and books under shade trees.

Time didn't matter. It just didn't. I was healing. Isaac and I both were.

I talked to Isaac not long after my meeting with Father Jacobs. I answered all his questions with the same answers I had been given. The truth in them was so simple now that I'd heard them. I watched the same peace come over Isaac's face as I felt in my heart after crying in Father Jacobs' arms.

I knew God loved us—that He wanted us to be happy. And I knew the loss of Mason was only short-term. I was grateful for that. The knowledge of it helped me take in each moment of each day and find the good in it.

Soon, I was in agreement with Isaac. Why go home? We could just stay in Terrebonne Parish and live happily, day after day, with people who knew and loved us.

We could just stay. I'd stay and watch Isaac ride Nightmare. Stay and watch a mother bird feed her chirping babies while Helen recited poetry under the big shade tree. Stay and have another cup of tea with Grams.

The days in Terrebonne Parish were filled with serenity—something I hadn't felt in a long time, so when Isaac came to me one evening asking if he could go fishing with Charles for a couple of days, I had no qualms allowing it. No worries or fears anything bad would happen. Terrebonne Parish brought that peace. Father Jacobs brought that peace. And God. God brought that peace.

"Where's Isaac?" Lawson asked one evening.

I jumped, nearly dropping the cup of tea I was holding as I stood leaning against the porch post after supper and staring up at the night sky.

"Whoa," Lawson said, lunging forward to catch the cup before it fell. "I didn't mean to frighten you."

"You didn't. I mean, you did, but—" I stumbled with my words and balanced the cup in my palm.

The more comfortable I got around Lawson, the more nervous I became. I didn't understand it, except that the more I got to know him, the more I liked him.

"I frighten you?" He raised his eyebrows playfully.

"Not at all." I looked down at my cup to avoid his gaze. If he saw my eyes, surely he'd see I was lying.

"Good to know. Nor you me."

I dared to look up. "Did you think I was trying to scare you?"

"Not that you were trying to—" He cut himself off midsentence as if he had more to say but chose not to. "Shall we take a walk?" He motioned with his hand the way one motions a lady through a doorway.

"I would like that," I said, setting my cup down on one of the glass tables on the porch.

Lawson took my hand and assisted me down the stairs, and I hooked my arm in his as we began walking.

"You were admiring the stars?" he asked as we strolled toward the garden where we had taken our first walk together.

"The stars?"

"That's why you didn't see me walk across the lawn, I'm assuming. You were looking up, and when I followed your gaze, all I saw were stars. No bats or hoot owls," he joked. "You were admiring the stars, then?"

I'd been paying no mind to the stars. I had been thinking about God and Mason somewhere beyond the stars—together. I smiled softly. "Just admiring in general, I suppose."

"You didn't answer my question."

"I believe I just did," I corrected.

"Not that question," Lawson countered.

"Which question are you referring to?"

"Where's Isaac?"

"Oh," I said, realizing he was right. "He's gone fishing with Uncle."

"So," Lawson began hesitantly, "Isaac has gone fishing, and you are calmly sipping tea, admiring the night sky?" He sounded skeptical.

"I suppose so," I answered, straightening with pride at how far I'd come.

"And you're not worried?" He looked at me with the knowing eyes of one who saw my angst and annoyance when Isaac had "gone fishing" the last time.

"No," I answered. "Not in the least."

He shook his head and laughed. "You do continue to surprise me, Miss Karla."

"I'm going to assume that's a compliment."

"How could it be anything but?"

We reached the water fountain that stood in the center of the garden, and I was about to ask him about his day, when . . .

Chirp.

First one cricket, joined quickly by a chorus of others. A beautiful melody of nature's music.

I closed my eyes for a brief moment and smiled.

"Crickets," I whispered, opening my eyes.

Lawson looked at me questioningly.

"Um—" How could I explain? The idea that crickets were talking to me in Morse code sounded simply ludicrous now. I shook my head, embarrassed at the notion.

Lawson stared. His beautiful brown eyes held only curiosity—no judgement.

"When Mason died," I began. "One appeared at his grave. I thought—" Nope. I couldn't do it. Lawson would think I was complete bonkers if I told him.

The silence lasted an awkward minute, and then Lawson spoke. "Mine was a bird."

I looked up at him.

"I thought Albany was sending them. Or God." He glanced up. "There was this one bird that kept coming to my window every morning. A hummingbird. This little tiny bird with big powerful wings. I'd watch it every morning and wonder what it was trying to tell me."

"Did you ever figure out what it was trying to tell you?"

"Maybe nothing," Lawson said. He ran his fingers through his dark hair. "Maybe it was just me *hoping* for a sign . . . some kind of message."

"You don't believe that," I said. And he didn't. It was written all over his face.

"When Albany died, I felt so small. I'd never felt like that before—"

I still had my arm looped in his, and I rubbed his arm to comfort him. To encourage him to continue.

"The world suddenly seemed so big, and I was just this little . . . this little . . . *thing* trapped inside of it. I felt so helpless. I couldn't do anything to save her. I'd have done *anything*. But there was nothing—" He took a deep breath. "That hummingbird outside my window was so tiny, just like I felt. But those wings—"

I smiled.

"Those wings were so powerful! Those wings lifted that little creature with such force." He looked at me. "And hummingbirds can fight!" His eyes grew large, as if still astonished at the thought of their strength. "Have you ever seen them fight over a honeysuckle?"

I shook my head, smiling. His face had a subtle hint of the same emotions I felt when the purpose of the crickets' song became clear to me.

He shook his head in amazement at their tenacity. "I realized that, despite feeling small, I still had power. Maybe not power over the things I wanted, but I was a fighter. So . . . I found my wings, and I began to fight my way out of the deep dark hole I'd found myself in."

"Good for you!" I tapped his arm encouragingly.

"And what about you?"

I sighed. "It was crickets. I always felt they were taunting me."

"And now?"

"Evelyn says that it's God's way of bringing music back to my life."

"Do you believe her?"

Chirp! Chirp! An entire orchestra of crickets was now performing under the dark, starry night, louder and more beautiful than I'd ever heard them.

I nodded my head. "Yes. Yes, I believe God's trying to tell me that life is full of music, if I will just listen for it."

"Or," Lawson suggested, "that life is a dance. And sometimes, we have to switch partners."

Any other time, such a statement would have offended me. But I knew, as did Lawson, that neither of us had *chosen* to switch partners. Our partners had been taken.

But then, why should we sit the next hundred dances out?

He turned and faced me formally. "Might I have this dance?" he asked, bowing at the waist and holding out his hand, palm up, waiting for my acceptance.

"I'd be honored." I laid my hand in his as he pulled me close. The warmth of the July night could not compare to the heat penetrating from his body as we danced under the star-lit sky.

We didn't know it, but the crickets were performing their last song of the season.

CHAPTER 29

A Grand Ball

It was the first week in August when Grams called everyone into the parlor. There was to be a grand ball at her good friend Captain John Muggah's hotel, and we were all expected to be in attendance.

"I have not been there in some years," Grams exclaimed, very much excited. "It is time, don't you think?" Grams asked with so much resolve that it was not really a question. "We will leave for the ball this morning, so let's all get packed quickly," she instructed.

"This morning? So soon?" I asked.

"Yes, dear. Now, hurry up!" She laid her hands on my shoulders and pointed me toward the parlor door.

"But what about Isaac?" I asked, looking back over my shoulder as she steered me closer to the hallway.

Isaac was still off on a fishing expedition with Charles, and I had no idea when to expect him back.

"We'll only be away for a few days. He'll be fine while we're gone. He's with Uncle, and if they return before we do, Evelyn will tell them where we've gone. Besides, a ball is no place for a child." She patted me on the bottom as she shooed me into the hallway. "Now, go pack. Hurry, dear." She was beaming. Excited was an understatement. Grams was elated.

I wasn't worried about Isaac. I truly wasn't. We'd been in Terrebonne Parish long enough to know there was a calm about the place. There wasn't the slightest chance of anything bad happening. It was simply impossible.

And yet, *something* was making me uneasy.

"Go on, dear," Grams encouraged, turning me toward the staircase to hurry me up the stairs.

I sulked as I headed upstairs obediently.

Evelyn was already in my room when I got there, pulling out travel bags from the armoire and placing them on the bed.

I was grateful for her help considering I had no idea what to pack for a ball. I gathered items from the dresser—lotion, perfume, a hairbrush—but I hesitated before laying my hairbrush in the bag.

"What's wrong, chil'?" Evelyn asked. "Ain't you 'cited?"

"Well, yes. But Isaac left to go fishing with Uncle, and—"

"He be alright," Evelyn said, laying a nightgown in my bag, then placing her assuring hands on my shoulders. "I'll takes care of him when he returns. I promise."

"It's just—" I wasn't nervous to be separated from him for a time—I'd already learned I could do that without worry—but something had my stomach uneasy. I didn't know what or why.

"You want to leave 'im a note?" Evelyn asked.

That was it! I'd gotten onto him for taking off without letting *me* know where *he* was going, and now I was about to do the same.

"Yes, that would be great." I sighed with relief.

Evelyn shuffled out of the room and came back quickly with a piece of paper, a fountain pen, and a bottle of ink.

I scrawled a brief note to Isaac letting him know where I'd be and when I expected to return. Then, I reminded him how much I loved him. I laid the pen down, immediately aware that it didn't relieve the uneasiness I was feeling.

"You all packed, Miss Karla?" Jeremiah poked his head into the bedroom. "Grams says to load up yer bags. The ferry will be arriv'n soon, an' you'ns don't wanna miss it."

It was all happening so fast. Why couldn't we have planned this trip out better? Why so sudden?

Evelyn closed up the bag containing my hair brush, hair pins, and rouge, then closed a smaller one with my nightgown and a few undergarments. Finally, she latched a fairly large chest where she had packed enough clothes for two days, including an exquisitely embroidered ball gown with a hooped petticoat she'd somehow managed to cram in.

"She's all set," Evelyn said to Jeremiah, who quickly stepped across the floor.

"See you downstairs at de carriage," he said, carrying the small bags in one hand and dragging the chest behind him.

I gave Evelyn a worried look.

"Go," she said, shooing me out the door. "It's all gonna be alright."

***

We stood on the docks where the Star, the steamboat ferry that would shuttle us to the island, was docked and people were beginning to board.

Helen fanned herself gracefully and held her head high as she walked down the dock, several young men noticeably admiring her sophistication. Emma and Ann, on the other hand, ran giggling past Helen, nearly knocking her over, but Helen recovered nicely, making her that much more admirable.

"Karla?" Jeremiah had come up behind me and was speaking in the quietest voice I'd heard him use since my arrival.

I turned to look at him. "Yes?"

"Do you 'member da story of da starvin' woman outside da king's castle?"

"Of course. The story you never explained."

"Do you need me to 'xplain it now?" He was waiting patiently, the way a school teacher gives their pupil plenty of time to recall the correct answer.

"I think I got it." I smiled. "The woman was simply grateful for the food. She didn't ask too many questions about where it came from. That's how life should be—living in the moment and not questioning everything."

"Well, dat sounds like a good 'xplanation, an' may be dat's what some folk get from de story, but dat's not de *point* of de story."

"It isn't?"

He shook his head firmly. "Not at all. See, de woman prayed to God fer food and she received food." He took a handkerchief from his pocket and wiped sweat from his brow.

"Thanks to the king," I interceded. "Or, I mean, Lucifer."

Jeremiah began to smile. "No. Thanks to God."

I stared at him blankly.

"Dat ol' Lucifer is a *nasty* fella." He shook his head and tucked the handkerchief back in his pocket. "But what he . . . and de king . . . and alotta folk don't know is God is always in control. *Always*." He began to laugh. A laugh that started low and grew. "So much so," he said, starting to double over. "So much so," he repeated, now holding his tummy in laughter, "that when God gave an order, *de devil himself had to obey*!" He laughed so hard that his dark face turned a hue of red. "I bet," he bellowed, taking gulps of breath between words and laughter. "I bet dat ol' Lucifer didn't even know he been tricked. God got 'im!" he said, shaking his finger. "God got 'im good!!"

His hearty laugh was contagious, and I felt myself smiling. I imagined how angry Lucifer must have been when he realized he'd done exactly what God had ordered. How angry he must always be that God is more powerful than he is.

"Whew-ee!" Jeremiah said, wiping his forehead with the back of his hand and straightening up from his doubled-over position. He took out the handkerchief and wiped his forehead and temples one more time before tucking it away again.

He took a few more breaths to compose himself, then placed his firm, rugged hands on my shoulders. The gleam of laughter was replaced with compassion as he looked me in the eyes. "You 'member dis, Karla. All dose times in yer life when you feel like de devil is getting de upper hand, you just 'member dat God is in control of e'erything. He's even in control of de devil, 'tho de devil don't know it. 'Cause God takes e'ry bad an' evil thing de devil does an' uses it fer His good, even if you don't see de good right away. You understand?"

I nodded.

"Don't you ever doubt it. You hear me?"

I nodded again and impulsively hugged his neck.

He patted my back, his large, strong hands radiating warmth.

I pulled away and looked into his dark, wrinkled face. "I'll see you soon." I winked.

He smiled and winked back.

But as I boarded the ferry, it began to feel like the kind of goodbye you'd share with someone you'd never see again. I deliberately brushed the idea aside. After all, Isaac was still in Terrebonne Parish, so of course I'd be back. Of course I'd see Jeremiah again. And Isaac. Right?

Right?!?!

I turned suddenly to run back. To get off the ferry. To change my mind. But when I turned, I saw we had already pulled away from the dock and were at least one hundred yards from the shore.

But how??

I stared across the distance toward Jeremiah, who was standing on the dock, waving goodbye.

CHAPTER 30

Transit

Grams and I stood on the balcony of the Star as it made its way from Terrebonne Parish to the island where the much-anticipated ball would be held. The wind whipped heavily at our hair—a refreshing change from the humid temperatures we'd been experiencing.

"I left Isaac," I mumbled.

Grams turned to me but didn't say anything. Her blue eyes were smiling, introducing brand new life lines to a face that seemed to only get younger because of them. Gray strands blew across her forehead, and she reached up with one hand and tucked them away as best she could. Just as she did, the ferry bounced gently against the water's current, causing the strand of hair to find its way back across her forehead. She turned her face into the wind, the breeze momentarily keeping her flyaways back.

I put my hands on the rail beside Grams', each steadying ourselves against the mild but steady crash of waves hitting the side of the ferry.

We stood for a long time without speaking.

Finally, a soft chuckle. I turned to see what Grams found humorous as she stared out across the crashing waves.

I followed her gaze, but there was nothing to see except the meeting of water and sky.

"Eleven miles," Grams said tranquilly.

I looked at her, then followed her gaze again. "I beg your pardon?"

"Look out, Karla, dear." She pointed ahead of us. "Look out, and what do you see?"

I looked. I saw an ocean of water. I saw a bird swoop down

and come up with a fish in its beak. I saw a sun setting on the horizon.

"Tell me. What do you see?" Grams repeated.

"Water. Birds. The sun. The horizon."

"What do you see *past* the horizon?"

I squinted. "Nothing. It's too far away."

"It's eleven miles," Grams said simply.

That looked about right. No point disputing that.

"There are eleven miles between us and the Earth's horizon," Grams explained. "For eleven miles, we can see things clearly; but beyond that, it's a mystery. I've heard explorers talk about it—those eleven miles. They say those eleven miles are the reason they push on, eleven miles at a time, anticipating what's past each new horizon."

Grams put her left hand on top of mine. "No one knows what's on the other side of the horizon. It's always a surprise. Sometimes a pleasant one, and sometimes unpleasant. But always a surprise." She patted my hand. "You stay dear. Enjoy the fresh air. I'm going to head in out of the wind for a bit."

"I won't be long," I replied, kissing her cheek.

She smiled, giving my hand a gentle squeeze. "Take your time."

I stood, staring out across the water. Not long ago, I would have disagreed with those explorers—that the anticipation of what's ahead is worth the journey. But now, I was grateful for each new horizon. And eleven miles at a time was about all I could handle.

***

It was midday when the Star made its approach to the shoreline. Unlike the floating docks and wood-planked walkways of Bayou Boeuf, where we'd boarded the Star, the sight before me screamed vacationer's paradise. White beaches with crystal clear water greeted us. A gentle, continuous breeze filled the salty ocean air—a welcoming contrast to the often-stifling heat of Terrebonne.

The island had appeared fairly small as we approached, but it now seemed much larger as we docked. I took note of the many structures on the island. The most obvious was a large two-story hotel. Grams nudged me as she nodded at it, explaining that was Captain John's hotel and where we'd be staying. It was also the location of the grand ball that had brought us to the island.

To the west of the hotel were at least one hundred upscale homes clustered together—a small village for the elite who could afford to travel regularly from the marshy mainland to the resort island.

"Our bags will be brought to our room," Grams said, exiting the ferry and heading toward the hotel. "Come. This way, dear."

Helen hooked her arm in mine, and Ann and Emma followed closely behind in similar fashion. "Are you happy, Chuckaboo?" Helen asked, staring ahead at the hotel.

I smiled. There was a sliver of concern for Isaac being an ocean away, but there was also an eagerness surrounding the hustle of people making their way toward the hotel that felt exciting. I allowed *that* excitement to overshadow my concern. After all, how often would I get to experience the thrill of attending an actual Victorian ball?

"Very," I answered truthfully.

Had I stalled a moment along the shoreline and took notice of the dimming sky, or the darkening waves—or had I had the experience to know the continuous wind I was so fond of had a little more gusto than was typical—I may have seen warning signs of what was to come.

Then again, hooked arm and arm with Helen, and gleefully mingling with a rush of people eager to dress for the upcoming jubilee, I probably would have missed them still.

CHAPTER 31

Reflections

"You have a passion for mirrors." Grams nodded to the mirror in my hand she'd pulled from her purse upon my request.

"A bit."

We were sitting on a bench outside the hotel as music drifted across the lawn. The breeze coming off the water was a welcome delight from the muggy but joyous ballroom full of merry laughter and dancing.

I held the mirror in my hand. Embroidered gold vines circled the glass then entwined, coiling down the length of the handle. I stared at the reflective silver, inadvertently tilting it back and forth to see if it shifted.

Grams rubbed the edge of the mirror. "Why?"

Should I tell her? I knew by now that with Grams the truth was always best. So, I took a quiet breath and answered with the best truth I could. "I sometimes imagine that what I see in the mirror is not what it seems. That what reflects behind me is actually in front of me."

Grams appeared to be thinking about it. "I can see how that could seem so," she said after a moment. "But it is always *you* in the mirror."

I moved the mirror closer. "Is it?"

"Yes." She nodded, softly touching my cheek with the back of her hand. "It's a reflection of who you are."

"Or who I want to be," I said softly.

"No," Grams insisted. "It's always *you* in the mirror—exactly the way God designed you. Your *perception* of your reflection may change, but your reflection doesn't."

I didn't respond. She was talking in riddles, and I didn't have the desire to decipher them. Holding the mirror, I realized I didn't care if Isaac and I ever went back home . . . and that realization both scared me and brought me peace.

"Mirrors," I mumbled, amused at how their reflective surfaces display qualities we don't always want to see, but, more
importantly, at their apparent ability to become a portal—a time
warp of sorts.

"And mirrors aren't the only thing that reflect who we are,"
she continued.

"I know."

"Do you?" Grams pressed.

"Yes," I answered quickly. I wanted to reveal that, for once,
I knew the answer to the point she was trying to make. "Our *actions* reflect who we are, as well."

"Yes," she said, patting my leg. "But still, there are other
things."

I waited for her to elaborate, but she didn't.

I handed her the mirror, acknowledging her silence as an
end to the conversation.

She tucked the mirror away and we sat quietly for a few
minutes.

There was often so much quiet between us. Not an uncomfortable, awkward silence, but, rather, a calming quiet. The sort
of quiet when deep thoughts develop and brilliant ideas form.
They were my favorite moments with Grams, and I didn't want
them to ever end.

"Grams?" I finally began.

"Yes, dear?"

"I have been so comfortable since I arrived—" I paused. I
longed to tell her so much. Still, I wasn't sure how much to share.
"When Mason died, I didn't have anywhere to go to get away from
the pain. It's been years . . ." I trailed off, not knowing how to put
into words what I wanted her to know. That home was no longer
home without Mason. That the world I once lived in died when
Mason died. But here in this world—in Terrebonne Parish—everything was okay. *I* was okay. Isaac was okay. "Home doesn't

feel like home anymore," I finished. "*This* feels like home."

Grams nodded that she understood.

"I mean, *you're* here, and Uncle and Nightmare . . . but it also feels like Isaac and I are in our own little world here."

Grams laughed out loud. "You and Isaac were in your own little world long before you came to Terrebonne Parish." She picked up my hand and laid it in hers.

I looked down at her flawless, wrinkled hand, fascinated by how, like her eyes, even her hands seemed to hold so much knowledge and wisdom.

"Yes," she continued, "you went about your daily business. But you were only going through the motions. You weren't *living*."

I looked at her, poised to defend myself.

"You and Isaac *both*," she said in a manner that didn't allow dispute. "Yes, you occupied the same space as the world around you, but you were not living *in it*. Not really." Her voice was so kind, but her face was firm, as if she needed to know I was listening and comprehending fully what she was saying. "Did you *participate* in others' lives? Did you interact with those around you?" She was speaking sternly, but not accusingly. Her words were weighted more with concern that allegation.

I knew she was speaking the truth, but I fought against it anyway. "Once," I defended, "I bought a lantern from an old man. He told me about his grandpa who had owned the lantern, and I patiently listened."

"Because you cared about the old man?" She narrowed her eyebrows, wanting me to think before answering. "Or because you needed to know as much as you could about the lantern?"

I looked away, feeling like a child who had just got caught in a lie. It's true, I had wanted to learn all about my precious lantern. That was why I had given the old man so much of my time. The lantern—which had lived in the past and would live in the future. The lantern—which would always be, and could never die.

Grams nodded knowingly. Kindly.

My heart knew only the consistent ache of losing Mason. I never once thought someone else might understand. I never considered others might be hurting about their own losses—their own struggles.

But I hadn't just stopped living, I had stopped caring. I'd stopped caring about anything and anyone that reminded me of living.

Anyone, except Isaac. Isaac had been my saving grace. If not for the fact that Isaac needed me to greet him each morning with a smile, I would have contentedly given in to an endless slumber, relieved that thinking about living was over.

Grams cupped my hand in hers and raised it to her chest. The simple movement was instantly calming.

"Karla, listen to me carefully. The day you arrived, Lawson stopped by to check on you. He was worried because you had taken such a frightening fall, but when he witnessed you were well, he was going to leave. You stopped him. Why?"

"Because . . ." I grappled for the right words. Could I tell her that I had needed to find out how much he knew about my arrival? How much he had actually seen?

Grams waited patiently.

I couldn't lie to her, but I didn't feel I could tell her everything, either. "Because I had a lot of questions when I first arrived," I answered honestly.

"You were looking for *answers*?" It was more of a clarification than a question.

I nodded.

She cupped my chin with her hand and forced me to look at her.

"And you found them," she said. Her eyes were so blue. So gentle.

I nodded slightly. It was true. I had found answers. Answers that confirmed God loves me . . . and because He loves me, I'd see Mason again. I'd discovered family is the gift God gives us to pull us through our worst times, and family comes in all shapes and sizes.

I stared across the lawn to the lighted ballroom windows. I'd learned life goes on. Birds flutter. Crickets chirp. The music plays on and the dancers dance, sometimes switching partners as they twirl and shift across the dance floor.

As if Grams heard my thoughts, she continued. "It's okay to keep living, Karla." The corners of her mouth turned upward. "And," she encouraged, "it's okay to love again."

I flinched. I wasn't looking for love. Not the kind Grams was implying.

My hand was still in hers and she must have felt me tense up because she quickly added, "Not today, perhaps. But someday."

I stared blankly, not ready for this conversation.

"Do you think God wants you to be happy?" she asked.

I nodded.

She looked down at my hand. Her timeless fingers began gently turning the gold band on my ring finger. "Do you think Mason wants you to be?"

I pulled my hand to my chest, protecting the ring. It was the only Earthly connection I had to Mason—the only sign to the world that he was and will always be my husband.

But Grams gently took my hand back in hers and held it softly, waiting.

Yes. The answer was yes. Mason would want me to be happy, just as I would want him to be happy if the roles were reversed. I wouldn't want Mason to carry the burden of sadness I've carried. I wouldn't want my death to stop his living.

"You're still here, Karla. *Mason's* gone. *You* are not."

"But why?" I asked. "Why Mason? I could accept my death. I could accept that. But why Mason? Why did Mason have to die, and I get to live?"

Grams laughed. "Don't you know? You're alive because—"

I stared at her, anxiously awaiting an answer I thought would never come. But something must have changed Grams' mind because she appeared to think carefully before continuing. "God didn't give you the death you so desperately want because He's not done giving you the life you so richly deserve."

I shuddered. How did she know how badly I'd wanted death? How did she know how much I'd prayed for it—especially in the days after Mason's funeral? The only thing that kept me from it . . . the *only* thing . . . had been Isaac.

"Jesus died so you could live," Grams said, squeezing my hand. "So *live*, Karla."

The wind began to pick up, and Grams looked at the sky. "You will need to go home soon." Her statement was abrupt and flat, as if she was relaying an order.

I furrowed my brow. "No." I stood up. "No!" I said again. Louder. Protesting. "I don't want to! I don't want to go home!" Saying the words out loud made me realize how true they were. "We can just stay here—me and Isaac. We can just stay here!"

The sky was growing dark. Grams looked up at it.

"Isaac and I can stay here forever." I was begging now. Begging for whoever had say to allow it.

"No," Grams said, turning to look me squarely in the eye and pulling me back to her. "Derniere is not a place to stay." She held my gaze, as if she wanted to say more but couldn't. Or *wouldn't*.

Derniere. Why did that sound familiar? Mason shared his wealth of historical knowledge all the time. What had he said about Dernier?

"*Today*," Grams said. "Today would be a good day to go home." She looked again at the sky, then out onto the water.

I followed her gaze to find an ocean and sky that had eerily morphed into one body. As if noticing it gave it power, the sky grew darker and the temperature began to drop rapidly. The wind picked up, pushing against an unseen force. Aching to be let free. Howling in anticipation.

"Esi! Esi! Come inside! The weather is turning unkind!" a voice called out. "Karla! You, too! Come!" It was Captain John. He stood at the entrance of the hotel motioning for us to join him.

"Esi?" I questioned, looking at Grams.

Grams leaned in and whispered, seemingly a bit embarrassed, "Esi is my first name. Nobody calls me that except John, and only when he's calling out my name as if he has authority over me." She winked before calling in a firm voice to Captain John, "I am not a child, John. You'll do well not to speak to me as such." But she stood up dutifully and made her way inside, Captain John escorting her through the door.

Derniere. Derniere.

I sat on the bench as the name kept gnawing away at me.

Derniere. Derniere.

Okay, think. We're on an island, near Louisiana.

Island.

Derniere.

Island.

Derniere.

"Isle Derniere!" I yelled out as it flooded back to me. Isle Derniere was an island on the south shore of Louisiana. It had been destroyed by a hurricane in 1856. It was more commonly known as Last Island—the name it took on after the hurricane.

"Oh no," I began mumbling. "Oh no. Oh no." I was shaking my head, trying to grasp what I had just realized. Hundreds of people had died when the hurricane hit!

But surely that wasn't happening *now*. It *couldn't* be. Not *here*. Not in Terrebonne.

I closed my eyes and recalled Mason telling the story across the dinner table.

When, Mason? 1856 when? What month?

It was August, so there were a lot of vacationers on the little island, he'd said.

No. No. No. No.

I ran after Grams and caught up with her just inside the lobby. I ripped her from Captain John's arms and turned her to face me. "Is this Isle Derniere??" I asked, both my hands firm on her shoulders.

Grams smiled calmly. "Yes, dear. It is."

Panic swept over me. "We have to leave. There's a storm coming!" I made no attempt to hide the urgency of the situation.

Grams continued smiling, unphased by the insistence in my voice. "It will be okay. You'll see. Come, we are missing a lavish ball that I intend to be a part of."

"You don't understand—" I began.

But Grams patted my panicked hand with her calm one and whispered, "I do, Karla, dear. I *do*. It will be okay. I promise." She turned, strolling casually with Captain John into the ballroom.

Helen would listen. I needed to find her and warn her!

I searched for Helen for longer than I felt time would allow, finally finding her sitting beside a small three-tiered indoor fountain.

"Helen! I've been searching for you everywhere! There's a storm coming. A *dangerous* storm!"

She pulled at my arm to sit beside her. "It's okay, Chuckaboo. The hotel is aware of the weather. The Star will arrive soon and take us from the island. In the meantime, enjoy yourself."

But the Star *wouldn't* arrive in time. The hurricane would arrive first, and nearly everyone and everything on the island would be destroyed. I recalled Mason's dramatic telling of it. At the time, the rise in his tone and broad arm movements seemed a bit theatrical, but now . . .

The only reason the Star wasn't destroyed, Mason had said, *is because it never made it to shore. The roaring tides washed it to the far east side of the island. Dragging all its anchors. Turning and creaking in the surging waves! The captain yelling out, "God help them! God help us all!!"*

Few, Mason had reported, *would fight their way across the turbulent waves to the Star and climb aboard to safety. But* very *few. Others would be found clinging to trees or whatever floating scraps of debris they could find. Some,* he'd said, *had hunkered down behind large wooden cisterns and attached themselves to their overturned remains after the surge. Still, others were found clinging to a piece of rotating playground equipment, gripping it desperately as it turned and swiveled in the aftermath.*

But how could I tell Helen? How could I make her believe me?

She sat coolly at the base of the fountain, oblivious of the danger.

The top tier of the fountain spouted water into the second tier, which in turn spouted water into the bottom tier, acting as a catch all. The water in the bottom tier, the base, was dark and appeared bottomless.

"Sit," Helen insisted, pulling again on my arm to join her, but I continued to stand.

"Fine." Helen shrugged, gazing at the fountain and twisting her hair around her finger, perfecting an already perfect curl. "But you really have no control over the weather outside, do you?"

I blinked incredulously. In my panic, I hadn't even thought about the words she said so simply, *You really have no control.*

I felt temporary panic followed, unbelievably, by a sense of calm. Helen was right. I couldn't stop the hurricane that was going to tear away at the island. I couldn't rush the steamer to come quicker. I knew how this ended, and there was nothing I could do about it.

I should have felt helpless, but instead I felt relieved. By realizing I had no control, I realized I could hold no blame. I had no responsibility to make it right.

There were so many things I had no control over. So many things I had to just let happen.

I reluctantly sat down beside Helen on the fountain's edge—not defeated, but at peace. It was a strange feeling. A storm was brewing outside that could kill us all, but I had no control over it. Not only could I not stop it, but it wasn't my job to. And it wasn't my fault that it was happening. I took an unexpected comfort in that knowledge.

Helen huffed. "The ladies' restroom was so crowded. I

couldn't see past the hair and hats to check my own. *This* is much better." She shot me a quick glance, holding my eye for a brief second.

"What is much better?" But as soon as I asked the question, I knew the answer. It suddenly occurred to me what she was doing at the fountain. She wasn't staring *at* it, she was staring *into* it. She was using it as a mirror!

I stared into the dark, bottomless tier of the fountain, the still water reflecting our faces clearly. I drug my fingertips across the surface.

"Karla!" Helen groaned as the water rippled under my fingertips and distorted our reflections. "I can't see!"

"Sorry," I mumbled, dumbfounded.

"No matter," she said, using the palm of her hand to push up on her curls. "I was done, anyway."

What was it Grams had said? *Mirrors aren't the only things that reflect who we are.*

All this time, I had been searching mirrors, but what if it wasn't a mirror that would get me and Isaac back? What if it was water?!

CHAPTER 32

A Message Home

In the lobby of the hotel, guests were waiting patiently for a ferry that would never arrive. Outside, the sound of crashing waves grew louder. There was no way off the island. No way to escape the storm.

I'd given in to the fact I had no control over what was about to happen, but I knew also that I absolutely had control over what I did when things happened out of my control.

My thoughts instantly turned to Isaac. Mason had said that the hurricane not only destroyed Isle Dernier, it also caused severe damage to parts of Louisiana, and Isaac was still there somewhere, off fishing with Uncle.

I ran to the hotel clerk where a short line had formed of guests who were waiting to check out, grumbling that the storm had cut their vacations short. I didn't know how much time I had, so I went directly to the front of the line, apologizing and explaining that I had an emergency. The guests smiled and nodded sympathetically when I mentioned my son, graciously allowing me to step in front of them.

Unlike me, they had no sense of urgency. Had they known what was to come, they surely would have been pushing and shoving, dispensing with niceties altogether.

"I need to send a telegram," I told the clerk.

The clerk looked at me, baffled. "But Madam, I cannot send a telegram."

"What? Why not?" I demanded.

"Because it's not possible. There are no cables that run from the island to the main land."

This was not happening! How was I going to warn Isaac of the storm?

And once again, not having control was not okay. Panic and anger set in. I beat my fists on the counter. "You find a way! Use Morse code or whatever you have to do, but you do it!"

Those who so politely let me pass in line with courteous smiles now shot me looks of concern.

I felt a man's arm wrap around my shoulders and try to pull me away, but I paid him no mind as I glared at the clerk.

"It's okay," the man with his arm around me said to the clerk. "I'll take care of this."

"Yes, sir," the clerk said, directing his attention to the next guest in line.

The man again tried to draw me away from the counter, but I pulled away, wanting desperately for the clerk to help in some way.

"I may be able to help you," he whispered in my ear. "Please, come with me."

I turned to look at him. To argue with him. To pull away. But it was Captain John! I stood staring at him wide-eyed. Confused.

A smile stretched across his face. "I think I can help." He leaned in close. "I have been working with the government to secretly install submarine cables to transmit telegrams across the ocean." He whispered, apparently set on keeping his secret as long as possible. "I don't know if they'll work, but there's no time like the present to test it."

"Thank you! Oh, thank you!" I wanted to hug his neck, but I composed myself as a lady should. "You are too kind." I said, continuing with formalities, even though in a few hours—minutes even—formalities would no longer matter.

He directed me away from the rest of the guests down a set of stairs that ran under the main floor of the hotel. Clearly, the stairwell was never intended for guest's eyes because they were quite a contrast to the shiny marble floors and decorative wall paper the upper floors of the hotel boasted. The dingy concrete steps and yellowed walls lacked any sign of housekeeping, and a foul odor implied food or other waste was stored somewhere just out of sight.

When we reached the bottom of a third set of stairs, Captain John guided me down a long hallway. Various-sized pipes, wires, and hoses ran along the ceiling. Discolored paint was peeling from the wall in large sections.

At the end of the hallway, Captain John opened a door and stepped aside proudly to display a contraption that took up a considerable portion of the room. It was large, spanning from floor to ceiling, with numerous knobs, switches, and wires across its front. It resembled an Alexander Graham Bell Museum piece—a far cry from the compact wireless phones and computers I'd grown familiar with.

I had real doubt the contraption could do what we needed it to, but Captain John beamed over his shiny new toy as he rushed over and began flipping switches and turning knobs. Numerous lights flickered several times before remaining permanently on, and he grinned at me, encouraged by the first indications of success.

I returned his smile. "Thank you for this." Whether it worked or not, I had to appreciate his effort. And his excitement alone made it worth giving the experiment a try.

He sat down on a stool in front of the machine and picked up a thick instructional manual, which he skimmed quickly, proceeding with each step as he read, flipping a few more switches and turning a couple of knobs. "There," he said, after flipping a final switch. "We should be ready. You do know this is a historical day, don't you?" The seriousness of the moment meshed with excitement on his face—each emotion not sure which should take precedence.

"You have no idea," I replied, forcing another smile.

"Alright then, madame, what would you like me to send?"

"It is for Isaac Garrison in Terrebonne Parish," I said. "Please send this: Hurricane coming. Stop."

"Whoa, whoa, whoa," Captain John interrupted. "A bad storm does not classify a hurricane," he interjected, apparently amused by my level of worry.

"Captain John," I said, firmly, "it is for my son. I must exaggerate the situation so he will take it seriously. Children can often be without worry when worry is sometimes required."

Seeming to understand, he began working at the machine, repeating, "Hurricane coming. Stop."

I continued, "No mirror. Stop"

He creased his brow and glanced over at me.

"Just send it. Please, sir," I begged.

He nodded, but he had a look about him that he thought he may have picked the wrong person for a trial run of his new machine.

"Water may be the way out. Stop."

Again he looked at me, but he repeated the message as he sent it.

"Look for your reflection. Stop."

Captain John, now visibly annoyed, typed the sentence, then asked, "Is that it?"

"Yes, sir. And thank you," I answered, leaning in to kiss his cheek.

His annoyance left him quickly, and he stumbled with his next words. "Well, now. Again, I can't say with certainty it will work. It's new and—"

"I understand," I interrupted.

We quickly retraced our steps down the hallway and up the stairs back into the lobby where people were running out the large entrance doors of the hotel.

"What's going on?" Captain John asked the desk clerk.

"They're going out to see the waves. I understand it to be quite a sight," the clerk answered, clearly disappointed he was missing the spectacle.

As the guests were running by, one of them bumped my shoulder quite hard.

"Ow!" I rubbed my arm and looked up just in time to catch a glance of the guest before he turned his face away and ran out the front door. "Wha—?!" My mouth dropped open. It was him! It was the man from Crawley Antiques! The man who had been there and then was gone. He was here!! I ran after him. "Hey, wait!!"

"Madame?!" Captain John yelled, chasing after me. "Wait! Where are you going?"

The draping layers of my dress kept me from running at top speed, allowing Captain John to catch up with me quickly, and I exited the hotel with Captain John directly behind me.

The violent wind hit me instantly as I stepped onto the hotel's porch, tearing my hair forcefully from its neat upsweep as rain and sand beat ruthlessly against my face. As if working as a team to hold me back, the rain drenched my dress while the wind encircled my legs, entangling the fabric so I couldn't take another step.

I steadied myself against the railing, swiping my hair from my face and searching for the man from the antique store. But it was too dark, and there were too many people. All I could see were backs of heads staring into the coming terror with fascination.

It was early evening, but black clouds swirled above, forcing the entire island into early nightfall. The only light came from the constant but flickering flashes of lightning that could be seen just on the other side of the clouds. It was a beautiful and frightening sight that made me both want to run and stand in awe of it.

Captain John joined me at the railing as a gust of wind nearly knocked him down.

The weight of my soaked dress made it difficult to stand as the force of the wind grew. Captain John wrapped his arms around me from behind just as I was about to stumble backwards, grasping the railing with both his hands, sandwiching me between him and the railing for protection.

A mixture of water and sand pelted against our bodies, the sharp, tiny darts aimed directly at our faces. The smell of salt in the mixture told me it wasn't just rain that was taking aim. The ocean was coming for us, as well.

I struggled to see through the darkness. Squinting. Trying to adjust my eyes to the dark and protect them from the hail of painful darts. I stared deep into the shadows toward where I knew the ocean to be, seeing only a wall of black.

Then, in an instant, I realized it wasn't darkness I was looking into, at all. It was the ocean! Stirred. Angry! Towering a hundred feet above us!

"Can you swim?!" Captain John yelled into my ear as the massive wave seemed to pause in midair, swelling in size and height, just before plunging in our direction.

I hunkered down, wrapping my arms fully around the banister as the furious wave barreled toward us. It hit hard. Crushing me with a force I didn't know water could exert. I felt Captain John struggling to keep his grip around me. Around the railing. But his struggle was ever so brief. Then, he was gone.

I held on tight with both arms to the railing as the impact of the water subsided as quickly as it had come. Still hanging on, I wiped strands of hair from my face and pulled hair from my mouth, spitting out a mouthful of salty, grainy water.

Then, a thunderous roar rose—a hollow, moaning sound that grew louder and sounded as if it were directly overhead.

I looked up.

An immense wave, this one bigger than the first, towered overhead. Threatening. Groaning. Snarling.

I grabbed tighter to the railing, closing my eyes and bracing for impact, and I waited. But nothing happened. The wind and water threw itself in all directions around me and at me, but the ominous wave never came.

I dared to lift my head. To assess the threat. But just as I did, my mouth dropped in horror. The massive wall of water hovered above me, as if it wanted me to see it, and I screamed as it came plummeting down, filling my open mouth with water. I was ripped from the railing, tossed in turbulent water, slammed against debris and into currents that hit harder than the debris.

Swim!

I kicked my feet and flailed my arms desperately.

Swim!

The shifting water turned me in every direction, not allowing me to surface for air.

Swim!!

I fought the undertow as best I could, but I was quickly losing strength and breath. And just as quickly, I was losing desire.

Swim! So loud. So clear.

I opened my eyes in the water and gave one final kick toward what I thought might be the surface, as the force of the relenting current fought against me. Just as I thought I might finally surface, a massive surge forced me further under.

CHAPTER 33

Resurrected

"Karla?" I heard a distant voice.

I tried calling out, but I was lost in the turbulence that surrounded me. I was twisting and turning. Tumbling and drowning.

Swim!

"Karla?"

Swim, Karla! Swim!!

I felt a hand near mine and I grabbed it, clutching to anything that could pull me out of the water.

"She's squeezing my hand."

More voices.

"That's a good sign."

Slowly, the water receded. Slowly, my breaths evened out. Slowly, I opened my eyes.

"Karla. Can you hear me?" I recognized the voice instantly. It was my sister, Cheryl. She sat staring at me, her hand still gripping mine as worry and sleepless nights showed in deep lines all over her face.

"Where am I?" My voice was hoarse. Dry.

"You had an accident. You're in the hospital."

"What?" I tried to sit up, but Cheryl put her hand on my chest.

"You were on your way back from Morgantown and you went off the road," she explained. "Don't move. Just relax."

Panic overtook me. "Where's Isaac?"

Cheryl's worried eyes told me more than I wanted to know.

"Where's Isaac?" I asked again, pushing against her hand.

"Just take it easy," she said, moving one of her hands gently to my shoulder in an attempt to calm me. "You've been out for a while. Just take it easy."

I felt a tube around my face, forcing air into my nose. My head hurt. My ribs hurt. I moved my hand to my waist as I continued trying to sit up, wincing in pain.

"You broke some ribs and you have some stitches, but you're going to be fine," she said. She was obviously trying to control her emotions, but her voice betrayed her. I knew she'd been sitting with me every second for however long I had been here.

"Where's Isaac?!" I demanded.

If my sister was here, who was with Isaac?

My sister looked down, away from my gaze.

"Where is he?!" I said, panic filling my chest and stomach.

"He was in the car with you," she said, looking at me for only half a second before looking away again. She pulled at a loose string on the hospital bedspread. Her hands were shaking and her nails, usually long and manicured, were bitten down to the quick.

"Karla," she started, "he's not well."

"Where is he?!" I screamed, pulling the oxygen tube from my face.

She looked past me to another bed in the room. The curtain that typically separates beds in a shared hospital room was pulled back. Machines beeped and hissed, making thunks and clicks as if it were all they could do to keep the person attached to them alive. It only took a second for me to realize who they were working so hard for. Isaac!

"No!" I yelled.

My sister wrapped her arms around me, holding me in the bed. "Karla," she said, "he's going to be okay. I know he is. I *believe* he is."

"What's wrong with him?" I was shaking. "What did I do to my baby?"

"*You* didn't do anything," she tried to assure me. She held my shoulders firmly, trying to get me to look at her. "It wasn't your fault. Do you hear me? You hit a deer. It wasn't your fault."

I sobbed, aware of the stabbing pain in my ribs between breaths.

"Your car went over a hill and into the river. By the time they reached your car, Isaac had been under water for a long time. He wasn't breathing."

"What?! No—"

My sister lifted my chin and forced me to look at her. "Pastor Dan has been here, and he says that all hope is not gone. We have been praying so hard, Karla. *So hard*! And I know God is listening. I *know* He is." She hugged me as she whispered, "He brought you back. He'll give us back Isaac."

***

Several days had passed since I awoke to the horror of what had happened. Progressively, I began moving easier. I graduated from sleeping in a hospital bed near Isaac to sleeping in a chair right beside him.

Now, I sat by his bed and stared at his beautiful face. I brushed his hair from his closed eyes. Wires ran from under his gown to machines on each side of his bed. A breathing tube was down his throat.

I'm so sorry, baby boy!

My thoughts raced with all that had happened since our car accident. I had been over it so many times, trying to analyze what was real and what wasn't.

But it was all real. I knew it beyond any doubt. I had rushed through a mirror into a world that didn't exist—not in the time and way we know, at least—and I spoke with people who knew me by name and embraced me as long-lost family. I made friends with emotions I had allowed to become strangers, and I reconciled with God for the loss I had been dealt.

And Isaac was there, too. He was there!

So, if I believed all of it as it was, then I had to believe that Isaac was *still* there, waiting for me to return from a ball that I would never return from.

I pictured his face the last time I'd seen him, trotting off on another fishing expedition. He was so happy in Terrebonne Parish. He loved it there! It was I who had spent too much time pushing on mirrors looking for a way home. Not Isaac. Isaac had been busy riding Nightmare and taking off with the boys. He had no desire to come home.

I held his warm hand and remembered the last time I held Mason's warm hand. It was in a hospital room just like this. I hadn't been ready to let Mason go, and I *hadn't* let him go. I didn't want to make the same mistake with Isaac.

But how could I let my own son go?! The doctors had said his prognosis was grim . . . that even if he woke, it was hard to predict what level of brain damage he might have after going so long without oxygen. That would be no life for Isaac—a boy who loved the outdoors and couldn't sit still for anything.

Hadn't Terrebonne Parish taught me that death is not the end, but a gap in time before once again being reunited with our loved ones? Hadn't I learned, without question, that life continues for the living? That those who pass on are happier than they'd ever been during their time among the living? Hadn't Terrebonne Parish taught me that letting go is *part* of living, not an excuse to join the dead?

But let Isaac go?

I listened to the machines breathing for him here in this world, and I thought of him in Terrebonne Parish taking deep breaths of sweet air as he ran through yellow fields and soaked up the sun.

The sun. The memory came quickly, destroying the picture I'd recreated of Isaac in Terrebonne Parish—of Isaac happy—because it wasn't sunny when I left Terrebonne Parish. It was raining. It was storming! In fact, a hurricane was destroying entire islands!!

Had Isaac gotten the warning I'd sent? Had the trial-by-desperation telegram successfully reached him?

I raced through the different timelines, trying to understand how it worked. Weeks here were only days in Terrebonne Parish, but weeks in Terrebonne Parish were only days here. I couldn't decipher the time differences. There seemed to be no rhyme or reason to it.

How long had passed for Isaac from the time I sent the telegram, assuming he received it? Days . . . weeks . . . hours?

I put my arms around Isaac and laid my head on his chest. "Isaac, I need you to come back," I whispered. "I know you may not want to, and I don't blame you, but I need you to come home."

Nothing.

I lifted my head and looked at him. "Isaac? Can you hear me?"

Still, nothing. I put my lips to his ear and whispered, "Isaac."

Isaac made a sound! It sounded like a gurgle. The rhythm of the machines changed from fixed beeps and clicks to irregular beeps and clicks as alarms went off.

Three nurses rushed into the room and quickly surrounded him. One of the nurses began looking at the monitors and reading numbers to another nurse, while the third nurse rushed to a machine that was above Isaac's head. She pushed a few buttons, and the machines stopped their chaotic beeping. She placed her stethoscope on Isaac's chest and frowned.

"What's going on?" I demanded.

The nurse continued to listen through the stethoscope, but she didn't reply.

I stood up. "What's going on!"

She took Isaac's hand in hers and said, "Isaac, can you squeeze my hand?"

I looked at their hands. Nothing.

"Is he okay?! Tell me, what's going on?"

"Squeeze my hand if you can hear me," the nurse repeated.

Again, nothing.

Finally, she turned to one of the other nurses and said, "Page the doctor, I think he has pulmonary edema."

"What's that?" I asked. "What does that mean?"

"He has fluid in his lungs," one of the nurses answered.

"Fluid?" I asked. "Like water?" I turned to the head nurse. "He has water in his lungs?"

The nurse kept working with Isaac and didn't reply. The nurse she had instructed to page the doctor picked up the phone.

"Do you mean water?" I asked again, going frantically from nurse to nurse, begging one of them to answer me.

The third nurse put her arm around my shoulder. "Yes," she said. "He has water on his lungs. It's not a good sign."

My mind was racing. Water! Water had brought me back from Terrebonne Parish. Would it bring Isaac back, too?

"No, it's good!" I exclaimed, pushing the nurse aside and grabbing Isaac's hand.

I pulled on his hand gently. "I've got you Isaac. Grab my hand!"

The nurses looked at me with sympathy. I heard the nurse's voice over the loud speaker, "Doctor Wheeler to room 407. Doctor Wheeler to room 407."

"Grab my hand, Isaac," I said more loudly. "Grab it!"

One of the nurses put her arms on my shoulders and tried to pull me away.

"Isaac!" I said, keeping a tight grip on his hand. "I'm here. I've got you!"

The nurse pulled at me more firmly, but I fought her, not letting go of the grip I had on Isaac.

"Let us take care of him," she said, as her hold became more forceful.

But I kept hold of Isaac, determined not to let him drown. The second nurse hung up the phone and began to help the other nurse pull me away. I struggled to keep hold of Isaac's hand, but his hand was growing clammy and damp. I felt my hand slipping from his as our outstretched hands were being pulled farther and farther apart.

"Swim, Isaac!" I yelled in desperation. "Swim!!"

Isaac's hand grabbed mine! His eyes shot open and he began pawing at the tube in his throat, desperately trying to remove it.

The nurses swarmed around him as he fought to get the tube out. They shoved me against the wall and grabbed Isaac's hands to restrain him. He made gurgling sounds and continued fighting them, grabbing at the tube.

"Get the tube out!" I yelled. "Take it out!!"

The doctor rushed in and, quickly assessing the situation, pushed the nurses away. He looked at the machines. He talked to Isaac calmly, telling him what he was doing, and Isaac's breathing went from quick breaths to slow even ones. Finally, the doctor gently pulled the tube from Isaac's throat, talking to him softly the entire time.

I made my way to Isaac's side and grabbed his hand again.

The doctor turned to the nurses. "What happened?"

"Pulmonary edema," one nurse answered.

The doctor's eyebrows rose and concern covered his face. He quickly took out his stethoscope and laid it to Isaac's wet chest.

Isaac was soaked—his hair, his cheeks, his entire body. Drenched.

Worry left the doctor's face as he listened. "Sounds clear to me."

The nurses looked confused.

"We'll send him down for a chest X-ray, but I think he'll be just fine." He winked at Isaac. "Welcome back. You gave us quite a scare."

The doctor left the room with the nurses, and I heard him in the hallway giving instructions as to what tests he wanted run. He must have walked off after that because I heard the nurses in the hallway bickering about what had just happened. They sounded confused and astounded at the same time.

"I know what I heard . . ." one nurse was saying.

Another nurse chimed in, "By all indications . . ."

I sat staring at Isaac.

"Sore," he whispered hoarsely, pointing to his throat.

"Yea." I smiled.

Isaac licked the moisture from above his upper lip and whispered something else.

"What?" I asked, leaning in closer.

"Salty," he whispered.

"Salty?" I asked. "Like the ocean?"

Isaac smiled and gave me a wink.

"Yea," I said. "I know." Tears streamed down my cheeks. Sweet, salty tears.

Isaac healed quickly and was out of the hospital just a few short days after waking. The doctors and nurses were surprised he had no permanent damage of any kind, but I wasn't.

We went home and started our lives again. This time, with a different purpose. We went home not to think about death, but to appreciate life.

Sometimes, when two people go through something as dramatic as what Isaac and I went through, it takes those people a while to talk about it. Isaac and I weren't those people. We talked about Terrebonne Parish like it was a place we'd visited and hoped to one day visit again.

In the quiet of my room, just before peacefully dozing off each night, I thought about it. I didn't know what Terrebonne Parish was, but I understood it wasn't heaven because if that were the case, I knew without any question Mason would have been there with us.

Anyone else may have considered it a holding place—somewhere you go when the decision has not yet been made whether it's your time to pass over—but I didn't believe that. I believed it was simply a gift from God. Not a holding place, but a learning place. A place to pause and take in all that happened. A place to make peace.

As I walked back through Grams' house each night in my memories, I recognized items at Grams' that Isaac and I had collected over time. The lantern hung in the barn where Nightmare was sheltered. The crate was the same one Evelyn used to take apples to the cellar the day she picked a peck with Jeremiah. The large mirror had hung in the dining room. I paid the items no mind when I was in Terrebonne Parish. They hadn't caught my eye there the way they had here when I first saw them. I wondered if I created them in Terrebonne Parish, or if they had survived all those years just to one day reunite with me here. I also wondered how everyone in Terrebonne knew me and Isaac. Try as I might, I couldn't place any of the beautiful souls who had been there—not Grams or Charles, nor Ann or Emma. Not even my precious Helen. Perhaps, if I searched the family tree far enough back, I could make some sense of it, but I never bothered. They were family . . . and that was enough for me.

And then there was Lawson. I missed him terribly. It wasn't the same kind of longing I had when I thought of Mason; it was different. I realized Lawson had been in Terrebonne Parish not for me to fall in love, but to show me it was possible. To suggest that, perhaps, one day, someone may come along to help fill a hole made when Mason left. It would not be Mason, but that would be okay. They would not completely fill the hole, and that would be okay, too. They would be another piece of the puzzle that is life.

Isaac and I continued antiquing, but Isaac's interests shifted from nutcrackers and cowbells to vintage fishing paraphernalia. Sometimes, he'd find a fishing lure of great interest and say, "Wouldn't Uncle love this one?" And I'd nod and say, "Yes, he would."

I started writing again—a passion I had as a child and lost somewhere between the ages of imagination and adulthood. It started as short sentences, writing all I could remember about Terrebonne Parish, jotting down names of places we'd been and people we'd met, and it turned into journal after journal of words that time and again brought me comfort.

As I sat on a blanket, journal in lap, I watched Isaac ride across an empty field on a horse belonging to a long-time friend of Mason's. When he first saw how disciplined Isaac was with the horse, he told Isaac he could come over to ride anytime he liked. He said it was as good for the horse as it was for Isaac.

I laid my journal down on the blanket and walked over to the fence as Isaac rode up, his hair bouncing in his eyes with each trot.

I rub the horse's nose. "She's beautiful, isn't she?"

"Uh huh," Isaac answers softly.

I detect something in his voice. "But?"

Isaac hesitates. "She's not Nightmare."

I pat her mane. "I think she knows."

Isaac smiles, indicating he understands. He leans down and rubs the horse's neck. "Let's go, girl," he says, giving the reins a gentle tug.

I sit back down and pick up my journal, reading the most recent entry:

The past is delicate. But like a rusty lantern or a tarnished mirror, its beauty will forever exist for anyone who chooses to see it.